RETRIBUTION

Recent Titles by Anthea Fraser from Severn House

The Rona Parish Mysteries

BROUGHT TO BOOK
JIGSAW
PERSON OR PERSONS UNKNOWN
A FAMILY CONCERN
ROGUE IN PORCELAIN
NEXT DOOR TO MURDER
UNFINISHED PORTRAIT
A QUESTION OF IDENTITY
JUSTICE POSTPONED
RETRIBUTION

Other Titles

PRESENCE OF MIND
THE MACBETH PROPHECY
BREATH OF BRIMSTONE
MOTIVE FOR MURDER
DANGEROUS DECEPTION
PAST SHADOWS
FATHERS AND DAUGHTERS
THICKER THAN WATER
SHIFTING SANDS
THE UNBURIED PAST

RETRIBUTION

Anthea Fraser

This first world edition published 2016
in Great Britain and 2017 in the USA by
SEVERN HOUSE PUBLISHERS LTD of
19 Cedar Road, Sutton, Surrey, England, SM2 5DA.
Trade paperback edition first published
in Great Britain and the USA 2017 by
SEVERN HOUSE PUBLISHERS LTD

British Library Cataloguing in Publication Data
A CIP catalogue record for this title is available from the British Library.

ISBN-13: 978-0-7278-8670-5 (cased)
ISBN-13: 978-1-84751-773-9 (trade paper)
ISBN-13: 978-1-78010-841-4 (e-book)

All Severn House titles are printed on acid-free paper.

Severn House Publishers support the Forest Stewardship Council™ [FSC™],
the leading international forest certification organisation.
All our titles that are printed on FSC certified paper carry the FSC logo.

Typeset by Palimpsest Book Production Ltd.,
Falkirk, Stirlingshire, Scotland.
Printed and bound in Great Britain by
TJ International, Padstow, Cornwall.

PROLOGUE

Chrissie Palmer stared moodily out of the car window as they left the London suburbs behind. Glancing over her shoulder, she checked that her daughter's headphones blocked out any conversation before saying testily, 'I really do think it's time all this stopped.'

Her husband sighed. 'Not again, Chrissie, for God's sake!'

'But it's so *morbid*, Alan. Damn it, thousands of other kids have died and I bet their families don't go through this gruesome ritual every year.'

'It's not gruesome,' Alan said doggedly, keeping his eyes on the road. 'And it's a comfort to the parents.'

'Damn it, it was nearly thirty years ago!'

'Twenty-six,' Alan corrected.

'Exactly! And keeping her room like a shrine, everything as she left it. It's creepy!'

He didn't reply and she felt a stab of pity, knowing that because, that day, he'd not walked his sister home from school, he felt responsible for her murder. But God! Every year at the end of November, when there were a million things to do, they had to make this sombre trek up to Buckfordshire, usually necessitating a day off work. At least this year the anniversary fell on a Saturday, though the downside was having to drag Amanda along with them.

And every year they visited the cemetery and laid fresh flowers on the grave, which inevitably led to her mother-in-law breaking down, before returning home to eat Tracy's favourite meal of roast chicken with, bizarrely, Yorkshire pudding, followed by apple crumble. If *that* wasn't morbid, Chrissie would like to know what was.

Alan glanced sideways at his wife's set face. 'Try to understand, love,' he said. 'Tracy was the same age as Amanda is now. Just imagine if—'

'Stop it!' Chrissie cried, putting her hands over her ears.

'I'm only saying—'

'Well, don't!'

'OK, OK. Just try to be a bit more understanding, that's all.' She didn't reply and he added, 'I think we should stop for a coffee break at the next service station. We could all do with stretching our legs.'

Chrissie drew a deep breath, then patted his hand on the driving wheel. 'Good idea,' she said.

ONE

Five months later

Lindsey Parish, skimming through the glossy pages of *Chiltern Life,* glanced up as her twin put a mug of coffee on the table. 'Nothing of yours in this month?'

'No.' Rona brought her own mug and sat down opposite her. 'Barnie wants to spread them out a bit.' Barnie Trent was the magazine's features editor.

'But you're still on the single-mothers series?'

'Only just, I'm reaching the end of the line. Possibly one more, to round it off.'

Lindsey's continued flicking brought her to the cookery feature and she paused, tapping a nail against the writer's name. 'I appreciate you never read this . . .' Rona's dislike of cooking was legendary and Max was the chef in that household, '. . . but do you know Nicole Summers? Personally, I mean?'

Rona shook her head. 'I'm freelance, remember. I don't come into contact with the other contributors.'

'Apparently she also runs a cookery school,' Lindsey said. 'I met her ex last week. Steve knows him from work and we bumped into him and his girlfriend at a concert.'

In the last month or so Steven Hathaway had featured more than once in Lindsey's conversation, but Rona had forborne from commenting, fearful that an inadvertent remark might put her sister on the defensive. Lindsey, who'd reverted to her maiden name after her divorce from Hugh Cavendish, had had several disastrous liaisons over the past few years – due, as she freely admitted, to falling for unsuitable men – and Rona hardly dared hope that Steve might prove her salvation. Both sisters had met him before Christmas, when his father, Frank, who was a friend of their own father, had featured in Rona's previous series on life-changing experiences.

In the interim, their lives had been dominated by the weddings of both of their parents – their mother Avril's to Guy Lacey and their father Tom's to Catherine Bishop – and it was on the latter occasion, to which the Hathaways had been invited, that Rona had begun to suspect a growing interest between Steve and her sister.

'In fact,' Lindsey was continuing, 'we're all going out for a meal on Friday.'

'How do you know he's her ex?' Rona asked curiously. 'It seems an odd thing to come out at a first meeting, specially with his girlfriend there.'

'Steve told me later. He wondered if you knew her. I only mentioned it because presumably Nicole's now a single mother herself and might be of interest.'

'Now that's an idea! Thanks, sis!' Rona spun the magazine round, scanning the relevant pages.

'Only problem is,' Lindsey continued, 'she mightn't appreciate a feature on herself appearing in a mag she writes for.'

'True. As it happens, I'm seeing Barnie this evening. I'll sound him out.'

Finishing her coffee, Lindsey pushed back her chair. 'I must go, I've a client coming in at two.' She was a partner in Chase Mortimer, a firm of solicitors in Guild Street. 'Thanks for lunch.'

'Such as it was.' It had been a simple salad, hastily thrown together on her sister's arrival.

'Well, I did only drop in to borrow this book.'

Rona accompanied her up the stairs to the hall. 'What's he like, the ex?' she asked, opening the front door.

'We only met briefly, but he seemed OK. Bit of a hunk, actually.'

'You can fill me in at Mum's birthday do on Saturday. If I approach Nicole it might be helpful to have some background info.'

Returning to the kitchen, she sat down and pulled the open magazine towards her. Although, as Lindsey had guessed, she didn't normally read the cookery section, she was aware that Nicole Summers was regarded as an authority on matters culinary and it would be useful to have some idea of what she actually wrote about.

In fact, the scope of the feature surprised her. There was a review of a restaurant that had just opened in Woodbourne, a listing of the month's cookery programmes on television and a note of new ingredients now available in the shops, alongside a column headed 'The history of the food on your plate' which gave the country of origin of each item. There were also suggested menus for a week, and the illustrated recipes were so appetizingly described that even Rona felt a momentary impulse to try them.

Although she'd been a sporadic contributor to the magazine over the last few years, usually in the form of series on local interests, Rona considered herself a biographer by profession and had four highly acclaimed 'lives' to her credit. It was in fact only six months since she'd finished the last one, on the life of the artist Elspeth Wilding, and at the time she'd been more than glad to put it behind her. Her husband, Max, maintained that death and disaster seemed to follow whichever genre she worked in, but after the traumas of the last bio he'd gone so far as to advise her to write only about people who'd been safely dead and buried for a hundred years. Perhaps she should take his advice.

Max himself was an artist with a studio across town, a measure that became necessary when, early in their marriage, it had become evident they couldn't work in the same house – he needing loud music to inspire him and she requiring complete silence for her writing. Furthermore, to their family and friends' initial disquiet, he also slept there three nights a week following his evening art classes. Early morning was his preferred painting time, and this way he was able to make full use of the light without the need to rush back across town at daybreak, having returned home merely to sleep. The arrangement, though unorthodox, suited them both admirably and they spoke on the phone at least twice a day.

Rona closed the magazine and sighed. Over the last few weeks she'd become increasingly restless as she worked on the undemanding series and, eager now to begin looking for another life to research, she was anxious to bring it to a close. Nicole Summers would be an excellent example with which to finish.

She flipped open her laptop, googled her and was interested to see she had a web page and blog as well as Twitter and Facebook accounts. So at least she wasn't averse to publicity. Rona studied her photograph judiciously: brown hair curling on her shoulders, oval face with well-defined brows above dark eyes, and an enigmatic Mona Lisa smile.

Thoughtfully she closed the laptop and loaded the lunch dishes into the dishwasher. As she'd told Lindsey, she would speak to Barnie and see what he advised.

* * *

Barnie and Dinah Trent lived in a sprawling bungalow on the north-eastern fringes of the town, a route increasingly familiar to Rona since not only was Lindsey's flat also off this road but so was the new home of their father and Catherine. She was still coming to terms with no longer being able to phone him on the spur of the moment to suggest lunch, as she frequently had both during his tenure at the bank and after his retirement, when he'd moved out of the family home in Belmont to a furnished flat in the centre of town. She missed those impromptu meetings.

She turned into Hollybush Lane and, as the five-bar gates were open, drove through them and pulled up in front of the house, closing the gates behind her before releasing her dog from the car. Despite this being home to three Siamese cats, Gus, her golden retriever, was a welcome visitor, a non-aggression pact having been agreed early in their acquaintance.

'Rona!' Dinah came hurrying to greet her, her rich, deep voice, as always, at odds with her diminutive height. 'Lovely to see you!'

Rona bent to return her hug and Gus, not to be left out, leapt up with an excited bark. By the time they'd disentangled themselves, Barnie had appeared to add his welcome and they all moved inside.

Rona loved this house with its relaxed, homely atmosphere, and over the years had grown fond of the two very disparate people who lived here. Barnie, a bear of a man with a high domed forehead, stood six foot two in his stocking feet, while Dinah, wiry-haired and dynamic, was under five foot. Yet despite their differences, they'd been happily married for thirty odd years – a stark contrast to her own parents.

She seated herself in her usual chair, looking about her with a contented sigh, and Barnie put a glass of Vodka and Russchian into her hand. 'So? How are the newly-weds?'

Rona smiled. 'As far as I know, very well. I haven't seen a great deal of them.'

'Well, that's the way with newly-weds, whatever their age!' Barnie bent to pat Gus, who was easing his way between the cats in front of the fire. After a mild day, the evening had turned chill. 'I promised Dinah there'd be no shop talk,' he went on. 'But before she comes back, how much mileage do you reckon is left in the single-mothers series?'

Rona shrugged. 'To be honest, I think it's run its course – perhaps just one more to finish it off. Which reminds me, I presume you've actually met Nicole Summers?'

Barnie raised a bushy eyebrow. 'Once. Why?'

'What's she like?'

'Efficient. Always meets her deadlines, and provides consistently good copy.'

'I meant personally?'

'I'm hardly in a position to judge. Why?'

'Lindsey pointed out that she's a single mother. I was wondering how you'd feel about my approaching her?'

Barnie whistled tunelessly. 'A bit incestuous, isn't it?'

'Not really. Magazines do sometimes run profiles on staff members.'

'Well, I suppose I've no objection, though whether you'd be able to twist her arm is another matter.'

'I looked her up online and she seems pretty publicity-conscious.'

'Concerning her work, yes. But from what I recall, there's no personal stuff.'

'You think she'd object?'

Barnie shrugged. 'As a matter of interest, how do you know she's a single mother?'

'Pure fluke, really. Lindsey met her ex.'

'She might have replaced him.'

'I hadn't thought of that,' Rona admitted.

'Well, if you want to approach her you have my blessing, for what it's worth.'

'Great. Have you by any chance got her mobile number?'

'It'll be on file at the office. I'll email it to you tomorrow.'

On cue, Dinah came bustling into the room. 'Dinner in ten minutes!' she announced. 'I'll have that sherry now, thank you, darling.' She perched on the arm of a chair and turned to Rona. 'Right, tell me all the news!'

'So how's Mel?' Rona enquired over dinner, adding with a smile, 'No more babies on the way?' The Trents' daughter lived in the States and her third child had been unplanned.

There was a pause and Rona, surprised Dinah hadn't launched into a detailed report as usual, looked up in time to catch an exchange of looks between husband and wife.

'Is something wrong?' she asked quickly.

It was Barnie who replied. 'She and Mitch are going through a bad patch, I'm afraid. Things are a little rocky at the moment.'

'Oh, I'm so sorry. Is it with his being away so much?' Melissa's husband was in the oil business, which necessitated long assignments overseas.

'That doesn't help,' Barnie said, but did not elaborate. Dinah offered more vegetables, and the subject was firmly closed.

Rona related the news to Max when he made his bedtime phone call. 'I hope it's not serious,' she added. 'It must be worrying for them, knowing Mel's unhappy when she's so far away. Oh, and I forgot to tell you earlier, Linz came up with a suggestion for another single-mother article – the last, I hope – someone who writes food articles for the mag. I'll give her a ring in the morning and see if she's willing to cooperate.'

But before she could do so, Rona's plans took an unexpected turn. The next morning she'd just read Barnie's email giving Nicole's number when her phone rang. She lifted it to find Prue Granger, her editor, on the line.

'Rona, how are things?'

'Fine, thanks, Prue.'

'Busy?'

'So-so,' Rona answered cautiously.

Prue hesitated. 'I have a proposition I'd like to run past you, but not over the phone. Will you be coming to town in the next few days?'

'I hadn't planned to, but of course I could if—'

'Tomorrow? Eleven o'clock at my office?'

Rona raised her eyebrows. 'Yes, I could manage that.'

'Excellent! See you then.' And she rang off.

Rona's curiosity was piqued. What could possibly have arisen that required her immediate presence? Well, she'd find out tomorrow.

Unlike the bigger firms with their open-plan offices and ranks of desks and computers, Jonas Jennings, an independent publisher specializing in non-fiction, still retained its small cluttered rooms up a winding staircase, and Rona was out of breath when she was shown into her editor's office.

'Rona, good to see you!' Prue came round her desk to greet her. Small, with curly hair and extra-large spectacles, she looked more like a precocious child than the competent businesswoman Rona knew her to be. She put her head round the door and called, 'Frances, be a love and bring in two coffees, will you?' before turning back into the room. 'Sit down, Rona. Journey OK?'

'The usual crush on the tube,' Rona replied. 'I can't imagine how you cope, commuting daily.'

'Needs must,' Prue answered vaguely, reseating herself and pulling some files towards her. 'Now, I wasn't quite clear from your reply on the phone. Are you working on anything at the moment?'

'A series for *Chiltern Life*, *comme toujours*,' Rona said lightly.

'Ongoing?'

'Just coming to an end, actually. Why?'

A knock on the door heralded a girl bearing a tray with two mugs of coffee and a plate of Marie biscuits, which she set down on the desk. As she left the room, instead of answering, Prue asked abruptly, 'Have you read any Russell Page?'

Rona looked surprised. 'Certainly – it was he who inspired me to write biographies. Wasn't he killed recently, in a car crash? I saw his obit in the paper.'

Prue nodded and Rona awaited her next comment with some interest.

'He was one of ours, of course,' she said at last. 'And apart from grieving for him as a friend, his death has left us in a somewhat parlous position.' She nibbled on a biscuit, then looked up, meeting Rona's eye. 'Do you remember Gideon Ward?'

Another unexpected and seemingly irrelevant question. 'Of course – the Jeremy Paxman of his day. He caused all sorts of upsets, didn't he? Members of Parliament resigned and business moguls were brought low. And wasn't there one interview in particular that caused a storm – something to do with a Nigerian food crisis?'

Prue nodded. 'It won him the TV Presenter of the Year Award.'

Rona eyed her curiously. 'Why did you bring him up?'

Prue sighed and leaned back in her chair. 'The point is that Russell had been working for the last eighteen months or so on his bio. It was scheduled to come out in March next year, which will be the tenth anniversary of Ward's death. And, well, now we're left high and dry, as it were.'

Light began to dawn. 'You're not by any chance suggesting I take it on?'

Prue leaned forward. 'Would you, Rona? Most of the research has been done and we have all Russell's notes, plus DVDs of Ward's interviews and so on. It would get us out of the most enormous hole if you'd agree.'

She took a quick drink of coffee, and when Rona didn't immediately comment went on. 'I appreciate this initial approach should have come through Eddie. I did email him, but he's out of the country dealing with the estate of one of his authors. We agreed that in view of the urgency I should outline the proposal and you could contact him after we've spoken.' Eddie Gold was Rona's agent.

'Actually,' she said slowly, 'I *was* starting to think about another bio, but this one would be extremely high-profile. Russell Page is a hard act to follow, and my style is very different from his.'

'Of course it would be *your* book, albeit with acknowledgment of Russell's initial input.'

'And from what you say, the schedule's pretty tight?'

'Well, as I said, originally publication was scheduled to coincide with the anniversary of Ward's death, but to be realistic few people would be aware of that.'

She glanced at Rona's still-doubtful face. 'I don't want you to feel under pressure, Rona. You have your own method of working and I appreciate biographies can't be rushed. A bonus is that most of the groundwork has been done, which should be a time saver.'

Rona sipped her coffee, her mind whirling off at a tangent. 'How would Page's wife feel about someone else taking it on?'

'Actually it was she who first mentioned your name. She knew we publish you, has read your books, and suggested you might be the person to do it.'

'That's kind of her.'

Gideon Ward! An interesting, larger-than-life character, a gift for any biographer, and falling neatly into her hands without her so much as lifting a finger, let alone having to beg for the privilege! Rona felt a growing excitement. Nonetheless, she wouldn't commit herself until she'd had time to consider it from every angle and discuss it with both Eddie and Max, though she knew in advance what her husband's reaction would be.

'How soon do you need an answer?' she asked.

'Yesterday!' Prue said with a laugh. 'Seriously, as soon as

possible. If you turn it down, we'll have to approach someone else. There are other possibilities, but you're our first choice.'

Rona rose to her feet. 'Provided I can get hold of Eddie, I'll let you know tomorrow,' she said. 'But whatever my decision, I'm very grateful for being given the opportunity.'

'No!' Max said forcefully. 'Absolutely and categorically not!'

On Wednesdays, when he had afternoon rather than evening classes, he took the opportunity to return home, and as usual had prepared and cooked a delicious meal. Rona, who'd already had a long conversation with Eddie Gold, had postponed her announcement until they'd finished eating, hoping that mellowed by food and wine he might be more amenable. In vain, as she now realized.

'You know how emotionally involved you get with your subjects,' he went on. 'And this man was a controversial character to start with. God knows what you'd stir up! Anyway, I thought you were going to do a piece on this woman food writer.'

'There's no hurry for that,' Rona said feebly. She paused. 'Eddie's in France, but I had a long chat with him on Skype and he advised me to go for it.'

'*He* doesn't have to live with you while you're writing it!'

'He says it's bound to be high-profile,' she went on, 'with a lot of kudos attached, which wouldn't do my career any harm. And as it's ten years since Gideon Ward died, it won't be as raw for the family as it was with Elspeth.'

'But from what you say the original biographer's death was only weeks ago, and you'll presumably have to meet *his* widow too. God, you'd be taking on a double whammy – grieving relatives on all sides!'

Rona didn't reply, her eyes on the coffee spoon she was twisting in her saucer.

Max leaned back in his chair, folded his arms, and said bluntly, 'It doesn't matter what the hell I say, does it? You've already made up your mind.'

She looked up, meeting his eyes. 'It would be so much nicer to have your blessing.'

'Darling, how can I give it, when the last two you did put you in actual physical danger? The mere thought of it scares me to death.'

'But I've always escaped unscathed!' she said, hoping to make him smile.

'So far,' he retorted grimly.

'Please, Max.'

He sighed, leaned forward, and reached for her hand. 'You know you always have my blessing, even if it's given through gritted teeth. Just – take care.'

'Of course I will,' she said.

Rona phoned Eddie Gold the next morning to inform him of her decision.

'Excellent!' he enthused. 'A ripe peach falling into your lap, if ever there was one. I'll get straight on to Prue and start the ball rolling. But there's no need to wait for the contract – I gather time is of the essence, so the sooner you can get down to it the better. And the best of luck, dear girl. You've made the right decision!'

Rona's next call was to Barnie.

'Did you contact Nicole Summers?' he asked, when she'd told him her news.

'No, I was just about to when all this came up.'

'But surely you'll fit her in first, to finish off the series? Providing she's amenable, of course.'

'I'm not sure, Barnie. The publishers are anxious to make up for lost time.'

'But once you're bogged down in a biography you'll be *hors de combat* for the foreseeable future, whereas this would take ten days max. At least find out if she'd be agreeable.'

Rona hesitated. It went against the grain not to finish one assignment before embarking on another and, as he'd pointed out, work on a bio was long-term. Prue had assured her the deadline was reasonably flexible, and ten days here or there wouldn't make a difference.

'All right,' she said, 'I'll see if she's agreeable. But if she isn't, could we bring the series to an end without having to search for anyone else?'

'Fair enough. Thanks, Rona.' He paused, then went on awkwardly. 'By the way, sorry to have cut you off the other evening when you asked about Mel. The fact is she and Mitch are on the verge of splitting up.'

Rona gave an exclamation of concern and he continued. 'She discovered he's been seeing someone, and she's coming home with the children next week for an indefinite stay. As you can imagine, Dinah's very upset about it – though of course she'll love having them here.'

'I'm so sorry,' Rona said inadequately. 'Is he serious about this other woman?'

'He says not, but Mel's hurt and bitter and is refusing to speak to him. Perhaps a spell apart will bring them to their senses.'

'Well, thanks for telling me. I do hope things work out.'

When the call ended, she glanced at the clock on the wall, before scrolling through her emails till she came to Barnie's giving Nicole's number. It was still only ten o'clock – she might possibly catch her at home. Without giving herself time to consider, she punched the relevant keys.

The call was answered at once, taking her by surprise. 'Nicole Summers,' said a crisp voice.

'Nicole, good morning. I'm Rona Parish. Of *Chiltern Life*,' she added awkwardly by way of introduction.

'Of course, I know who you are. As a matter of interest, how did you get my number?'

'Barnie Trent gave it to me – I hope you don't mind. I was wondering if I could . . . come to see you?'

'Why?'

'Well, I've been doing an intermittent series for the magazine . . .'

'On single mothers. Yes, I know.'

Rona felt oddly gratified. 'Those who've made a notable success of their lives,' she added diplomatically.

'Ah!'

'And I was wondering if you'd agree to contribute to it,' she finished quickly.

There was a pause. Then Nicole said slowly, 'I don't see why not. *Pour encourager les autres,* and all that.'

Rona released her breath, unsure whether or not she felt relieved. 'That's great. Thanks. So when and where could we meet? Do you live in Marsborough?'

'No, I'm in Woodbourne. Is it the writing or cooking you're interested in?'

'Both, really.'

'Well, you could sit in on one of my classes, if that would help. Or would you prefer a straightforward interview?'

Rona gave a little laugh. 'Again, both. How often do you hold your classes?'

'Tuesday mornings and Thursday evenings. In fact, I have one this evening.'

'I think, if it's all the same to you, I'd rather we spoke first.'

'Fine. Well, I'm at home tomorrow, if that would suit you.'

'Yes, indeed. That would be great.'

'It'll take you about half an hour to get here, so say ten thirty? The address is fourteen Norse Crescent – postcode MB45 7JL, if you have a satnav. See you then.' And she ended the call.

Rona leaned back in her chair and drew a deep breath. At the beginning of the week she'd had no work in prospect. Now she was committed to two separate projects, one of which would keep her busy for an indefinite period. But first things first. Switching on her computer, she began to compile a list of questions to put to Nicole Summers.

TWO

As Rona had guessed from the address, Nicole's home was in a small development of Scandinavian-style wooden houses that she'd visited once before. They'd been built in the seventies, incorporating features revolutionary at that time in the UK, such as triple glazing, wood-burning stoves and solar panels.

Like the rest of the estate, the front gardens in Norse Crescent were unfenced, and as there was no car in the drive of number fourteen Rona drove straight in. She turned from locking the car to see Nicole Summers standing in the doorway watching her. Feeling at a disadvantage, she went to meet her with outstretched hand.

'Good morning! It's good of you to see me.'

Nicole's hand was cool and swiftly withdrawn. 'My pleasure,' she said. Following her inside, Rona saw that, as in the house she'd visited previously, the ground floor was open-plan with floor, walls and ceiling composed of rich golden pine, which glowed in the spring sunshine that flooded through the windows.

'Please sit down,' Nicole invited, indicating a comfortable-looking sofa upholstered in oatmeal tweed, in front of which a low glass-topped coffee table bore a tray set with heavy ceramic mugs and a cafetière that was emitting an appetizing aroma. There was also a plate of tiny delicious-looking cakes.

As Nicole seated herself in a matching chair and busied herself pouring coffee, Rona covertly studied her – dark eyes, a mouth that looked unused to smiling, and a cloud of hair that framed her face without softening it. When she bent forward, a small butterfly shape was visible below her right ear, and Rona wondered fleetingly if she had other tattoos on her body.

Though undeniably an attractive woman, there was a cool reserve about her that Rona, who was used to striking up an almost instant rapport with those she interviewed, found faintly disconcerting. Still, rapport or no, she had an interview to conduct and she extracted her recorder from her handbag.

'Have you any objection if I use this?'

'None at all.' Nicole handed her a steaming mug of coffee and pushed the milk jug and cakes towards her. 'Please help yourself.'

Rona smiled as she did so. 'If I were any kind of a cook, I'd be asking you for the recipe!'

Nicole raised her eyebrows. 'But you're not?'

She shook her head. 'Fortunately I'm married to a man who's a great chef. Otherwise I'd live on takeaways, restaurant meals and convenience food.' As in fact she did when Max wasn't home – a point she forbore from mentioning.

'And you're not interested in learning?'

'I'm afraid not.'

'Well, your talents lie in other directions. So . . .' Nicole leaned back in her chair, crossing her long legs and cradling her mug between her hands. 'What is it you want of me?'

'Basically the story of how you started out on your career. For instance, did you always want to start your own business? Or only after your marriage broke down?'

Again a raised eyebrow. 'If that's a tactful way of asking if it was a financial necessity, the answer is no. My daughter and I are well provided for.'

Embarrassed, Rona started to apologize, but Nicole brushed her protest aside. 'I'd always enjoyed cooking and experimenting with food from different cultures, and after a particularly boring week at work I decided to leave my part-time job and strike out on my own. The fact that this happened shortly after Patrick and I separated was entirely fortuitous.'

'So how did you set about it?'

'I began by studying nutrition, comparing the proteins, carbs and fats in different foods and working out the best ways to combine them. The next stage was to devise meals based on these principles. And when friends kept asking for recipes I decided to collate them, possibly with a view to publication. I was also intrigued by the way our diet had evolved as new ingredients were discovered, so I gave the date a particular fruit, vegetable or seasoning first appeared in the UK and where it originated. It involved fascinating research, on among other things the spice trade dating from antiquity.' She smiled fleetingly. 'To be honest, at one time I was more interested in the research than the cookery!'

'I can imagine,' Rona said, remembering the interesting information alongside the recipes.

'I sent my first attempt to *Chiltern Life*,' Nicole continued. 'Barnie Trent took it, and we were both amazed at the positive feedback. Then the series was commissioned and the idea of holding cookery classes stemmed from that. And now a publisher has suggested I put the recipes together in a series of paperbacks – cakes, meat, fish, and so on – which is rather gratifying.'

'How does Barnie feel about that?' Rona asked.

'He's quite happy as long as it's made clear the recipes first appeared in *Chiltern Life*.'

Rona nodded, glancing down the length of the open-plan area to what looked like the corner of a kitchen unit. Catching the direction of her gaze, Nicole gave a short laugh.

'You won't be surprised to hear I don't teach from home. We have a Community Centre in Woodbourne, and I rent their kitchens twice a week. It's the ideal solution.'

'How many are in the classes?' Rona asked.

'As the kitchen has only four stations we're limited to eight at a time, but I wouldn't want more. With that number I can follow the progress of each pupil, and it's interesting to see how they differ in approach. The afternoon classes tend to be composed of retired people while the evening ones have a younger age group, mainly those with jobs who can't get there during the day.'

Which also applied to Max's art classes.

'And do the same people come back week after week? Or do you have a set number of lessons?'

Nicole made a mock grimace. 'I can't get rid of them! I have a waiting list, but I'm reluctant to limit the number of lessons because one leads on to another in a natural sequence. Also everyone knows each other and they work well together. It would be a pity to disband them.'

Remembering Barnie's comment about the dearth of personal information, Rona said tentatively, 'You mentioned a daughter.'

'Venetia, yes. She's eight years old and a very self-sufficient young lady, I'm glad to say. A lot of children would have played their parents off against each other in our situation, but she spreads her favours equally.'

'She sees her father, then?'

'Of course, every weekend. He collects her from school on Friday and brings her home on Sunday evening. All very civilized.'

Rona wondered how his girlfriend felt about that. Surveying the glowing wood-lined spaces, she said artlessly, 'This is a lovely house. Have you lived here long?'

'Since we were married. I drew the long straw when we separated, mainly due to Venetia's school but also because Patrick was moving to a new job.'

Though she wanted to know more about this oddly intriguing woman, Rona felt she'd used up her ration of personal questions and was about to return to more general topics when Nicole pre-empted her.

'So, would you like to sit in on one of my classes? It might even tempt you to have a go yourself.'

Rona laughed. 'I'd be delighted to watch, but I'm afraid I'm beyond hope on the cooking front.'

'Well, since you've some way to come, you'd probably prefer the afternoon session. The class runs from two till four on Tuesday afternoon, so I suggest you call here at one thirty and we can go along together.'

Smoothly though it was done, it was a dismissal. Rona switched off her recorder, slipped it into her bag, and rose to her feet.

'That would be great. Thanks so much, and also for the cakes and coffee.'

As she drove home, Rona thought with satisfaction that, as she'd anticipated, Nicole Summers was the perfect subject with which to finish the series on a high note – a single mother who had not only succeeded in making a new life for herself but in the process had become that much-maligned word a 'celebrity'. It would be interesting to hear Lindsey's assessment of her ex-husband.

Avril Lacey, previously Parish, stared balefully at the puppy, and the puppy stared balefully back at her. It was a battle of wills – had been from the first – and she resented having met her match in this tiny King Charles spaniel. The truth was that she didn't care for dogs, a fact that had never occurred to her new husband, who'd blithely announced that he and his first wife had always had one and once the wedding was over it would be good to rectify that omission.

Why, she asked herself now, hadn't she been brave enough to confess her shortcomings in this area? Though he'd have been disappointed, Guy wouldn't have tried to force her.

She sighed, looking down at the offending puddle.

'I put you out five minutes ago,' she said severely, 'and all you did was sit on the mat till I let you back in. Then you go and do this – on purpose!'

With some vague idea of puppy-training she reached forward, grabbed him by the scruff of his neck, and forced his nose down into the still-warm liquid. 'Bad dog!' she scolded. 'Now you can go out again, and stay there till you learn your lesson.'

She picked up the wriggling bundle, opened the back door, and deposited him outside, shutting the door quickly as Guy came into the kitchen.

'Where's Rex?' he asked. His eyes fell on the puddle. 'Oh dear! Never mind, it's early days.'

'He'd just been out, but he waited till he came in again,' Avril said crossly. 'I've better things to do than mop up after him a dozen times a day.'

'Not a dozen, darling, surely! Where is he now?'

A piteous whimper sounded from outside and Guy threw her an amused glance.

'Shutting the stable door?' he asked, and opened it. Rex scuttled quickly inside and licked Guy's shoe in gratitude. He laughed and picked him up.

'He's gorgeous, isn't he?' he said, allowing the puppy to lick his face and ear. 'You can't really be cross with him.'

'He'd just been out,' Avril repeated, not to be won over.

'Well, he'll learn. We'll just have to be patient.'

We! She thought as she went for a cloth, but she held her tongue.

'Have you finalized the numbers with Serendipity?' Guy was continuing. They were holding her birthday dinner at that acclaimed restaurant the following evening.

Avril's face cleared. 'Yes. Did I tell you Lindsey phoned? She asked if she could bring Steve Hathaway. I hadn't realized they were seeing each other. I'm so glad – she did so hate being the odd one out. So that brings it to eight, a nice, round number.'

She had spent the last few years worrying about her twin daughter, who after her divorce had become involved with one unsavoury man after another, suffering heartbreak as each relationship inevitably broke down.

Hopefully, though, Steve Hathaway was of a different mould. His father, Frank, had been at university with Tom, and they'd bumped into him and his wife at irregular intervals until Ruth's death shortly before she and Tom separated. Though Avril had never met Steve, she'd heard about him from Rona and he sounded a much more suitable prospect.

'Excellent!' Guy said, still fondling the puppy. 'It should be a good evening.'

The following morning Rona received two communications that pushed Nicole temporarily out of her thoughts. The first was a letter from Phyllis Ward, forwarded from her publishers, expressing pleasure that Rona would be taking on the interrupted biography of her husband.

'*Although Mr Page made copious notes and to the best of my knowledge I handed over all relevant documents, I hope you will agree that a meeting would be helpful to us both. I should be delighted to meet you at your convenience, either here or in London.*'

'Where's "here"?' Max asked, as Rona read the letter aloud at the breakfast table.

'Richmond.'

'I should opt for London. You can go by train and get the tube or taxi to wherever you're meeting. Less hassle.'

'But seeing his home would give me the chance to soak up the atmosphere, imagine him *in situ*. That's always helpful, and it's only about an hour's drive via the M1 and the North Circular.'

Max shrugged, returning to his newspaper. 'What time are we due at Serendipity?' he asked after a moment.

'Eight o'clock. Guy has booked one of the gallery tables.' She flicked a glance at her husband. 'Lindsey's bringing Steve Hathaway,' she added.

'To meet the family? Well, well!'

'Don't read too much into it,' Rona warned. 'It's only natural when they're seeing each other. Don't go making any pointed remarks, or you might put him off.'

Max raised a pained eyebrow. '*Moi?*' he said.

The second distraction came in the form of a phone call.

'Ms Parish? This is Esmé Page. I hope you don't mind my phoning. As it's quite urgent, I persuaded Prue Granger to let me have your number.' She'd been speaking rapidly, and paused for breath.

'The point is,' she went on more slowly, 'I'm going away next week and in view of the publication deadline wanted to hand over all Russell's notes and papers to you before I go. Incidentally, I should say I'm delighted you've agreed to take on the biography.'

So, Rona reflected ruefully, despite her promise to Barnie she was not to be allowed to forget her other commitment.

'Thank you,' she said. 'When are you leaving, Mrs Page?'

'On Wednesday. My son came home for the . . . funeral.' Her voice shook slightly. 'And he's taking me back to Scotland for a few weeks. He thinks it would do me good to have a break.'

'Of course. I quite understand.' On Tuesday she would be with Nicole in Woodbourne, which left only Monday. 'Where exactly do you live?'

'Just outside Merefield. I hope that's not too far from you?'

'No, not all.' In fact it was only a half-hour drive. 'Would some time on Monday suit you?'

'Perfectly, yes. I've some last-minute things to see to, so could we say three o'clock? If you've a pen, I'll give you the address and postcode.'

Rona wrote them down. 'I look forward to meeting you,' she said as the call ended. But did she? It was clear Mrs Page was still shaken by her husband's death; she could only hope she wouldn't break down, and be thankful that Mrs Ward at least had had time to come to terms with her widowhood.

The Serendipity restaurant was noted for three things: its unusual layout of waist-high partitions snaking in and out of the tables, giving each the illusion of privacy, its magnificent animal sculptures carved out of ice, and the counters on either side of the room displaying raw meat and fish from which guests could choose their meal and watch it being cooked on the grills set into the wall behind. A short flight of steps to the right of the entrance led up to a gallery running the length of that wall, so that those seated there had a bird's-eye view of the main floor.

When Rona and Max arrived that evening Avril and Guy were already there, with Sarah, Guy's daughter, and her new husband, Clive. Rona kissed her mother and handed over a small package.

'Happy birthday, Mum!' she said.

'Thank you, darling! We've decided to delay the present-opening till after the meal, but we'll start on the champagne as soon as Lindsey and Steve arrive. And,' she added as they came up the steps, 'here they are now!'

Everyone stood as the couple approached the table and introductions were performed. Rona was the only one who'd already met Steve, and she was glad to see how easily he was absorbed into the group. There'd been a time when he was reserved and reportedly antisocial. Obviously, Lindsey was good for him.

'We'd a great evening with Patrick and Samantha,' Lindsey told her under cover of the general conversation. 'How did you get on with Nicole?'

'Fine. I'm going to sit in on one of her cookery classes on Tuesday.'

Lindsey gave a choke of laughter. 'That'll be a new experience for you! We can't talk now, but I'll phone tomorrow and we can swap news.'

* * *

The food was, as always, excellent, the conversation lively. And when coffee was served Avril opened her packages, exclaiming with delight over each of them. It had been a relaxed and happy evening.

'How's your father?' Rona asked Steve as they were preparing to leave.

'In fine form, thanks. He sends his best wishes. We were very grateful for the way you portrayed his experiences.'

Frank had been involved in a failed rescue attempt after a car crash that proved not to have been accidental; and his memory recall had finally brought the criminal to justice.

'He sent me a note,' she said, 'which was sweet of him. I'm so glad everything worked out in the end.'

'He's in better form than I've known him for some time. Once everything had been brought into the open, it was as if a great weight had been lifted from him. And as a bonus,' Steve added with a smile, 'Monica and her family have more or less adopted him!'

Rona's article had also coincidentally reunited him with her next-door neighbour, who as a child had been involved in an earlier event in his life.

'All in all, a good result, then,' she said with satisfaction.

As promised, Lindsey phoned the next afternoon. Max was watching sport on TV and Rona took the call in the kitchen.

'So what did you think of Nicole?' Lindsey asked.

'Hard to say. She's not easy to get to know.'

'You should hear Samantha on the subject!'

'If that's the girlfriend, it'll hardly be an unbiased opinion!'

'Actually, she's very nice. We got on really well.'

'And Patrick?'

'Handsome, charming, pretty laid-back. Mind you, he's quite a strong character. And if Nicole is too, I can imagine sparks flying.'

'Well, at least they had an amicable divorce. Apparently their little girl spends every weekend with her father.'

'Yes, I gathered that.'

'Actually, Linz, this will be the last in the single-mother series. I've been asked to do another bio.'

'Asked to?'

'Yes, on Gideon Ward. Russell Page was going to do it and had made all the preliminary notes, but he died suddenly and Prue wants me to take it on.'

Lindsey gave a low whistle. 'Well, Ward was a big name. It should be quite a coup for you.'

'The trouble is they want it pretty soon, to coincide with various anniversaries, so it will be all systems go once I've done the Nicole article.'

'Well, that's great. Congratulations, sis. You probably won't want much input on Patrick after all.'

'Oh, anything you've got will be grist to the mill. I still have to write the article. How does Steve know him?'

'Initially through business – Sedgwick Hotels are his clients and Patrick's the manager of the new one in Marsborough – but they became friends.' The Sedgwick was the town's latest hotel, having taken over the ailing Lansdowne in Alban Road.

'I suppose you didn't glean the cause of the divorce?'

'Have a heart, Ro! That's not exactly dinner-table conversation, but if I get the chance, I'll try to suss it out of Sam. I have to go now – Steve's calling for me in fifteen minutes. Let me know how the cookery class goes.' And she rang off.

Mentally switching from one project to the other – a process she was becoming adept at – Rona went up to her study to prepare for the interview with Mrs Page. Her first task was to discover exactly when her husband had died, and having gone online to read his obituary, she learned that the fatal car crash had been less than three weeks ago. After skipping through the list of books written and awards received, being already familiar with them, she was shocked to read that he'd died at the early age of fifty-four – and felt a stab of guilt that she was going to reap the benefits of his last research.

As she switched off her computer, she accepted that the following day's interview would be a difficult one.

Ottersmere, twelve miles long and at its widest point three across, was the only natural lake in Buckfordshire. It lay in the south-east corner of the county and, although a favourite destination with those interested in sailing, that Monday afternoon the grey water was clear of boats and a lowering sky gave promise of rain.

The small market town of Merefield had developed alongside it and, following the directions given to her, Rona found the Page home on its fringes, set on a slight hill overlooking the lake. She turned into the open gates and drove up the sloping gravel drive to the front door, apprehensive at the prospect of meeting such a recent widow.

The door was opened by a man in his thirties clad in T-shirt and jeans. 'Ms Parish?' He shook Rona's hand. 'I'm Josh Page. Please come in, my mother's expecting you.'

As Rona walked into the hall a young woman appeared briefly in a doorway, smiled at her, and disappeared again. The daughter-in-law, no doubt. Rona had no time to speculate, as Josh was opening a door on the far side of the hall.

'Ms Parish is here, Mum,' he said and, having stepped aside for her to enter, withdrew, closing the door behind him.

Rona found herself in a large, light room with bay windows overlooking the lake. It was comfortably furnished with sofas and easy chairs covered in a pale-blue material, and although it was the end of April a small fire burned in the grate. The woman seated beside it rose as Rona came in and held out her hand. As Rona took it, she estimated that Esmé Page was in her early fifties, but her face was sunken and she seemed somehow diminished.

'So good of you to come at such short notice,' she said. 'Please sit down.'

Rona did so, unsure how best to convey her sympathies. 'I'm sorry we're meeting in such sad circumstances,' she began hesitantly.

'Yes,' Esmé said distractedly, 'it's been a great shock.'

There was a brief knock on the door, which opened to admit the young woman Rona had briefly glimpsed, bearing a tray laden with cups and saucers, teapot and milk jug. No home-made cakes on this occasion, but there was a plate on which triangles of shortbread were neatly arranged.

'Thank you, dear,' Esmé said, adding by way of introduction, 'My daughter-in-law, Caitlin.' And the two nodded to each other as she left the room.

Esmé's hand was shaking as she poured the tea. 'It was so sudden, you see,' she said jerkily. 'No long illness to prepare us – though I suppose I should be thankful for that.'

Her eyes strayed to the silver-framed photograph on a side table and Rona, following her gaze, recognized the lean, clever face with the small moustache. It was the same image that appeared on the jackets of his books.

Since Esmé had broached the subject, she asked gently, 'How exactly did it happen?'

'A car crash.' Esmé's voice shook. 'He'd set off early for the reference library, intending to spend the whole day there. He said he'd had enough distractions so was going somewhere he wouldn't be disturbed.' She dabbed her eyes with a handkerchief. 'Which is why I can't understand how he came to die in a country lane miles from anywhere. I'd give anything to know how he spent those last few hours.'

'Was another car involved?' Rona asked.

'No, he . . . went into a tree head-on. It was after a bend and the accident people think he must have misjudged it, been going too fast and not had time to pull out of it. Which seems quite likely – I was always telling him to slow down but he never did. Like all men, he wouldn't accept any criticism of his driving.' She gave a sad little smile.

'No one saw it happen,' she went on after a moment. 'The next car to come along phoned for help, but by then he was beyond it. I can only pray he was killed outright.' Her hands were twisting in her lap. 'I was expecting him home for dinner, but instead it was the police who came.'

'I'm so terribly sorry,' Rona said inadequately.

'And to add insult to injury,' Esmé continued, her voice shaking, 'we were burgled during the funeral. What kind of people would do that?'

Rona regarded her with horrified pity. 'That's appalling! Were they caught?'

Esmé shook her head. 'They didn't take much – the police think they might have been disturbed, though I don't know who by – but the house was turned upside down.'

'I can see why you need to get away for a while.'

Esmé belatedly remembered her duties as hostess. 'I'm so sorry – would you like some shortbread?'

Rona took a piece, murmuring her thanks, and Esmé drank her rapidly cooling tea.

'But down to business,' she continued. 'I've put all his papers in a suitcase for you, together with his memory sticks and the DVDs of Ward's TV interviews. There might be other bits and pieces as well that aren't relevant – I didn't go through them all – so just select what you need.'

She paused. 'It seems almost indecent to be handing them over so soon, but Russell was a stickler for deadlines and I knew he'd want me not to waste time. On the other hand, I also knew Prue would be embarrassed to approach me too soon, so I took the initiative at the funeral, told her I understood her position and suggested you took over the book. Russell and I both enjoyed your work and I'm sure he would approve.'

Amazed that the man she so revered should have read her own books, Rona could only murmur a subdued 'Thank you.'

Esmé frowned thoughtfully. 'There's just one thing perhaps I should mention. He'd had something on his mind those last few weeks, concerning one of the TV interviews. I asked him about it, but he wouldn't discuss it. He said it was a delicate matter and that anyway he might be mistaken. Then quite out of the blue he decided to visit his old school, which he'd not been back to in years. And when I asked him why, all he'd say was that it was a nostalgia trip.'

She glanced at Rona apologetically. 'I'm probably making a mountain out of a molehill and the two things might not be connected, but I thought you should know in case they were important.'

'Have you any idea whose interview was worrying him?'

'Unfortunately not.'

Rona thought for a minute. 'Which school did he go to?'

'Buckford College.'

Rona knew it, having visited it during a previous assignment. 'Is that where Gideon Ward went?'

Esmé shook her head. 'That was my immediate thought, but he was at Winchester.'

'Did he say anything about the visit when he got home? Who he'd seen or anything?'

'No, he was very non-committal. But there wasn't a reunion or anything, it was in the middle of term and a weekday at that. Which struck me as odd.' She shrugged, spreading her hands. 'But then again, I might be attaching too much importance to it.'

'Thank you for letting me know. There might be something in his notes that would explain it.'

'That's what I wondered. I had a quick look through them – but seeing his handwritten scribbles and memoranda was . . . upsetting, so I didn't pursue it.'

She lifted the teapot enquiringly, but Rona shook her head.

'Thank you, no. I'm sure you've a lot to do, Mrs Page. I won't take up any more of your time.'

'Very well.' Esmé stood with her. 'Would you like my mobile number, in case you need to contact me?'

'Thank you, that might be useful.' Rona wrote it down.

Hearing the sitting room door open, Josh emerged from the kitchen carrying a bulky-looking case. 'I'll take this to the car for you,' he offered. 'It's quite heavy.'

Rona took Esmé's hand. 'I feel very honoured to be taking over from your husband,' she said sincerely. 'I hope I don't let either of you down.'

Esmé's eyes filled. 'I'm sure you won't,' she said.

Alan Palmer put down the phone and turned to his wife, his eyes troubled. Chrissie, who'd been listening to his side of the conversation, waited with bated breath. A call at six in the morning did not bode well. 'How bad is it?'

'I don't know – Dad doesn't know. Bad enough for her to be rushed into hospital. And today, of all days.'

Chrissie nodded. After twelve years of marriage she was well aware that it would have been Tracy's birthday. Incredibly enough, her thirty-sixth.

'He wants you to go up there?'

Alan nodded, starting to dress. 'Could you call the office and let them know? Luckily I've no appointments today.'

'But you'll be home tonight?' Chrissie asked anxiously.

'I can't promise, love. I'll let you know.'

Twenty minutes later he was backing the car out of the drive, fearful of what lay ahead. His sister's birthday had a different ritual from her anniversary but had been followed just as rigorously down the years. His parents would visit her grave, taking the flowers he and Chrissie had sent, and in the evening an emotional phone call would be made. Not this evening, though. Had the flowers arrived? Would his father take them to the hospital instead?

'She doesn't seem to know what's happening,' George Palmer

had said on the phone, his voice breaking. 'She keeps asking for Tracy, Alan. Subconsciously she must know it's her birthday.'

Rush-hour traffic was heavy, and as he inched his way towards the M1 Alan's mind slid inexorably back twenty-six years to the day when his world fell apart. Although his parents had never hinted that they blamed him, he knew he was responsible for his sister's death and every detail of that day was imprinted on his mind in merciless detail.

The normal practice had been for his mother to meet Tracy from school, while he and his friends dawdled their way home via the sweet shop, swapping marbles and discussing the local football team. It was the best part of his day, a brief interlude of freedom between the rigours of school and obligatory homework. But that afternoon his mother had a job interview, and he'd been charged with escorting Tracy home.

It had put him in a bad mood all day, earning him a detention at break, and when the final bell rang and his friends gathered in the playground he slouched over to join them. Then Tracy had come skipping up, her plaits coming unwound as usual and a graze on her knee.

'What's *she* want?' Dave Forrester had asked.

And he'd replied, 'Dunno. Go home, Tracy.'

Her face had fallen. 'Mum said you were taking me.'

'You're not a baby!' Dave had jeered. 'Don't you know where you live?'

Tracy's lip quivered. 'I'm not allowed to cross the main road by myself.'

The others were losing patience. 'Come on, Al, tell her to get lost!'

And, to his lifelong regret, he'd succumbed. 'You'll be OK if you look both ways,' he'd told her gruffly, and had gone off with his pals leaving her staring after him with tear-filled eyes.

That was the last time he'd seen her. Agonizingly he fast-forwarded the rest of that day – the frantic questions from his parents, the neighbours' and then the police searches, and finally the discovery of her small limp body, a knife wound in her chest.

Alan drew a deep, shuddering breath. For no obvious reason, as sometimes happened, the traffic jam suddenly eased and the cars in front of him began to move again. With his eyes full of tears, he continued his journey home.

THREE

Catherine Parish looked a little despairingly at her husband, still seated at the breakfast table behind his newspaper.

'Any plans for today?' she asked brightly.

'Nothing special, my love,' he answered without looking up. 'I'm entirely at your disposal.'

And that was the trouble, she thought, carrying the dishes through to the kitchen and slotting them into the dishwasher. Much as she loved him, after fifteen years of widowhood she was used to having her own space. And to her distress she found herself half-wishing the status quo of the last two years had continued – when they'd met frequently, and frequently made love, but she had still been free to follow the pursuits that interested her before, returning at the end of the day to the quiet solitude of her bungalow.

But, bless his heart, Tom seemed to assume that now they were married they'd spend all their time together and, though she hated herself for it, she was beginning to feel suffocated. It was essential to find a remedy before that feeling led to resentment, and she'd spent the last week mulling over possibilities.

The best solution, she'd decided, was to suggest that Tom, a retired bank manager whose only outside interest appeared to be golf, should embark on some project that would absorb his time and energies before he, too, began to feel disillusioned. For that matter, she could do with one herself.

She walked to the window and stood looking out at the garden. Crocuses and daffodils provided splashes of gold, purple and pink along the borders and new green spikes were beginning to appear. It would be exciting, this first spring in the house, to see what came up and perhaps plan a new layout. But she couldn't spend all her time in the garden, and as she began reviewing possible activities an idea suddenly came to her.

While at St Stephen's Primary in Buckford she'd initiated a project for ten-year-olds that had involved compiling, in scrapbook form, a record of the school over the last hundred years with, on opposite pages, a list of events that had taken place worldwide on the same dates. She had become so intrigued by it that she'd set to work producing a fully researched history, and this had been so well received that she was persuaded to undertake the same for the renowned Buckford College and, following that, the local grammar school. What she didn't know about educational development over the last century, she thought humorously, was negligible.

So how would the authorities in Marsborough react if she suggested doing the same for the schools in this area? Remembering how totally immersed she'd been in her research, the prospect of resurrecting that passion was invigorating. If permission were granted, it would certainly fit the bill for her – but what about Tom?

Why not, she thought suddenly, suggest something similar for him? A history not of the branch where he'd spent most of his working life but of the National Banking Group, when it was established and how its fortunes had fluctuated through economic growth and recession up to the present day?

She hurried back to the dining room, seated herself opposite him and, leaning forward, gently lowered his newspaper with one finger.

'Tom . . .' she began.

Rona spent that morning rereading Nicole's website and flicking through the cookery pages of the latest *Chiltern Life*, hoping that her abysmal lack of knowledge on the subject would not be too apparent when she sat in on the class later. It was only as she logged off to prepare an early lunch that she caught sight of the handwritten letter on top of her in-tray and realized she'd not replied to Phyllis Ward.

The printed letterhead did not provide an email address so would necessitate either a phone call or letter. To gain extra time for her article on Nicole, she opted for the latter. She'd write it when she returned this afternoon.

'Sorry, boy,' she told Gus when he greeted her, tail wagging, as she came downstairs. 'That early walk will have to last you till I get back, but I promise we'll go up to the park then.'

Though she took the dog with her on some of her trips, the two-hour cookery class was too long to leave him in the car and he'd be more comfortable at home. An option would have been to take him to Max at the studio, but he had a sitting this afternoon and the distraction would not be welcome. Gus would have to make do with his basket till she returned.

It was a beautiful spring day, and Rona's spirits rose as she turned off the main Marsborough to Buckford road on to the more rural one leading to Woodbourne. She was anxious now to complete the magazine series and turn her attention to the engrossing prospect of another biography. She'd not had a chance even to open the suitcase Mrs Page had given her and was eager to discover why the TV interviews had caused Russell such concern. Had his unexpected visit to his old school been connected with them? It was hard to see how.

Resolutely she turned her thoughts back to Nicole, and Barnie's comment that despite her readiness to publicize her work nothing of her personal life had emerged. Which could prove a drawback for the article. The whole point of the series had been to portray how these single women had faced up to their new state, the battles they'd fought to overcome feelings of rejection or loss and the positive results that had been achieved. She mustn't let the article turn into just another advertisement for the cookery school. Perhaps, she thought hopefully, after the class there would be an opportunity to enlarge on Friday's interview.

Her musings had brought her to Norse Crescent, and this time there was a blue Toyota in the driveway of number fourteen. Rona pulled in alongside it, locked her own car and went to ring the doorbell. It was exactly one thirty.

A couple of cars went past behind her, and somewhere close by a dog barked. The front door remained closed. Rona frowned slightly and glanced again at her watch. Surely Nicole would be ready to leave? Perhaps she'd not heard the bell, though in the open-plan house it should be audible anywhere. She rang again, pressing it for a little longer.

When there was still no response, she moved sideways to look through the window. The hall and sitting room stretched away, but there was no sign of life. In a moment of panic, Rona wondered if she was late. Had Nicole said one o'clock and, giving up waiting for her, gone on ahead? But that must be her car in the drive, since she was the only occupant.

Perhaps the bell was out of order? She lifted the brass knocker and let it fall three times, confident this would bring a response. It didn't, and she stepped back a few paces, looking up at the first-floor windows. One was open, a flimsy curtain fluttering in the slight breeze.

Slightly concerned now, Rona looked about her. A path at the side of the house led to a wooden gate and, finding it unlocked, she pushed it open and walked through into the back garden. It was small and neat, fenced on three sides, with a child's swing at the far end. There was a patio outside the house, and glass doors that presumably led into the kitchen.

Feeling a little like Peeping Tom, Rona walked over to them. Shading her eyes to deflect reflection, she peered inside – and gasped in consternation. Nicole was lying face down on the floor, one arm flung out. Rona rapped sharply on the glass, but could discern no movement in response.

With trembling fingers she fumbled in her bag for her mobile, tapped out 999, and requested an ambulance. 'Please ask them to hurry,' she added when she'd given the address. 'I don't know how long she's been unconscious.'

With the assurance that help would soon be at hand, Rona knocked on the glass again, still hoping to rouse Nicole, but again without success. She turned away distractedly, at a loss what to do. The students would be on their way to the Community Centre, but she'd no way of letting them know there'd be no class today.

After another despairing glance at the prone figure, she hurried back to the front of the house to await the ambulance, whose siren she could now hear approaching.

Rona stared at the paramedics in disbelief. 'But you *have* to break in! Suppose she's had a stroke or a heart attack? Surely time is crucial?'

They shook their heads. 'Sorry. It's frustrating for us too, but we have to wait for the police. Strict orders.'

'But goodness knows when they'll get here!'

'They won't be long, love,' said the male attendant soothingly. 'Member of the family, are you?'

'No, I only met her last week, but that's hardly the point! She's in urgent need of help, you must see that!'

She became aware of another siren in the distance, growing

progressively louder, and slowly released her breath. Thank God! Now at last they could do what was necessary.

The woman attendant had gone to meet them and came hurrying back with two uniformed police officers. Having checked there was no other means of gaining entry, the decision was taken to break the small side window and everyone stood back as the glass was shattered. A wad of material was positioned to provide protection and, given a leg up by her colleague, the woman officer wriggled her way inside. Seconds later she slid back the glass door and the paramedics hurried in, followed by the other officer.

Rona, under strict orders to remain outside, watched with quickened heartbeat as they bent over the inert figure and from their body language realized with a sickening lurch of her stomach that help had come too late. She'd *told* them, she thought frantically, instinctively taking a step forward. But her way was swiftly barred. Someone had moved to screen her from the figure on the floor, but not before she'd seen the pool of blood.

She raised horrified eyes. 'Is she . . .?' and received a sombre nod in reply. Then both paramedics were ushered outside as the senior police officer took out his phone and began speaking rapidly into it.

Rona put out a hand to steady herself, and felt someone take her arm. It was the female paramedic. 'Come and sit down for a while, love. You've had a shock. I'm Daisy and this is Joe. What's your name?'

'Rona.' The word came out in a whisper. She allowed herself to be led back past the two cars to an ambulance that waited with its rear door open in preparation for the unneeded stretcher Joe was carrying.

Daisy helped her into it and seated her on one of the bunks that lined the walls. Rona found she was shaking uncontrollably. This couldn't be happening – it just couldn't – not again! But even in her shocked state she'd known that the blood hadn't come from any natural haemorrhaging.

'Now darling,' Daisy was saying encouragingly, 'take a drink of this. It will help to steady you.'

A polystyrene cup was put into her hand and she obediently sipped the cold water. She was still holding it when the female police officer appeared at the open door and, nodding at the paramedics, turned to Rona.

'I'm PC Lesley Johnson,' she said by way of introduction. 'Do you feel able to answer a few questions, ma'am?'

Rona nodded. 'Though I can't tell you much, I'm afraid.'

'Let's start with your name and address, and the name of the person you were visiting.'

Those at least she could supply, and also the reason for her own presence. However, having unfortunately been in a similar position before, she was well aware that she was a possible suspect herself until she could prove otherwise.

'Are you aware of Ms Summers' next of kin, Ms Parish?'

Rona stared at her blankly. God! She'd been worrying about the cookery class, without any thought of those who'd be most affected. 'She's divorced, but she has an eight-year-old daughter.'

'Any idea which school she attends?'

'No, only that it's local.'

'And her ex-husband?'

Rona moistened her lips. 'Patrick Summers. He lives in Marsborough now. You should be able to contact him at the Sedgwick Hotel.'

PC Johnson nodded and returned to the house, presumably to report her findings. Minutes later she was back.

'Is one of those cars yours, Ms Parish?'

'Yes, the Audi.'

'Do you feel up to driving it?'

Beside her Daisy made a quick movement and the policewoman raised a hand in acknowledgment. 'We'd like you to come to the station to make a statement, but I'll drive you there if you'd prefer it.'

'I think I would,' Rona acknowledged.

During the last few minutes she'd been aware of more cars drawing up, but the solid sides of the ambulance prevented her from seeing outside. Reluctantly she stepped out of its protective shell, thanked the attendants for their care of her, and slid into the passenger seat of her own car to be driven to Woodbourne police station.

An hour and a half later, and with two calming cups of tea inside her, Rona insisted that she was capable of driving back to Marsborough. The police had, of course, been uncommunicative about the cause of death, but as she left the house she'd seen the yellow tape being put in place and knew it was regarded as a crime scene. Somehow, in either her private or her professional life, Nicole Summers had made a dangerous enemy.

As she drove home, more slowly than she would normally have done, Rona's chaotic thoughts veered from Nicole herself to her daughter and to Patrick, who was a friend of Steve's. Would Venetia now live with her father? Who would break the news of her mother's death? And – frightening thought – how long before her own arrival had Nicole been killed? Suppose she'd arrived while the murderer was still in the house?

She shuddered, pushing away the thought. But – a point she'd not considered before – how had he or she got in? As she had reason to know, all the doors and ground-floor windows had been securely locked. Had Nicole herself admitted her killer? It was another thought to shy away from, and she was relieved to see she was now approaching Marsborough.

Rona frequently didn't use the car for weeks on end and, as the Georgian houses in Lightbourne Avenue had no garages and on-street parking was a nightmare, she rented a garage in the next road. Still partly on autopilot, she drove into it, locked up and, on slightly shaky legs, walked home.

Her key was still in the lock when Gus's nose inched impatiently round the door, and she remembered her promise of a walk in the park. She edged into the house, pushing back the excited dog with one foot, and closed the door behind her. Yes, he'd need a walk, but first she needed to speak to Max. And, she supposed, to Barnie.

The clock in the hall was showing four forty-five, exactly four hours since she'd blithely set out to attend the cookery class. She wondered if the students had had access to the Community Centre and how long they'd waited before dispersing and going home. They'd learn soon enough what had happened to their instructor.

She went down the basement stairs to the kitchen, Gus nearly tripping her up on every step. 'Soon,' she told him, and by way of apology dropped a couple of the treats she kept as rewards into his dish. Then, picking up the phone, she seated herself at the kitchen table and braced herself for her husband's reaction to her news.

'Max?'

'Hello, love. Good timing, my sitter has just left.'

She'd forgotten all about the sitter.

'Well,' he continued, 'are you sufficiently inspired to cook me a three-course meal tomorrow?'

'I never got to the class, Max,' she said sombrely. 'Nor did Nicole.' And she told him how she'd spent the afternoon.

When she came to the end, there was a moment's disbelieving silence. Then he said explosively, 'My God, Rona, how do you *do* it? Every bloody time—'

'If you shout at me,' she said carefully, 'I might burst into tears.'

Immediately he was contrite. 'Darling, I'm sorry. Of course you've had a tremendous shock. Look, I'll come home.'

She closed her eyes on a wave of relief but made a token protest. 'There's no need—'

'There's every need. I'll be back in twenty minutes.'

'Gus needs a walk.'

'We'll take him together. In the meantime, pour yourself a brandy or something.'

'Max, it's only five o'clock!'

'Medicinal. I'm on my way.' And he rang off.

In fact, with Max at her side and Gus running joyously ahead, as so often in the past the park proved a welcome catharsis. Its stretching slopes above the town provided a sense of space, of being beyond the reach of the trials and tribulations of daily living, and in consequence gave her a clearer perspective.

They stopped at their usual spot, the wind blowing her hair as they stood gazing across the roofs and steeples of the town.

'Will you look for another subject?' Max asked, breaking several minutes' silence.

Rona shook her head. 'I arranged with Barnie that this would be the last, and that if Nicole didn't consent to it we'd just end the series.'

'So you're free to get down to the bio.'

'I suppose so. It's odd, Max, I hardly knew her and, to be honest, didn't particularly like her, but she was an interesting character and I was looking forward to trying to discover what made her tick. Now, we'll never know.'

'I wonder who the hell killed her.'

Rona shivered. 'I hope they find out soon, and let me off the hook.'

'They can't seriously suspect you.'

'Max, they suspect *everyone*! Often the person who reports a crime proves to be the one who committed it. Come to that, my fingerprints will be in the house from my visit on Friday.'

'But you told the police about that?'

'Of course I did.'

'Then I'm sure you've nothing to worry about.' He tucked her arm through his. 'Come on, home beckons. It's starting to get chilly. And since this is an extra home visit, instead of digging in the freezer for something to cook, I think we should go to Dino's.'

Dino's was an Italian restaurant five minutes' walk from their home. She and Max were regular customers, and Rona frequently went there alone when he was teaching and the prospect of a salad or takeaway had lost its appeal.

'That would be good,' she said.

To Rona's relief there'd been only the briefest mention on the news that evening and the dead woman hadn't been named, so after a good meal and some restorative lovemaking she slept better than she'd dared hope. Only when she stirred, around seven, did the horrendous memories of the previous day resurface. She thought again of the eight-year-old daughter and wondered if Nicole's parents were alive and whether she'd had siblings, and was again frustrated by how little she knew of her.

She had not after all felt up to contacting Barnie the previous evening. As soon as Max left for the studio she went up to her study and reluctantly picked up the phone, wondering if the news had already reached him. From his breezy greeting it was obvious that it hadn't, and she broke in quickly.

'Barnie, I have some terrible news. Nicole Summers has been murdered.'

There was a stunned silence. Then he said, 'Come again?'

'She's been murdered, and – oh Barnie! – I was there. I'd gone to attend one of her cookery classes.'

'For God's sake, Rona, start at the beginning and tell me everything.'

So she did. As she came to an end, he said anxiously, 'But you're all right, aren't you? You weren't in any danger?'

'I don't think so, but it must have happened not long before I arrived.'

'My God! What was Max's reaction?'

'Much as you'd expect.'

Having satisfied himself she was unharmed, at least physically, his thoughts turned to Nicole. 'That poor girl! She'd so much to live for. What a terrible waste! But why the hell would anyone want to kill her? Was it a robbery gone wrong?'

'I suppose so, but I was shunted off pretty quickly so I don't know any details. There'll no doubt be more online.'

'I didn't hear or see the news this morning,' Barnie admitted. 'There was a minor panic because Mel's flight has been delayed and we couldn't find out when she's likely to land. In the end we gave up, and Dinah just set off for Heathrow. I hope she hasn't too long to wait.'

'Give Mel my love,' Rona said. 'And I hope things work out with Mitch.'

'Thanks.' He paused. 'At least you have the bio to help take your mind off things.'

Her mobile started to ring and Barnie, hearing it, said quickly, 'I'll sign off for now, but we'll talk again soon.'

The ID showed her twin was calling. 'Ro! Thank God you're OK!' Lindsey's voice was shaking. 'You said you were seeing Nicole yesterday. You didn't actually *go*, did you?'

Rona sighed, resigned to having to go through the whole thing again. 'I did, yes. In fact, I was the one who found her.'

'*My God!* You were actually in the *house*?'

'No, I saw her through the patio doors and phoned for help.'

'It said on the news she was stabbed. Could you tell that, from where you were?'

'No, I just saw her lying on the floor,' Rona replied, blotting from her mind the pool of blood she'd caught sight of later. 'How did you hear about it? From the news?'

'No, Samantha phoned me just now. We were supposed to be meeting for lunch, but she postponed it. She's in quite a state – the police are interviewing Patrick.'

'They questioned me too. But I shouldn't think he's got anything to worry about, being in Marsborough.'

'But he wasn't, that's the point! He went to see her yesterday.'

Rona drew in her breath. 'Did he, now?'

'Sam's out of her mind with worry.'

'I can imagine. Linz, do you know what's happened to their little girl? Is she with Patrick?'

'No, she's gone to his parents. She's very close to them, Sam says, though they didn't get on with Nicole.'

'What about *her* parents?'

'I've no idea, I've never heard them mentioned.' Lindsey paused. 'But are you OK, Ro? Really?'

'It was a shock, of course, and I'm desperately sorry for her, but I'd have felt much worse if I'd *known* her. This time last week, remember, we'd not even met.'

'Don't I know it! I brought all this on you and I wish to heaven I'd never mentioned her.'

'It's hardly your fault, Linz.'

'It certainly feels like it. Did the police give you much of a grilling?'

'They asked a lot of questions I couldn't answer, which didn't go down too well. They said they'll be in touch.'

'Have you heard from the parents?'

'No. That's one thing to be thankful for – neither of them know I'd any connection with Nicole.'

'Well, as you say, be thankful for small mercies. I'll let you know if I hear any more at this end.'

'Thanks, Linz. See you soon.'

No sooner had Rona put down the phone than it rang again, and her heart sank as she recognized the voice of her friend Tess Chadwick, who worked on the *Stokely Gazette*.

'Rona, hi!' she began breezily. 'I see this dead woman in Woodbourne was a *Chiltern Life* journalist.'

Trust Tess to be one of the first to pick up the news – she'd a nose like a bloodhound's. 'What woman would that be, Tess?' she asked, but without hope.

'Ah-ha! Such dissemblance leads me to suspect you know more than you're letting on. Come on – you work on the same mag, you *must* have known her.'

'Actually we'd never met till last week. I was going to do an article on her.'

Tess pounced. 'You saw her last week? Well, well! You really are the kiss of death, aren't you? You'll be telling me next that you found the body!'

Rona drew in her breath, and before she could formulate a reply Tess said softly, 'My God! You did, didn't you? How do you *do* it, Rona?'

'If you mention that to a soul,' Rona said with emphasis, 'I shall strangle you with my bare hands.'

'OK, OK. But at least give me some gen on her. We can just quote you as "a source".'

'I hadn't time to get any, Tess. Honestly. I should have gone to her class with her that afternoon – that's why I was there.'

'Well, at least tell me what she was like.'

'Pretty unforthcoming, actually. She was happy to talk about her work, but not her personal life.'

'She must have said *something.*'

'No, she didn't. Truly. I was as frustrated as you are, but I'd hoped to get more. Now, of course, I won't. I'm sorry, Tess.'

'Well, if you find out anything . . .'

'I know, I know.'

Rona switched off the phone and was turning away when she caught sight of the handwritten letter in her in-tray. Phyllis Ward! Someone else she should have contacted. Well, there was no need now to employ delaying tactics – in fact the sooner she saw her the sooner she could bury herself in her new project.

She lifted the phone again.

By that evening the news of Nicole's death had become widespread and on the six o'clock bulletin a reporter positioned outside her house ran through such facts as had been established, the yellow tape gleaming in the sunshine behind him. Two women who'd attended the cookery school were interviewed and expressed their shock and horror at the news.

'We were supposed to be having a class,' one said tearfully, 'and we couldn't think why she didn't come or answer her mobile. We waited nearly an hour before giving up and going home. I just can't believe what's happened – it doesn't make sense!'

Rona was watching the report when Max returned for his Wednesday night at home. He came to join her, and put an arm around her.

'Any further developments?'

'Not on the news, but Linz phoned and said her husband was being questioned. Apparently he visited Nicole yesterday.'

'Ah, well, that figures. The husband's always the prime suspect.' A photograph appeared on the screen, the one from Nicole's web page. 'Good-looking woman,' he added. Then the scene switched to the anchor in the studio, and Rona pressed the remote to turn it off.

Max glanced at her face. 'There's nothing you can do, love. Try to put it behind you and concentrate on this bio project.'

Rona sighed. 'Sound advice, but not easy to follow. I did ring Mrs Ward, but unfortunately she can't see me till Friday. Still, with all this happening I've not so much as opened the suitcase I brought back from Merefield. I can go through that to prepare for meeting her.'

'Good thinking,' Max said. 'So let's go downstairs and I'll pour us a drink before I start on supper.'

FOUR

'You were very restless last night, my love,' Max remarked over breakfast.

Rona sighed, brushing a hand over her eyes. 'Sorry, I kept dreaming about Nicole – odd, disjointed dreams that didn't make sense, and every time I woke I remembered she was dead.'

'Just as well you've something else to occupy you, then,' he observed.

'The trouble is the last thing I feel like doing is wading through Russell's mixed-up handwritten notes to learn what he found out about Ward.'

'Come on now, you've been wanting to write another bio,' Max rallied her. 'What's more, you've been handed an interesting subject on a plate and there's nothing to stop you getting down to it.'

He was right, of course, but his logic did little to lighten her mood. After he'd left, she vacuumed the kitchen floor and put an extra load in the washing machine. Then, when she could delay no longer, she went up to the study and the unopened suitcase that awaited her.

As a preliminary, though, she first went online to check Ward's CV and was disconcerted by the breadth of it. Among a variety of other undertakings, he'd played both cricket and rugby at international level, spent several years as a foreign correspondent, and lectured on economics at a well-known university. A man of many parts, it seemed, which made her task even more daunting. She could only hope Russell Page had indeed done most of the groundwork, as Prue had assured her.

It was with some trepidation that she finally turned to the suitcase, and her heart sank still further as she viewed its contents. It was packed full of bulging files, sheets of loose paper, memory sticks, ballpoint pens and tubes of correction fluid. She guessed that Esmé had simply cleared her husband's desk and bundled everything she could see into the case, with no semblance of order.

Nestling among the clutter were the promised DVDs, and they at least appeared well-organized, possibly thanks to Ward himself. They were in groups of six, each series held together by an elastic band and labelled with the year in which it had been broadcast, the earliest dated 2002, the last 2007, the year of his death.

Intrigued, Rona flicked through one set after another, thankfully noting that each disc was marked with the date of transmission and the name of the interviewee. And an imposing group they were. Members of Parliament, stage and screen stars, authors, business magnates and captains of industry had all been subjected to the needle-sharp questioning for which Ward was famous, and not a few had fallen at the first fence. One actress, she remembered, had stormed off the set mid-interview, and others had been reduced to tears.

As she came to the final set, she felt a quickening of interest. All the other series had been arranged in date order, but the disc that lay on top here was the interview labelled #4. Why? Was this the one that had caused Russell sleepless nights?

The subject, she saw, was Bruce Sedgwick – a name she'd already heard this week – and she wondered if he'd any connection with the hotel chain for which Patrick Summers worked. In any event it should be interesting, and she resolved to watch it as soon as she'd had a quick glance through the rest of the contents.

It was the pages of handwritten notes that she took out first, intrigued by the pointed, spidery writing with idiosyncratic doodles in the margins. The half-formed thoughts and jottings gave a revealing insight into the character of the author, who as she flicked through them struck her as both meticulous and impatient – qualities not always compatible. The pages were full of crossings-out and stars where insertions were slotted in, and notes to follow up certain lines which she would need to look into herself.

All in all, it was clear that taking over a book someone else had worked on was more of a hindrance than the help Prue had intimated. Russell Page's methods were not hers, and she'd need to go through everything he'd written and sort it out subject by subject before she could transmute it into her own words and style.

The telephone on her desk shrilled and the screen identified the caller as 'Magda'. Rona reached for it with a sigh of relief. Magda Ridgeway, a friend from schooldays, was the owner of a group of boutiques around the county much frequented by the great and the good of Buckfordshire and beyond, and by not a few from London.

'Magda! How are you?'

'Positively blooming,' Magda replied. 'How about you?'

'Wilting!' Rona replied with a laugh. 'I've been handed a poisoned chalice and I'm not sure of the best way to handle it.'

'Sounds interesting. How about telling me about it over lunch?'

'That would be great, Mags. I need to come up for air.'

'Well, I'm at the Marsborough shop today, so shall we say twelve thirty at The Gallery?'

'Perfect. See you there.'

Ending the call, Rona glanced at her watch. It was already eleven thirty; she'd just time to watch the DVD before going to meet her. Abandoning the morass of papers strewn all over her desk and the surrounding area, she went downstairs and slipped the disc into the machine. She'd seen several of the Gideon Ward interviews in the past – maybe even this one without particularly registering it – but the man had been dead for nine years and her memory of them was hazy.

She settled on the sofa and Gus, having heard her come down, padded in and settled at her feet. And there on the screen was the bearded, wild-haired figure she remembered, complete with the horn-rimmed spectacles and plaid sports jacket for which he'd been famous.

'My guest this evening,' he began in his deep, throaty voice, 'is Bruce Sedgwick, newly arrived from Australia to take over his late uncle's chain of luxury hotels.'

So it *was* the same Sedgwick. Rona wondered how he felt about one of his managers being a suspect in a murder case. She studied him with interest. Considerably younger than Ward – early forties at a guess – he was fair-haired and tanned, lounging back in his chair in a blue open-neck shirt that matched his eyes and to all appearances the genial, laid-back Aussie. But Rona, noting the tightness of his jaw and the guarded expression in those startlingly blue eyes, was not fooled.

'So, Mr Sedgwick,' Ward went on, with sarcastic formality, 'I hear this legacy came to you out of the blue. How so?'

Sedgwick laughed a little nervously. 'Yeah, I guess I buck the trend,' he replied, his voice a lazy drawl. 'Most folks over here have a rich uncle in Australia. For me, it was the other way around.'

'So how did your family come to be living half a world apart?'

'My dad emigrated to Oz in his twenties,' Sedgwick replied, 'preferring open spaces to sitting behind a desk – while his brother, my Uncle Jason, was the little piggy who stayed home. Dad got work on a sheep station and eventually met my ma. They were together a couple of years, and when they split she left me behind.'

'Hardly a maternal gesture,' Ward observed drily. 'Did she make contact later?'

Sedgwick shook his head. 'She was a no-strings gal. Didn't miss her, though. Dad and me got along just fine. Meanwhile, back home in the UK, Uncle Jason was making a name for himself as a TV chef. We'd get a Christmas update each year telling how many Michelin stars he'd collected as he progressed from owning a Mayfair restaurant to taking over first one and then a succession of hotels.'

'You and your father never considered returning to your roots?'

'Not for a minute. Uncle wrote once, years ago, asking if I'd go back with a view to taking over from him in due course. Him and his wife had no kids and he'd have liked the family connection to continue, but it didn't appeal. Then my aunt died a couple of years ago, so I guess he'd no one else to leave things to.'

'Your father's not still alive?'

'No, Dad copped it last year, only months before Uncle and also from a stroke. Genetic weakness, maybe. I'll have to watch it!'

'Did you ever tie the knot yourself?'

'Tried it once. Didn't last, and no kids. We're not a prolific family and I'm the last of the line.'

Ward took a long, slow drink from the glass of water in front of him. This was another trademark, a ploy to keep the interviewee waiting, wondering what would follow. Bruce Sedgwick was patently uncomfortable. He tapped the arm of his chair, shifted uneasily, and looked up at the ceiling.

'So, how does it feel to inherit a clutch of luxury hotels?' Ward continued then. 'Bit different from sheep farming?'

'Oh, that was the old man, mate. Me, I just bummed around turning my hand to anything going and ended up on a construction site in Alice. Yeah, it's different all right, but frankly I was just as happy being the wild Colonial boy. It's not as if I'm needed here – the hotels run themselves – but the will stipulated I live in the UK, so here I am, a kind of figurehead, I guess.'

Ward sat back, regarding him over steepled fingers. 'The hotels were, of course, only part of your uncle's estate. Your inheritance includes a couple of racehorses, I believe, not to mention his country home, Sedgwick Hall, which is open to the public. And since in his later years he was a noted art collector, you must have some very valuable paintings.'

'Oh sure, it's like the National Gallery. Trouble is they're all modern art – garish reds, greens and oranges that hit you right between the eyes. Can't be doing with them myself! Give me a decent landscape any day, something I can relate to.'

The interview was coming to a close. Ward had been less caustic than usual, relying on his tone of voice to needle his guest, and for the life of her Rona couldn't see what had caught Page's interest. She'd armed herself with a notebook and pencil to jot down anything she wanted to replay or look into, but it lay unopened in her lap. Was it, after all, pure coincidence that this DVD had been at the top of the pile?

Somewhat deflated, she switched off the set and stood up, stretching. Gus raised his head hopefully and she nodded. 'Yes, we're going to The Gallery for lunch,' she told him. Since he behaved impeccably and remained under the table, the cafés and wine bars of Marsborough condoned his presence. It would do them both good to get out of the house for a while.

It was a lovely spring day, and Rona's spirits rose as she and Gus set off. The trees lining Lightbourne Avenue and the lower end of Fullers Walk were in full leaf, with that lovely young green of new growth. As they neared Guild Street and the residential houses gave way to shops, she saw that the florist had set out stands of flowers to tempt passers-by, while a smell of newly-baked bread from the baker's next door awakened her appetite.

She rounded the corner into Guild Street, glancing into the windows of Willows' Fine Furniture as she passed. The firm had featured in one of her articles on local family businesses, and she hoped the various crises that had beset the family had by now been happily resolved. Alongside the main entrance to the store was the black iron staircase leading up to The Gallery café.

The walkway above housed several specialist shops, among them a delicatessen, a gift shop and one selling rare books. But The Gallery held pride of place since, like the furniture store below, it rounded the corner from Guild Street to Fullers Walk, thus offering its patrons a choice of view. Rona seated herself at a window table, settled Gus beneath it, and picked up the menu.

'What a gorgeous day!' Magda exclaimed, flopping into the chair opposite.

'Isn't it?' Rona agreed. 'I hadn't noticed till I came out, too busy poring over documents and old DVDs.'

Magda indicated the menu. 'Have you decided what you're having?'

'Cheese soufflé and a side salad. How about you?'

'The spring air's made me hungry. I think I'll go for the fish and chips. They use a lovely beer batter here.'

'Goodness! If I had that at lunchtime, I'd never get any work done.'

'Ah, but your work is more cerebral than mine!' Magda said smugly.

Rona raised her eyebrows. 'You're very chirpy today.'

'I told you I was blooming.' She looked up as the waitress arrived at their table, then, their order having been given, turned back to Rona.

'So, tell me about this poisoned chalice.'

Resignedly Rona did so, starting with the summons from Prue and taking in her visit to Esmé Page. 'I've just been watching Ward's interview with Bruce Sedgwick,' she ended. 'It looked as though Page might have found that particular one interesting, but I can't imagine why.'

'Bruce Sedgwick,' Magda mused, buttering the roll on her side plate. 'I met him at the opening of the new hotel.'

'Did you?' Rona lent forward interestedly. 'What's he like? Has he become anglicized over the years?'

Magda gave a short laugh. 'Quite the reverse! I think he deliberately lays on the strine!'

Rona smiled. 'Did you like him?'

'We only exchanged a couple of words. He was OK, though he rather fancies himself as a ladies' man – all that antipodean charm.'

'*Is* there a woman in his life?' Rona asked. 'He told Gideon Ward he was divorced.'

'According to gossip there are always glamorous ladies hanging around – he's as rich as Croesus, remember – but so far he's managed to hold them at bay.'

'I'll have to meet him and try to discover why Page thought him important. Lindsey's latest admirer knows the hotel manager, which might help.'

'Patrick Summers? Yes, I met him too. What a terrible thing about his ex-wife! It said in the press she worked for *Chiltern Life*. Did you know her?'

Rona sighed. 'I suppose I'll have to come clean,' she said, and explained her brief connection with Nicole.

Magda's eyes widened in horror. 'Oh, you poor love! What a ghastly thing to happen! Are you OK?'

'More OK than she is,' Rona said grimly. 'But I keep waking in the night and seeing her lying there.' She gave a little shudder. 'What makes it worse is that I probably only missed the murderer by minutes – or there might have been two of us!'

'For God's sake, Rona!' Magda exclaimed.

'Sorry, but it's true.'

'What possible motive could anyone have had? Was it a bungled burglary?'

'There was no forced entry and it was broad daylight, so I'd say that's unlikely. It's her daughter I'm worried about, that poor little eight-year-old having her whole world turned upside down.'

Magda nodded soberly. 'It hardly bears thinking about.'

Their food arrived and Rona took the chance to change the subject. 'Anyway, that's quite enough about me. What have you been up to? It's quite a while since I saw you.'

Magda didn't reply at once and, glancing across at her, Rona saw a smile spreading over her face.

'What?' she demanded.

Magda looked up. 'I do have some news, as it happens. That's one reason I wanted to see you.'

'So? What is it?'

Magda took a deep breath. 'I'm pregnant!' she said.

Rona laid down her fork and stared at her. 'You're not serious?'

'Oh, but I am. Twelve weeks. We were keeping it quiet till now because things can go wrong in the first three months. It's due in October.' She paused. 'Well, aren't you going to congratulate me or something?'

'Yes, of course, if that's what you want.'

Magda burst out laughing. 'Of course it's what we want! We've been talking about it for ages and decided it was time to do something about it.'

Rona was having trouble assimilating the news. It had simply never occurred to her that the Ridgeways would start a family. 'Then I'm delighted for you both.' She paused. 'Will you go on working?'

'Try to stop me! I might take a week or two off immediately afterwards, but then little one will come everywhere with me, like Mary's little lamb, and I'll park its car seat in one of the changing rooms. Gavin's like a dog with two tails!' she added.

Gavin, to whom Rona had been on the point of becoming engaged when she met Max.

She forced a smile. 'I suppose I'd better start knitting!' she said.

As she walked briskly home, Rona admitted to herself that she was upset by Magda's news. They'd been close friends for most of their lives, but a baby was sure to change things and, selfishly, she resented that. Magda wouldn't any longer be able to phone her at the last minute to suggest a cinema or theatre trip. There would be babysitters to arrange, feeding timetables to consider. And their lunches together – if they continued – would be dominated by talk of the baby's progress as it slept in its car seat beside them.

'Oh, *damn!*' she said aloud.

Having decided to look into the possibility of researching local schools, Catherine had faced a dilemma: whereas Buckford Grammar was co-educational, here secondary education was split between the High School for Girls and Marsborough Grammar for boys. With luck she might be asked to do both, but since Rona and Lindsey had attended the High School she elected to start there and made an appointment to call in the following week.

Tom, on the other hand, had been unimpressed with her suggestion that he embark on something similar. 'I thought retirement meant a life of leisure,' he'd protested. 'Now you're saying I should bury myself in papers again!'

'It'll keep your brain active,' Catherine had told him brightly. 'Be a love and at least give it a try.' Allegedly he was thinking it over but that morning, after some searching, she'd unearthed the records of the three Buckford schools, still in a packing case following her move from the bungalow, and after lunch she settled on the sofa and turned to the children's presentation of the story of St Stephen's.

She glanced across at Tom, who was flicking through a car magazine. 'It was through this that I first met Rona,' she said. 'Do you remember, she was writing the history of Buckford for its eight-hundredth anniversary and needed a section on the development of education? Gordon Breen, the vicar, told her I'd run this project and she contacted me.'

'God yes, I remember now. And when she mentioned your name over dinner, I told her you had an account with us.'

Catherine smiled at him fondly. 'And the rest, as they say, is history. But this really *is* history.'

She turned back to the book on her lap. A copy of the original, it was in the form of a scrapbook, with all the uneven writing, lopsided drawings and remnants of dried glue faithfully reproduced, and as she went through it a wealth of memories assaulted her.

Here was the poem Poppy Williams had written about school in Victorian times, alongside a sepia photo of a little girl in a pinafore and a boy in winged collar. And on the page opposite, in her own copperplate, were brief accounts of what was happening in the world at large – the passing of the Trade Union Act, the publication of George Eliot's *Middlemarch,* the foundation of the Rugby Union – a layout that was followed throughout the book. As well as world history, there were sections on health issues during the various periods and, more light-heartedly, hobbies and changing fashions.

Newspaper cuttings, yellow even in reproduction, advertised a variety of objects from carpet sweepers to leghorn hats, and a 'Ladies' Help' agency offered parlour maids of the highest diligence and respectability.

As she turned the pages, progressing through the decades, Catherine thought fondly of the children who had worked on them, remembering their enthusiasm and pride in the finished product. It was odd to think most of them would now be parents themselves. Then, turning another page, she came to an abrupt halt, coldness washing over her as she stared fixedly down at the photograph confronting her.

She must have made some sound, because Tom looked up. 'Anything wrong?' he asked. And, more sharply when she didn't reply, 'Catherine?'

She drew a trembling breath, still focused on the bright little face beneath a mop cap. 'It's just that I've come across a photo of Tracy Palmer,' she said unsteadily. 'A little girl who . . . died.'

Tom came to lean over her shoulder, looking down at the book. 'How very sad – she looks such a happy little thing, with her life before her. What happened to her?'

'She was murdered, Tom,' Catherine said in a low voice. 'On her way home from school.'

He exclaimed in horror. 'God, how awful! Was she molested in some way?'

'Thankfully no, she was at least spared that.' She drew a deep, convulsive breath and snapped the book shut, pressing her hands down on the cover.

'So what—?'

'Please, Tom, I don't want to talk about it.'

'But darling—'

'Please!' Her voice rose.

'All right.' He straightened, looking at her worriedly. 'Is there anything I can get you? A glass of water? Brandy?'

She gave a choked laugh. 'A cup of coffee would do wonders. We didn't have any after lunch.'

'But—'

'Just coffee will be fine, Tom.' Her voice was steadier now and he turned obediently and went to the kitchen to make it. When he returned, she took the mug from him with a smile.

'Sorry to be such a drama queen,' she said. 'You look at the past through rose-tinted glasses, don't you? Forgetting there were bad times as well as good. One of them caught me unawares, that's all.'

'You don't want to tell me what happened? It might exorcize the memory somehow.'

She shook her head, sipping at the hot coffee. 'When we've finished this, let's go for a drive somewhere. I won't do any more looking back today.'

'Fair enough. Where would you like to go?'

She smiled at him, and he saw that she was trying to reassure him, rather than the other way around. 'How about Penbury Court? We've not been there for a while.'

He returned her smile. That was the stately home in whose gardens he had asked her to marry him.

'An excellent idea!' he said.

Lindsey Parish sat alone in one of the booths in the Bacchus wine bar. Her morning appointment had overrun and she was snatching a late lunch before returning to the office, her thoughts, as always when alone, on Steve Hathaway.

They had now been seeing each other for several months, and she'd still no idea of the depth of his feelings for her. All her previous relationships had been based on physical attraction – and looking back, little else – that inevitably faded along with the initial passion. But she'd come to know Steve gradually, appreciating in the first instance his care and kindness when she sprained her ankle in town and he'd taken her back to his home, where she had been warmly welcomed not only by his father, Frank, but also by Luke, his twelve-year-old son. The downside of which was that she felt stuck in the role of family friend.

Their first dates had been meals at their house, evenings spent watching television with Frank or Luke, or outings that included the whole family. Steve knew of the string of affairs she'd embarked on since her divorce – she had blurted that out at their first meeting – and she, in turn, knew he was also divorced and had recently had an unhappy love affair during a spell in the States. It seemed, she thought impatiently, as though he was shielding them both from further hurt. His first kiss had come when she'd given up hope of receiving one and, like those that had followed, had been light and totally non-committal.

'Mind if I join you?'

She looked up with a start as Jonathan Hurst slid on to the seat opposite her. Had her thoughts of bad relationships conjured him up? she wondered fancifully. She and Jonathan, a fellow partner at Chase Mortimer, had a chequered history, having indulged in two abortive affairs, both of which she had ended. The last had caused a breach with his wife, but she gathered they were back together.

As though reading her thoughts, he gave her a twisted smile. 'It's all right, Lindsey, I'm not going to leap on you. As a matter of fact, I have some news you might find interesting.'

'Oh?' She was surprised at his amicable tone – he'd barely spoken to her for the last few months.

'In fact, you're one of the first to hear it.' He paused as a waiter brought over a plate of tapas and a half bottle of wine.

'I presume you won't join me?' Jonathan asked, glancing at Lindsey's water glass.

'No, thanks. So, what's this news?'

He took a drink of wine, swilling it round his mouth before setting down the glass. 'We're moving,' he said. 'I've applied for a transfer to the Brighton office. Carol and I talked it over and decided that if we were to make a fresh start we should begin it in new surroundings. It won't affect the kids as they're at boarding school.' Again the twisted smile. 'Well, say something. It must be a relief to know you won't have to keep avoiding me at the office!'

'Jonathan, I—'

He held up a hand. 'Joke, Lindsey,' he said succinctly.

She hesitated, not meeting his eyes. 'Did you ever tell Carol who you were involved with?'

'No, you can rest easy. She still insists she doesn't want to know.'

She looked up then. 'Well, I hope things work out for you. I'm sure new surroundings will help.'

He nodded and started on his tapas. 'We'll be having a farewell drinks party at the Sedgwick. I hope you'll come.'

'Oh, I'm not sure—'

'Look, to be frank it will seem odd if you don't. I'll be inviting all the partners and their . . . partners, so bring along this new fella of yours.'

'The Sedgwick rather than the Clarendon . . .' she commented, adroitly sidestepping. 'I wonder if that's a sign of the times?'

'The Clarendon's held sway as the premier hotel for aeons, but it'll have to look to its laurels now we have a new one. I thought it would be good to try it out.' He paused, looking at her consideringly. 'So you'll come? You'll get a formal invitation, of course.'

'Actually, Steve knows the manager,' Lindsey said. Then wished she hadn't, as Jonathan picked up on it at once.

'The bloke whose ex has been murdered? Hardly the kind of publicity they were hoping for! What's he like?'

'Very nice. I've met him a couple of times, but not since the . . . tragedy. How soon are you moving?'

'Can't wait to get rid of me? Don't answer that! Not for several weeks – there are a lot of loose ends to tie up. We sold the house straight away, which is a relief, but we still have to find a new one, so the contents will go into storage for a while.'

'Well, I hope you'll all be very happy.' Lindsey picked up her handbag. 'You'll have to excuse me, Jonathan. I must get back. Nice to have seen you,' she added automatically.

'Likewise, I'm sure,' he replied.

'You'll never guess what I heard today,' Rona said, when Max phoned her that evening.

'Then you'd better tell me.'

She took a deep breath. 'Magda's pregnant! The baby's due in October.'

She paused, waiting for a reaction as incredulous as her own. Instead there was a pause before he said quietly, 'Well, well!'

'Is that all you can say?' Rona demanded. 'It's Magda we're talking about, for God's sake!'

'I'm not really surprised, that's all. I thought they'd get round to it sooner or later.'

'Well, I certainly didn't! It was the last thing I expected.'

Max gave a half-laugh. 'You sound almost indignant!'

'I suppose I am. It will change everything.'

'Babies usually do, I believe, but usually for the better.' He paused, then went on, 'By the way, I had a call from Cynthia today. She's attending a reunion in London next week, and wonders if she could spend a night here on the way down and again on the way back.'

Cynthia Fielding, Max's elder sister, lived near their father in Northumberland.

'She's aware of our lack of guest room,' Max continued when Rona didn't immediately comment. 'I offered her the choice of a camp bed in the old studio or a more comfortable one here at Farthings. It would only be a sleeping arrangement, I could drop her off at bedtime and collect her the next morning.'

'Which did she opt for?'

'The studio. We can tart it up a bit at the weekend, set up the bed and so on.'

'Fine. It will be good to see her.'

Max said gently, 'Don't let it bother you about Magda, love. You've been best friends for most of your lives, and a baby isn't going to change that.'

'I hope you're right,' she said.

FIVE

The house in Richmond was tall and thin, set back from a leafy avenue up a long garden path. With no driveway available, Rona parked in the road, hoping there were no restrictions.

The path was bordered with brightly-coloured bedding plants, and two small bay trees in terracotta pots flanked the white-painted front door. It was opened by a woman in an overall, who smiled at her enquiringly.

'Mrs Ward?' Rona said uncertainly.

'Ms Parish?'

'Yes.'

The woman moved aside. 'Come in, she's expecting you.'

Rona was shown into the front room and Phyllis Ward rose to greet her, coming forward with hand outstretched. Tall and thin, like her house, she had a lined face, hair pulled severely back into a bun, and an unexpectedly sweet smile. She moved with unconscious grace, shoulders back and head high, unlike many of her generation who were prone to stoop. In her cashmere jumper and tweed skirt she looked, Rona thought with fleeting amusement, like what Granny Beecham would have called a 'gentlewoman'.

'It's so good of you to come,' she said in a low, pleasant voice. 'I'm aware, of course, that you're well qualified to take on Gideon's biography, but I wanted to put things on a more personal footing.'

She waved a hand towards a plaid-covered sofa. 'Please sit down, Ms Parish. Mrs Ledger will be in with coffee directly.'

Rona obediently seated herself and extracted her recorder from her handbag. 'Will it be all right if I use this?' she asked. 'It's so much easier than trying to make notes.'

'Of course.'

A tap on the door heralded the woman who'd admitted her, carrying a tray with a silver coffee pot and a plate of tiny buttered scones, still hot from the oven.

'Such a tragedy about Mr Page,' Phyllis Ward commented, when they were alone again and the coffee had been poured. 'He was a charming man.'

'I never met him,' Rona admitted, 'but I've always admired his books. In fact they inspired me to write biographies myself.'

'And you do so brilliantly. I made a point of reading a couple when I learned you were taking over from him. You bring your subjects very much to life.'

'Thank you.' Rona set down her cup and plate on the little table beside her. 'I have all the notes he made, of course, and the DVDs of your husband's interviews, but I've not had time to look through them yet. In any case, I've always found nothing can compare with hearing about my subjects first-hand from the people who knew them best, so may I ask you to imagine I know nothing at all about him and describe him to me?'

Phyllis took a sip of her coffee. 'I think he's best summed up as a man who lived life to the full,' she began. 'He'd never say, "I wonder what it's like to do such and such?" – he would go out and *do* it, discover it for himself, whether it was bungee jumping or learning Arabic. He was intensely curious about everything – how things worked, how people felt. On occasion it could appear intrusive, but that's what made him such a good interviewer.'

She smiled reminiscently. 'He'd often come home and regale me with the most scurrilous stories about those he'd met – and as you're aware, he met a great many well-known people.'

Rona made a mock grimace. 'Now I shall be wondering what he said about those on the discs!' She hesitated. 'Did he by any chance mention Bruce Sedgwick?'

Phyllis shot her a quick look. 'Curiously enough, Mr Page asked me the same question.'

Rona felt a quiver – of what, she wasn't sure. 'And . . . did he?'

She shook her head slowly. 'As I told him, I can't recall anything of significance. I don't think Gideon cared for the man – but then that wasn't unusual, I'm afraid. Why do you ask?'

'Well, the discs I received are parcelled together in series, all labelled and in chronological order.'

Mrs Ward nodded. 'Gideon was very methodical.'

'All, that is, except for the final series. The interview with Bruce Sedgwick was on top, though it was numbered #4. I wondered why.'

Phyllis frowned. 'How very curious. That must have been Mr Page's doing.'

Since it seemed she had no answer to the puzzle, Rona moved on. 'There was one interview that created a particular stir, wasn't there?'

'My dear, there were several! But no doubt you're referring to the Nigerian food scandal. It made a considerable impact, and as a result the distribution of supplies was radically reorganized. Gideon was credited with saving thousands of lives, and the interview won him an award.'

Her eyes went to the glass oblong with its gold depiction of Ariel, in pride of place on the mantelpiece.

Rona glanced again at the questions she'd prepared. 'I apologize if I'm going over points you've already covered with Russell Page. As I said, I've not read his notes yet. But to go back a bit, I believe in his younger days your husband played several sports internationally?'

'Yes indeed. In the early years of our marriage I travelled with him all over the world – South Africa, Australia, the States – but when the children began to arrive I had to trim my sails, as he would have put it.'

'How many children did you have?'

'Two boys and two girls. All married now, with families of their own. He was immensely proud of them, though when they were young I had to step in occasionally to prevent him bullying them into taking up some sport or interest that didn't remotely appeal to them. He'd an insatiable desire to widen his experience, and imagined everyone else felt the same. He devoured books at the rate of three or four a week, however busy his schedule. The classics, of course – often for the third or fourth time of reading – modern literature, travel books, biographies . . . he was quite voracious.'

'He sounds larger than life,' Rona commented. 'I wish I'd known him.'

'So do I, my dear.'

There was a brief silence, then she said tentatively, 'He died of a heart attack, I believe?'

'Yes.' Phyllis sighed, shaking her head. 'He'd had warning signs but persistently ignored them, and although I tried to monitor his diet it was a useless exercise. He loved food – the richer the better – and drank quite heavily, though in more than forty years of marriage I never saw him the worse for it.' Her mouth twisted. 'He was enjoying his after-dinner port when the attack came, so the taste of it must have been the last thing he experienced. I've often thought if he could have chosen how to die, it would have been exactly that – after a good meal and with me at his side.'

'Life must seem very tame without him,' Rona said.

Phyllis smiled fleetingly. 'A lot calmer, certainly. I adored him, but living with him could be quite challenging. And I've a lot to be thankful for. All my family live close by – they don't crowd me, but they're there if I need them.'

'Have any of them taken after their father?'

'Professionally, you mean? Not directly. Harvey works for the BBC but in an administrative role, and Alison is a journalist. If you mean temperament, the answer, thankfully, is no. More than one dynamo in the family would have been exhausting!'

Rona smiled with her, wondering how best to frame her next question.

'As you said, he could be quite astringent. Did any of his interviewees demand an apology or threaten to sue?'

Phyllis waved a dismissive hand. 'There were the odd murmurings on occasion, but they never came to anything. To be honest, it was not knowing what he would come out with that made the programmes compulsive viewing. And he did a lot of research before each interview, ensuring he had the facts right.'

She laid down her coffee cup, adding reflectively, 'There were several people he'd have liked to interview who for one reason or another were unavailable. Some he pursued for a year or more to no avail.'

'Did you meet anyone he'd interviewed?'

'Sometimes. And believe me it could be embarrassing, especially when details of their personal lives had come under discussion. Very occasionally it was obvious there were bad feelings and I had to steer Gideon away.' She gave a laugh. 'Believe me, life was never dull.'

The clock on the mantelpiece chimed twelve. 'I mustn't keep you any longer,' she said. 'It was good of you to come out here. I wanted to satisfy myself I could safely leave him in your hands.'

Rona switched off her recorder and stood up. She'd asked all her questions, and if she thought of more she could always contact Mrs Ward again. 'For my part, I feel I now know your husband much better,' she said. 'I'll try to do him justice.'

To her relief, there was no parking ticket on the windscreen. Rona drove slowly out of the avenue and headed for home, grateful for the interlude that had engaged her attention and temporarily blotted out thoughts of Nicole. Over the last two days this had been a constant struggle and now, alone again, she was vulnerable.

Coming to the main road, she switched on the radio and forced herself to concentrate on the political discussion in progress. Thank goodness it was the weekend and Max would be home.

The Sedgwick Hotel in Alban Road was only a few hundred yards from the Hathaways' home, and Lindsey and Steve had fallen into the habit of calling in there for pre-dinner drinks. They had not, however, done so in the three days since Nicole's death, and that Friday evening Lindsey felt less than comfortable as they went through the swing doors.

'Don't worry,' Steve had assured her, 'Patrick's not likely to be here. He'll be keeping a low profile, poor bloke.'

But Patrick *was* there, standing by the reception desk. He looked pale and drawn, but his eyes lit up at the sight of them. He came forward quickly and shook their hands.

'Thank God for friendly faces!' he exclaimed. 'The boss insisted I show myself to prove I've nothing to hide, but I can tell you it's a strain. The guests are polite, though I'm very conscious of surreptitious glances, and who can blame them? Come into my office and we can talk.'

They followed him down a corridor and into a luxuriously furnished room complete with sofa and easy chairs.

'Now, what are you drinking? G&Ts?' He lifted one of the desk phones. 'Michel? Would you send three gin and tonics to my office, please.'

He put the phone down and turned to them with a rueful smile. 'Sam's on a two-day course up in Doncaster,' he said. 'Just when I need her most!'

'We're terribly sorry about all this, Patrick,' Steve said quietly.

He ran a hand distractedly through his hair. 'It's the devil of a mess, I can tell you. Whatever her faults, Nicky didn't deserve that. And why the hell did it have to happen when I was in the vicinity? I'll always regret my last words to her.' He glanced at Lindsey. 'Sam said your sister was there that day?'

She nodded.

'She knew Nicky, then?'

'No, she'd only just met her, but she was hoping to do an article on her for *Chiltern Life*.' Lindsey swallowed. 'Actually, it was Rona who . . . found her. They'd arranged to go to the cookery class together.'

'Good God! What time was that?'

'I think Ro said she arrived at one thirty.'

'And I left the house about one. It's a tight time frame.'

There was a tap on the door and the barman came in with the drinks, laying the tray on Patrick's desk as he nodded his thanks.

'Have you any idea who could have done it, or why?' Steve asked, as the door closed behind him.

Patrick wiped a hand over his face. 'None. She wasn't everyone's flavour of the month – she could be quite cutting when she chose – but I can't imagine anyone going so far as to kill her.'

The fact that someone had done so hung between them. He passed them their drinks and, taking his own, sat down opposite them on one of the easy chairs. 'Naturally the police wanted to know if our meeting had been amicable,' he went on bitterly, having taken a long draught of his drink. 'I thought of lying, but it wouldn't have held water. Though we'd always maintained a civilized façade, it was common knowledge we were engaged in a bitter argument over Venetia, our daughter. Nicky was all set on sending her to boarding school, and I accused her of trying to offload her.'

He leaned forward, holding his glass between his knees and staring down into it. 'I feel disloyal saying this, especially now, but I sometimes felt the child was starved of affection. Oh, Nicky was fond enough of her, but she was never demonstrative and her business clearly came first. Venetia once said "Mummy doesn't like me to hug her!", which I thought inexpressibly sad.'

Steve cleared his throat. 'Perhaps that was the way she'd been brought up herself?' he suggested.

Patrick looked up. 'I wouldn't know. She refused to speak about her family or her childhood, insisting it was in the past and irrelevant.' He gave a brief laugh. 'I didn't – don't – even know if her parents are still alive.'

'But that's terrible!' Lindsey exclaimed. 'Suppose they read of her death in the papers?'

Patrick shrugged. 'All I can think is that they became estranged years ago, and Nicky was never one to forgive and forget. Nevertheless, I wish I'd persevered. It's bizarre that I haven't a clue who Neeshie's other grandparents are.'

'Rona said there was no sign of forced entry,' Lindsey said hesitantly. 'In fact the police had to break in.'

Patrick nodded. 'Another nail in my coffin! They reckon it must have been someone she knew, or at least admitted herself.'

'It's surprising no one in the road saw anything.'

'Not really. It's commuterland, everyone would have been at work. It said in the papers police made door-to-door enquiries to no avail.' He paused, staring into his drink. 'I think she was seeing someone,' he said.

Steve and Lindsey exchanged a swift glance. 'In a relationship, you mean?'

He nodded. 'I could be wrong – and even if I'm not, I'm not suggesting for a minute he might have anything to do with it – but once or twice Venetia' s mentioned "Mummy's friend, Uncle Rory".'

'You told the police?' Steve asked sharply.

'Of course.' Patrick stood up suddenly and started pacing the room. 'God, what I wouldn't give to put the clock back! This time last week everything was normal!'

There was a brief silence, then Steve asked, 'Did you go to Woodbourne specifically to see her?'

'Yes, it was my day off and there were a few of my things at the house I'd never bothered to collect. I decided to combine a visit with seeing if we could finally come to some sort of compromise about boarding school.'

'But you didn't?'

'Far from it. It developed into a blazing row. In fact if the neighbours *had* been home they might well have heard it, which wouldn't have helped my case. I finally stormed out of the house, accusing her of all manner of things, and left the scene in a cloud of dust.'

He stopped pacing and regarded them with a rueful smile. 'Sorry for bending your ears like this. Can't be what you expected when you came out for a quiet drink.'

'I wish there was some way we could help,' Steve said.

'You *have* helped, by letting me sound off like this. I feel better, having got it off my chest. Now I must let you go and relax in the bar, and return to my duties.'

'How's the sorting out going?' Max asked during supper. 'Are you beginning to see the light?'

'Well, I've managed to decipher a pile of his handwritten notes, but they've left me with more questions than answers. Several pages with paras beginning "Who was . . .?" and "Why did he . . .?" and "When was . . .?" etcetera are paperclipped together. And the most puzzling thing about it is that the "he" doesn't seem to refer to Gideon Ward.'

Max raised an eyebrow. 'How do you mean?'

'It's hard to explain, but he doesn't fit the context somehow.'

Max refilled her glass. 'If he was writing about Ward, he's hardly likely to have spent time researching someone else.'

'Unless it was Bruce Sedgwick,' Rona said.

Max stared at her. 'The hotel guy? How the hell does he enter the equation?'

Rona made a dismissive gesture. 'He probably doesn't, I'm just being fanciful.'

'But why should you even think of him?'

'It was just that his interview was out of sequence, the only one that was. Russell had placed it on top of the pile, as though he wanted to go back to it, and when I asked Mrs Ward if her husband had ever spoken about Sedgwick she said Russell had asked the same question. So I googled him. But there wasn't much personal stuff – it was nearly all about the various hotels he's taken over, the dates he acquired them and so on.'

She looked up, meeting Max's quizzical gaze. 'Look, will you do something for me? Will you watch the Sedgwick interview and see if anything strikes you as unusual?'

'Certainly, if you think it might help.'

When they'd finished the meal, Rona brought the DVD from her study and slotted it into the machine in the sitting room. Then she sat beside Max and watched it with more attention than she'd given it the first time, but again without finding anything exceptional.

She turned hopefully to Max. 'Well?'

'Well, he's pretty full of himself. But for the life of me I can't see anything of specific interest.'

Rona sighed. 'I was afraid you'd say that. But if Russell was so interested in it, we must be missing something.'

'Sorry, love, I'm afraid I can't help you. Nice to see old Gideon in action, though. I'd like to watch some of his other interviews sometime. He was always good value.'

Unlike Catherine, Avril's daily routine had changed little since her remarriage. As Guy had not yet retired, she continued to work at the library four mornings a week and alternate Saturdays, helped at the Save the Children shop on Wednesdays, and played bridge on Thursday and occasionally Monday afternoons. The only difference was that, having left Belmont, she was now based at the main library on Guild Street. And she happened to be on the desk that Saturday morning when Catherine came in.

Both women saw each other at the same moment and there was a brief awkwardness. Then Catherine smiled and approached the desk.

'Hello, Avril. I didn't know you worked here.'

'Just part-time,' Avril replied. 'I moved here from the Belmont branch.' She paused. 'Is there anything I can help you with, or are you just browsing?'

'Actually, I *would* be grateful if you could steer me in the right direction. I've embarked on a history of the grammar school, and I'm hoping there are some reference books I could refer to.'

'I'm sure there are.' Avril came round the counter. 'You could try the education section, but there should be something under local history too.' She gave Catherine a quick smile. 'I seem to remember Rona saying you did the same for Buckford schools.'

'That's right. We met when she was doing her project for the town's octocentenary.'

Which, as both women were tacitly aware, was also when Tom and Catherine's relationship developed.

'Here's the local history section,' Avril said quickly. 'It's subdivided, as you'll see, but there should be something to interest you. The section on education is farther down on the right.'

'Thanks so much,' Catherine replied. 'I'm sure I'll find something here.'

Avril nodded and turned away. This was, she realized, the longest conversation she'd ever had with Catherine, and she was surprised to find that the woman who for so long she'd blamed for the break-up of her marriage was someone who, under other circumstances, could have been a friend.

Catherine had reached a similar conclusion, and over lunch she said casually, 'I bumped into Avril at the library.'

Tom looked at her sharply. 'You went to Belmont?'

'No, she's moved to the central one on Guild Street. She was very helpful, and guided me to the sections I was interested in.'

He made no further comment, and after a minute she continued, 'You know, I think it's time she and I got to know each other. We've all moved on now.'

Tom smiled. 'I've been thinking that for some time, but I didn't want to force the issue.'

'Then how about inviting her and Guy to dinner? Perhaps with Rona, Lindsey and Max?'

'An excellent idea. We'll just have to hope Avril's ready too.'

'I think she might be. It would make things so much easier all round, especially for the girls. I'll give her a call next week.'

SIX

On Monday morning, Rona was surrounded by Russell Page's notes when the phone rang. She lifted it to find Barnie on the line.

'Are you knee-deep in research?' he greeted her.

'Pretty much, yes.'

'May I interrupt to make a request?'

'Not another series, Barnie?' she protested with a laugh.

'Nothing so strenuous.' He paused. 'Would you do me an obit for Nicole?'

She caught her breath, fumbling for excuses, but he was continuing. 'Really, Rona, I can't think of anyone else to ask, and you're ideally suited to the task.'

'But Barnie, I only met her once!'

'So what? Most obituary writers have *never* met their subject. You can look through back numbers to get the flavour of her work, speak to students at the cookery school and her ex-husband . . .'

'Even though he's the prime suspect?'

'Nevertheless, he knew her better than most. Come on, Rona, be a pal. A hundred words or so, and we can run it in the next issue. It's the least we owe her.'

'*You* might owe her,' Rona said flatly. 'I don't think I do. I've spent the best part of a week trying to forget my last sight of her.'

'This could be the means of drawing a line under it.'

'What's more, I'm probably under suspicion myself, as the one who found her.'

'Even so.'

She gave a choke of laughter. 'I notice you don't contradict me!'

Barnie refused to be diverted. 'So it's a yes?'

'Really, I don't—'

'You're a brick, Rona. Let me know what info you require and I'll have it scanned across. Sorry, must go – someone's on the other line.' And he rang off, leaving her staring at the phone in incredulous disbelief. How had he talked her into that?

With resignation and a heavy heart, she pushed Russell's papers aside and flicked through her storage container for the disc containing Nicole's interview. The coolly detached voice whisked her straight back to the elegant room in Norse Crescent, and to her consternation she burst into tears.

Idiot! she scolded herself, reaching for a tissue, but the tears kept coming, a culmination perhaps of the trauma she'd been trying to suppress, and they continued to pour down her cheeks as she listened to what had proved her only interview with the woman now being referred to as 'the deceased'.

She heard her own voice say, 'You mentioned a daughter?'

Then Nicole: 'Venetia, yes. She's eight years old and a very self-sufficient young lady.'

She certainly needed to be now, Rona thought, and again ached with pity for the motherless child whose father might also be taken from her.

The front door bell suddenly clanged through the house, and down in the hall Gus set up a frenzied barking. God, Rona thought in panic, I can't answer it with my eyes swollen and my face all red and blotchy! Hurriedly she blew her nose and wiped away the tears, which the shock of the doorbell had dried up at source.

The bell sounded again, this time three short rings and a longer one, and she breathed a sigh of relief. That was Lindsey's private signal. She ran down the stairs and thankfully opened the door to her sister.

'I just—' Lindsey began, and broke off as she saw her twin's face. 'Ro! Whatever's wrong?'

'Come in, Linz. It's nothing really, I'm just being a ninny.'

'I don't know when I last saw you cry. What's happened?'

'As I said, nothing. I've been replaying my interview with Nicole, that's all.'

'Ah. Well, let's go downstairs and have some coffee. I've a dental appointment round the corner in half an hour and slipped out early so I could pop in. Just as well I did, by the look of you.'

'Barnie's asked me to write her obit,' Rona told her as they went down the basement stairs, Gus, as usual, doing his best to trip them up.

'Unfeeling brute!' Lindsey seated herself at the kitchen table.

'And he calmly suggested I contact her ex-husband. As if I could, in the circumstances.'

'Actually, I doubt if he'd mind. That's one of the reasons I wanted to see you. Steve and I had a long talk with him on Friday. He's upset at what's happened, of course, but he isn't heartbroken. I'm sure he'd speak to you.'

Rona spooned coffee into the cafetière. 'So at least the police haven't arrested him.'

'Not so far, but I should think it's only a question of time. He's the obvious suspect, poor man. One thing that might interest you: he thinks Nicole had a lover.'

'Oh? Trying to deflect suspicion?'

'Don't be so cynical. He stressed that he wasn't suggesting he could be responsible.'

'But nevertheless planted the seed. So who was he, or doesn't Patrick know?'

'Rory someone. Anyway he told the police, so no doubt they'll be following it up.'

'No doubt.' Rona brought the cafetière to the table and sat down to wait for the coffee to brew.

'And I've more news,' Lindsey said. 'Though this doesn't affect you. Jonathan's transferring to the Brighton office. He and Carol have already sold their house.'

'So another of your lovers flees the scene,' Rona said caustically, then immediately regretted it. Months earlier Dominic Frayne, the man she'd expected Lindsey to marry, had moved to Paris with his faithful assistant, known to the twins as Bloody Carla.

'Sorry!' she said quietly.

Lindsey shrugged and, reaching across, pressed down the plunger. 'I haven't got long,' she said in explanation.

Rona brought over two mugs and poured the coffee. 'And not to be outdone,' she announced, 'I've some news myself. Prepare yourself for a shock: Magda is pregnant.'

Lindsey sat back in her chair, staring at her. 'No!'

'Very definitely yes. Let's hope Mum doesn't get wind of it, or we'll have no peace.'

'She can hardly have a go at *me*!' Lindsey said.

'Don't count on it. Anyway, I shall have to get out my knitting needles.'

'That'll be the day. Seriously, was it planned, do you think?'

'She swears it was, and that she and Gavin had been thinking about it for some time. They both seem delighted.'

'Well, I suppose that's as it should be.'

'Do you think the maternal gene was omitted from our DNA?'

'Could be. Watch out, though, once the baby puts in an appearance. Propinquity can, I hear, be lethal.' Lindsey glanced at her watch and stood up. 'I'd better go. Do you want me to put in a word for you with Patrick? He already knows it was you who found her.'

Rona's eyes widened. 'You told him?'

'You don't mind, do you? He knew you'd been there that day – Sam had told him – and it just seemed to follow on.'

'So he knows I was doing an article on her?'

Lindsey nodded. 'It should be a way in for you.'

'Then thanks, Linz, that might be a help.' She started to rise, but Lindsey waved her down.

'Stay here and finish your coffee. It will help restore your equilibrium. I'll see myself out.' And with a wave of her hand she was gone.

Lindsey was as good as her word, and a couple of hours later Rona had a phone call from Patrick.

'I hear you've been landed with Nicole's obituary,' he said, after introducing himself. 'If you think I could be of help, I'd be glad to do what I can.'

'That's very good of you. As Lindsey might have explained, I only met her once but we worked for the same magazine. And, of course, I've known *of* her for some time. I'm really terribly sorry about it all.'

'Thank you. It's been a shock, especially for our daughter.' He cleared his throat. 'I don't know how you go about these things, but if it's all right with you I'd prefer not to be interviewed at the hotel. Tomorrow's my day off, so I could come to you if you like – or we could meet somewhere neutral, though that might be tricky. My photo's been in the local press and I'm trying to keep my head down.'

'You're more than welcome to come here, Nineteen Lightbourne Avenue. Do you know where that is?'

'I'll find it. Would eleven o'clock be OK? There are a few things I have to do first.'

'Of course. I'll see you then. And thank you.'

It was only later that Rona realized it was on his free day last week that he'd gone to Woodbourne to see Nicole.

So once again the bio would have to be put temporarily on hold. Rona sighed; she seemed doomed never to have a clear run at it. Resignedly she gathered together Russell's papers, saved the notes she'd made on screen, and prepared a list of subjects she wanted to discuss with Patrick Summers. At least he should be able to give her some insight into the enigmatic woman who had been his wife.

'My God! Are you sure you're not Lindsey?' he exclaimed by way of greeting. 'She didn't tell me you were twins!' Then he smiled, holding out his hand. 'Forgive me, that was unpardonably rude. Ms Parish, I presume. Or—' He glanced at her wedding ring.

'Ms Parish professionally, but Rona will be fine.'

She led the way into the sitting room, where Gus came to greet him, sniffing at his trouser leg. Patrick bent to pat him and Rona studied him covertly. A bit of a hunk, Lindsey had said, and she had to agree. Tall and broad-shouldered, he had dark wavy hair and a lop-sided smile that was unaccountably attractive.

'Coffee?' she asked.

'Lovely. Thanks.'

She poured him a mug and he sat down, apparently quite at ease. 'So, what were you hoping to write about Nicole?'

Who was supposed to be interviewing whom? Rona wondered humorously. She said, 'I write for *Chiltern Life* occasionally myself and I've been doing a series on single mothers.'

That smile again. 'For which, thanks to me, she qualified.'

'Well, yes. I was interested in the column she wrote for the magazine and also how she'd set up her cookery school.'

'You said you'd met her?'

'The previous week – that was when she invited me to sit in on her class. I was to be at the house at one thirty on Tuesday.'

'Which I presume you were?'

She nodded.

'I'm so sorry. It must have been a hell of a shock.'

'It was,' Rona acknowledged. Then, before he could resume his questioning, 'Had you been divorced for some time?'

'Nearly three years, but I'd moved out before that. Things had been difficult between us for a while.'

'How did you meet?'

'I was working in the bar of a hotel in Stokely and she came in with some guy who began to hassle her. She seemed upset. I went to check she was OK and he became aggressive, so I asked him to leave. He blustered for a while but people were starting to notice, so he grabbed her arm and tried to pull her to her feet. She resisted, and rather than make any more of a scene he left.

'A few minutes later she came to the bar and offered to buy me a drink to thank me.' Patrick smiled. 'I said a better way would be to come out with me the following evening, and things took off from there.'

'So Stokely was Nicole's home town?'

He shook his head. 'It was where she was living at the time. She'd never stayed in one place for more than a year or so.'

Rona frowned. 'Then where were her parents?'

'Ah, well that's just it, I've no idea. She refused to speak about her family or her childhood. All she'd say was that it was unhappy and she'd broken all ties with them.'

'And in ten years you didn't learn any more?' Rona asked incredulously.

'Frankly, it didn't seem worth pursuing. She'd get upset if I tried to bring it up, and in the end I just thought "What the hell? It doesn't really matter anyway." Now, of course, I feel differently. As Lindsey pointed out, they might have read of her death in the papers, but I've no way of contacting them or even knowing who they are.'

Rona glanced at her list of questions. 'Where was she working when you met?'

'At a firm of accountants.'

'And she stayed on after you were married?'

'No, I was on the point of transferring to Woodbourne as assistant manager at the Sandon – which was great because my parents live in Nettleton. And as Nicole was pregnant, she didn't look for anything else.'

'It sounds as though you had a small wedding,' Rona said.

Patrick grimaced. 'The smallest legally possible. Stokely register office, with only my parents and brother to act as witnesses. Not that it worried me. I was in love and all I cared about was being married.'

'There was no one at all on her side? Not even friends?'

He shook his head. 'The only people she knew were from work, and she said they never discussed personal matters.'

'So there's no one I can speak to, to get an angle on her?'

'Oh, don't misunderstand me.' He bent forward to put his mug on the coffee table and sat back again. 'I was speaking of when we met. She came to know people in Woodbourne, especially after Venetia was born, and there were several couples we met regularly for meals at each other's houses. That's when her interest in cooking really started. Then later, after we'd split, there were her students. I believe she came to know them quite well.'

'Would any of them be prepared to speak to me?'

He shrugged. 'It's worth a try. I can email you our friends' names and phone numbers, though I don't know if she kept up with them after I left. And you could contact the Community Centre about her students.'

'Right, thanks.' She gave a little laugh. 'It'll be an unusual obituary, with no mention of her parents or where she was born.'

'I think it's her journalistic and cookery careers that will interest people.'

'Trouble is I don't know much about them, either. I'll have to hope I can glean enough to satisfy my editor.' She lifted the coffee pot enquiringly, and he nodded.

'Please.'

Rona refilled both cups. 'How's your little daughter coping with all this?'

Patrick lifted his shoulders. 'Children are very resilient, thank God, and she's with my parents. They've always been close, which is a tremendous blessing. When I left Nicole I moved into the hotel and, as I couldn't have Venetia with me there, she stayed with them during her weekend visits. This last week I've gone over as soon as I come off duty each evening, to spend time with her before she goes to bed.'

Rona wondered fleetingly how Samantha fitted in to this schedule. 'You said your parents live in Nettleton?'

'Yes. As you probably know, it's only a twenty-minute drive from

Woodbourne, so she's been able to continue at the same school. They'd only just gone back after the Easter break, and last week there was all the initial shock and upset, then the business of packing Neeshie's things and settling her in with her grandparents. But we thought it best for her to go back yesterday. It keeps her occupied, and the staff and pupils know the position and are all watching out for her.'

Rona nodded. 'To change the subject, I know this is an odd question, but how do you get on with Bruce Sedgwick?'

Patrick raised an eyebrow. 'OK. He gives me a pretty free rein. Why?'

'Well, it's an involved story, but I've been asked to write a biography of Gideon Ward, the television presenter. Do you remember him?'

'Certainly. Excellent interviewer. I didn't know you were a biographer, though. That must be fascinating.'

'The *Chiltern Life* work is really a stop-gap between lives, though admittedly the gaps have been pretty long on occasion. So I was looking through the DVDs of Ward's interviews and found one with Bruce Sedgwick. He hadn't been here long at the time, and I wondered whether he'd become at all . . . anglicized.'

Patrick laughed. 'Not really, though he seems quite at home here. He has nothing to do with the day-to-day running of the hotel, so I don't see that much of him. He's been pretty decent this last week, though.'

'Do you like him – as a person, I mean?' Rona asked diffidently.

'I've not really thought about it, he's just the boss.' Patrick considered for a moment. 'If he wasn't the boss, I doubt if we'd have much in common, though he seems well liked. Always has a glamorous woman on his arm, and seldom the same one! I hear riotous parties are held at Sedgwick Hall.'

Rona laughed. 'Sounds like the 1920s!'

'How did he come over in the interview?'

'As a bit of a rough diamond, I suppose. Somewhat resentful at having to leave Oz under the terms of the will.'

'Well, for a sheep farmer or whatever he was, I reckon he's fallen on his feet.' He glanced at his watch. 'Is there anything else I can help you with? If not, I should be on my way. I'm meeting my girlfriend for lunch.'

'No, you've been very helpful. Thank you.'

He smiled ruefully, getting to his feet. 'I doubt if you know much more about Nicole than before I arrived.'

'I've a rounder picture of her.' She walked with him to the front door. 'I do hope they find the culprit soon, so we can get on with our lives.'

He turned to look at her. 'God! Are you a suspect too?'

'There's always the suspicion that the one who finds the victim could turn out to be the killer.'

'I never thought of that. You have my sympathy.' He started down the steps. 'If there's anything else you think of, just let me know.'

Rona was closing the front door as the phone began to ring.

'Hello, Rona, it's Catherine. I'm wondering if you and Max could come for a meal next week? I know he's only free on Wednesday and Friday, but either would be fine.'

'Hi, Catherine. That sounds lovely.'

'I'm hoping it'll be rather a special occasion,' Catherine went on. 'Lindsey is coming, and I'm about to invite Avril and Guy.'

Rona drew in her breath. 'Wow!'

'I reckon it's time normal relations were established, if you'll excuse the pun.'

'That would be great.' She hesitated. 'I do hope they'll come.'

'I saw your mother at the library on Saturday and we exchanged a few words. I think the time is right, but I wanted to make sure both you and Lindsey – and of course Max – would be free before issuing the invitation. Shall we make it Friday week? That will be – let me see – the thirteenth.' She gave a little laugh. 'Oh dear, Friday the thirteenth! I hope that isn't an omen!'

'Only a good one, I'm sure,' Rona said.

'I'll come back to you when I've spoken to them, hopefully with confirmation of the date.'

Avril returned from her shift at the library to see the answerphone blinking, and was startled to hear Catherine's voice inviting herself and Guy to dinner. Thank God it had acted as an intermediary! If they'd spoken directly she wasn't at all sure how she'd have reacted. Now she at least had time to think about it and, when he came home from work, consult Guy.

The puppy was cavorting about her legs and she bent to unclip his lead. He ran ahead of her into the kitchen and could be heard lapping at his water bowl. She hung her jacket on the hook and followed him slowly, trying to analyse her feelings. The bitterness towards both Catherine and Tom had long gone, though awkwardness undoubtedly remained. She had, in the normal course of things, met Tom several times over the last year or so and accordingly felt more comfortable with him. And as she'd realized only last week, she no longer regarded Catherine as the hated 'Other Woman'.

Which, no doubt, was as it should be, but didn't mean she wanted any closer dealings with them. It had been fine meeting Tom on neutral ground; seeing him established in his new home with a new wife might be a totally different matter.

Rex was jumping up at her and she tipped food into his bowl. She and the puppy were growing used to each other and he was proving a great favourite at the library. Mostly he slept in a basket under her desk, and there was an enclosed yard behind the building where she let him out regularly. So far there had been no embarrassing puddles and, to be honest, she enjoyed their twice-daily walks in the park.

She sat down at the kitchen table, watching him eat while she wrestled with the problem which, she acknowledged, was hers alone. Guy, while welcoming Catherine's invitation, would leave the ultimate decision to her. And how would it seem, to the girls as well as Tom and Catherine, if she made excuses not to go?

So there it was – the decision had been made for her and she might as well accept it.

'Oh, *damn*!' she said.

SEVEN

It had been arranged that Max's sister Cynthia would arrive in Marsborough on Wednesday and, since he had an afternoon rather than evening class, it would be Rona who'd meet her at the station.

That morning she'd received the promised email from Patrick giving the names and phone numbers of the couples he and Nicole had been most friendly with, and she'd arranged to meet two of the wives the following day, after she'd seen Cynthia on to the London train.

Tracking down the cookery students, however, was proving more difficult. The spokesperson at Woodbourne Community Centre refused to give out students' particulars, but grudgingly agreed to ask one of the class to get in touch. Rona, who'd stressed the magazine angle, could only hope curiosity if nothing else would prevail.

Rona hadn't seen her sister-in-law since the previous October, when she and Max had flown to Tynecastle for his father's birthday celebrations, and she felt a rush of affection as she saw the small round figure bustling down the platform trailing her wheelie bag. Five years older than Max, Cynthia had more or less brought him up after their mother died young.

'Good to see you, Cyn!' she exclaimed, bending to kiss the rosy cheek. 'You look well!'

'So do you, my dear. That brother of mine not working you too hard, then?'

Rona smiled. 'I'd like to see him try! How are things up north?

'Jogging along nicely. Father seems to have a new lease of life and is painting again.'

Roland Allerdyce was a Royal Academician and still, though in his eighties, a regular contributor to their exhibitions. His initials, 'R.A.', coupled with the RA of his status had caused much amusement to Cynthia's sons when they were younger, and they'd irreverently addressed their grandfather as Rahrah.

'That's very good news,' Rona said. They'd reached her car, and she opened the boot for Cynthia's case.

'He sends his love, of course,' Cynthia added, 'as do Paul and the boys.'

'So what is this reunion you're going to?' Rona asked as they drove out of the station car park.

'I don't suppose you'll remember, but some years ago I attended an embroidery course.'

'I didn't know that, but I've always admired the work you've done.'

'Well, there was a group of us on the course who became friends. Over the years we scattered all over the country and only kept in touch via Christmas cards, then someone suggested we should make an effort to get together and have a celebratory lunch. It'll be lovely to see everyone again.'

She looked out of the window as they turned into Guild Street. 'I always forget what a gracious-looking town you live in,' she commented. 'All this Georgian architecture is to die for!'

'It has its disadvantages,' Rona said. 'Lack of garages, for one. I'll let you and your case into the house before garaging the car.'

They turned off Guild Street into Fullers Walk, and as they passed the turning to Dean's Crescent she added, 'Not wishing to subject you to my cooking, I've booked a table for the two of us at Dino's tomorrow, when Max is at his class. You're OK tonight – he's the chef when he's home on Wednesdays.'

Cynthia laughed. 'I'm continually surprised that a competent young woman like you never learned to wield a wooden spoon!'

'It's not that I can't, I just loathe it,' Rona said frankly.

Number nineteen, like the other Georgian houses in Lightbourne Avenue, was a handsome four-storey building, the interior of which Rona and Max had modified to suit their lifestyle, principally by removing interior walls to make one large room on each floor. The basement was given over to the state-of-the-art kitchen, the ground floor to the sitting room, while the first floor accommodated their en-suite bedroom and Rona's study.

The room at the top of the house was seldom used. It had been intended as Max's studio, but was abandoned when the two of them working under one roof had become an impossibility and he'd invested in a studio across town. The rather bleak space, normally used for storage, was all they could offer by way of a guest room and Rona, having struggled up the final staircase with Cynthia's case, surveyed it without enthusiasm.

'It's not exactly five-star,' she said apologetically, eyeing the camp bed she and Max had made up at the weekend. 'It's not been used since Lindsey stayed here a couple of years ago while her flat was being redecorated. We've rigged up a bedside lamp for you, and I hope that table and mirror will be OK.'

'It'll be fine,' Cynthia said comfortably. 'It's good of you to put me up at all, but I couldn't come all this way south without seeing you.'

'We'd never have forgiven you! Now I'll leave you to unpack. Come down when you're ready and we'll have a cup of tea while we wait for Max to come home.'

They spent a pleasant evening together – Max, as usual, producing a meal up to restaurant standards. They ate at the kitchen table, the candle flames reflected in the patio windows like a host of fireflies hovering outside.

Rona had asked him not to mention Nicole or her murder, so when Cynthia enquired what she was working on she simply outlined the biography she'd inherited from Russell Page.

'Good for you!' Cynthia exclaimed. 'I was so sorry to hear of his death. A relatively young man, too. But Gideon Ward is quite a plum to have fallen into your hands. I always enjoyed his interviews – he could be so acerbic and it was amusing to see the great and the good squirming under his questioning.'

'*Schadenfreude!*' Max said with a smile.

'That was half the fun of it! I should imagine he was a man who lived life to the full.'

'Oh, he was,' Rona confirmed. 'He had enough interests and achievements for half a dozen ordinary mortals.'

Later, as they went upstairs, Cynthia said, 'I promised Father I'd try to pin you down to dates for a visit. Any possibilities on the horizon?'

'Max should certainly go,' Rona agreed, 'but I really can't afford to take time off till I've got a lot more of this bio under my belt. At the moment my study's a welter of scraps of paper, notebooks, DVDs, cassettes and goodness knows what else, all of which need to be put into some sort of order before I can actually start on the writing.'

'I'll look in my diary tomorrow,' Max promised.

Cynthia caught the ten o'clock train to London the next morning; and Rona, with mixed feelings, set off again for Woodbourne and her meeting with the Summers' erstwhile friends.

They had arranged to meet at the Rendezvous café in the centre of town and Rona, having parked in the multi-storey, found it easily. She pushed open the door to be met with the hum of conversation, the clink of cutlery, and the enticing smell of freshly roasted coffee.

Across the room two women were sitting in a window alcove

and, catching her eye, one of them hesitantly raised her hand. Rona threaded her way through the tables to join them.

'Hello, I'm Rona,' she said, and they stood to shake her hand.

'Amy Thomson,' replied the shorter of the two, 'and this is my friend Flic.'

'It's good of you to meet me,' Rona said as they all sat down. 'As I mentioned on the phone, I work on *Chiltern Life* and I've been asked to write an obituary of Nicole. Which, as I only met her once, I'm finding difficult.'

'We were very shocked by her death, and especially the manner of it,' said the woman called Flic, and Rona was glad she'd not admitted finding the body. 'You don't expect it to happen to someone you know.'

'And so close to home!' added Amy with a shudder. 'Geographically as well as metaphorically.'

'You live on the estate?'

'We do, yes. Just along the road. Flic and Harry are ten minutes' drive away.'

'We didn't see her as often as when she was with Patrick,' Flic said. 'He was the driving force in arranging dinner dates and so on. Since he left, our contact has mostly been through our children, who still play with Venetia. Or did. They see her at school, but she's with her grandparents at the moment.'

The waitress approached and they ordered coffee and cakes for three.

'But when you met for dinner,' Rona said, returning to the subject in hand, 'you got on well together?'

The women exchanged glances. 'To be honest, we never felt we really *knew* her,' Amy said hesitantly. 'Oh, she was the perfect guest and hostess – but I, at least, always felt I was kept at arm's length, an acquaintance rather than a friend.'

Flic nodded. 'The rest of us used to chat about our families and so on, but she never did. In the early days we did ask the odd question, but Patrick had a quiet word with our husbands and said it upset her to talk about them, so we stopped.'

Rona repressed a sigh. It seemed she wasn't going to get much further in her attempt to fathom Nicole.

'And we saw even less of her after she started a new relationship,' Amy put in.

'Oh?' Rona prompted, suddenly more hopeful.

'It started about six months ago. We gathered he's a musician of some sort – plays in a local orchestra.'

'Was it serious?' Rona asked, remembering Patrick's oblique reference.

'No idea.' Amy again. 'Most of our information was gleaned from Venetia, who was always chatting about "Uncle Rory".'

'Did they live together?'

'Oh no. Although—' She flushed. 'I sound like the local gossip, but his car *was* there overnight at weekends, when Venetia was with Patrick.'

'Did you ever meet him?'

'Only once. Ted and I bumped into them coming out of the cinema.' She gave a little laugh. 'She didn't look too pleased to see us, but she'd no option but to introduce us. Rory Jesmond, his name was. He seemed pleasant enough – quite a bit older than her, I'd say.'

Rona considered for a moment, then reluctantly jettisoned him. There was no way she could approach this man and blatantly question him about his affair. Even if she did, she doubted she'd learn any more. And should he prove to be the killer, it was the police's job to nail him, not hers.

'Can you think of any anecdotes to make the obituary more personal?' she asked a little desperately. 'All I have at the moment is her column for the magazine and the cookery school. I'm hoping to meet some of her students, but they're not likely to have known her as well as you did.'

'She was a very private person,' Flic said, which, Rona considered, was an understatement.

The waitress arrived and for a moment or two they busied themselves pouring coffee and handing round the cakes. Flic selected an éclair and regarded it critically.

'Not up to Nicole's standard,' she said. 'She really was a fantastic cook. In fact, Amy and I pride ourselves on having launched her career – it was because we kept asking for recipes of dishes she'd served us that she decided to write them down.'

'Did she teach herself to cook?' Rona asked.

'Who knows? Perhaps the unmentionable mother taught her.'

'So there's really nothing personal you can tell me? For instance, if she had any other interests beside cookery?'

The two women looked at each other, thinking back. 'Well, she was quite musical. When we were round there, there was usually classical music playing in the background and she often mentioned going to concerts. Which is probably how she met Rory.'

'And she read a lot,' Flic added. 'My husband's very into books, and she always seemed to have read any he happened to mention and could discuss them in detail. I can't think of anything else, can you, Amy?'

'Only that she was quite strict with Venetia. Stricter than I am with my lot, at any rate.'

'In what way?'

'Well, she was only allowed to watch TV at weekends, which cut her off from chats about weekday programmes, and during the holidays she was packed off to summer school or whatever. OK, so Nicole was working, but it wasn't a full-time job. I probably shouldn't say this – speaking ill of the dead and all that – but I did suspect she just wanted her out of the way.'

Rona frowned. 'But she wasn't . . . unkind to her, surely?'

'No, just a bit offhand. I never saw her hug Neeshie, even when she was crying.' Amy smiled. 'There were times I had to stop myself from hugging her myself!'

'I think it was just that basically she wasn't fond of children,' Flic added.

Did Nicole's attitude to her daughter reflect her own upbringing? Rona wondered. It seemed she'd never know.

They talked for a further twenty minutes but nothing more of interest emerged, and when Rona left the two friends it was with a feeling of frustration. But just as she reached the car park her mobile rang, showing a number she didn't recognize.

'Is that Ms Parish?' asked a hesitant voice.

'Yes?'

'Someone at the Community Centre asked me to phone you.'

'Oh, yes. Thank you. Were you in one of Nicole's classes?'

'That's right.'

'Then could I come and speak to you?'

'Well, I don't know that I can tell you anything. We only knew her on a teacher–student basis.' A pause. 'Actually, we're all still in shock. We waited at the Centre nearly an hour.'

'I'm so sorry,' Rona said, recalling her frustration at being unable to notify them.

'For what? *You* weren't to blame.'

Hastily she backtracked. 'I meant for what you went through,' she amplified. This, after all, was the daytime class, composed mostly of pensioners. 'Would it be possible to have a word with you, and perhaps your friends? I'm here in Woodbourne at the moment.'

'Oh, I'm not sure . . .'

'It needn't take long,' Rona pleaded.

'But I'm not at home. I've just arrived at the Centre, that's how I got your message.' So the unobliging woman hadn't bothered to contact her. 'Some of us meet here for lunch on Thursdays.'

'Then perhaps I could join you, Mrs . . .?'

'Harris. Dorothy Harris. Well, I suppose so, yes.'

'Thank you, I'm very grateful. So where is the Centre, exactly?'

'In the market square, opposite the library.'

Within walking distance, then. Rona wondered if she dared feed the meter and leave the car where it was.

'Right. I'll be with you in about ten minutes. Thank you so much, Mrs Harris.'

An aroma of lunch came to meet her as she pushed her way through the swing doors, the source identified by a sign indicating the cafeteria on her right. Following it, she searched, for the second time in an hour, for an unknown person who she hoped might help her. And, as before, someone raised a hand to attract her attention.

The grey-haired woman was seated with two others at a table for four, and as Rona approached she indicated the free seat. 'I'm Dorothy Harris,' she said, 'and these are my friends, Mrs Digby and Mrs Sloan. We were all in Mrs Summers' Tuesday class.'

Three for the price of one, Rona thought. Perhaps her luck was at last changing.

'I advise you to order before we talk,' Mrs Harris continued. 'They get very busy, and it's first come first served. The cottage pie's always good, but you have to go to the counter and pay for it in advance.'

'Thanks.' Rona did so, having to queue a couple of minutes to place her order.

As she rejoined them, Mrs Digby, a tall woman with scraped-back iron-grey hair, said, almost accusingly, 'You work for *Chiltern Life*?'

'Freelance, yes.'

'So you knew Mrs Summers?'

'No. I'd only met her once, the week before she . . . died. I was going to write an article on her for a series I was doing.'

'About the cookery school?'

'Well, it was on single mothers, actually, and the success they'd made of their lives. Sadly that won't now be happening, but I've been asked to write her obituary and am anxious to speak to people who knew her.'

'I wouldn't say we *knew* her, exactly,' ventured Mrs Sloane, a birdlike little woman.

A familiar refrain. 'Did she talk to you about anything other than cooking? Give an opinion on current affairs, for example?'

They shook their heads.

'Three cottage pies and three teas!' called out a voice. Mrs Harris raised her hand and the food was brought to the table.

'Please start while it's hot,' Rona said.

Not needing to be pressed, they picked up their knives and forks.

'We never discussed politics,' Mrs Digby amplified, 'but we did occasionally talk about music. The Woodbourne Ensemble gives concerts in this building, and Mrs Summers knew one of the musicians. Sometimes our lessons coincided with a rehearsal, and afterwards we'd be allowed to go in and listen. I'm not musical myself, but it was restful to sit there for a while after slaving over a hot stove.'

Rona's ears pricked up. 'You say Mrs Summers knew one of the players?'

'Mr Jesmond, yes. He sometimes came over and talked to us, explained about the piece they'd been playing.'

'Cottage pie and ginger beer?'

'Yours, I think?' suggested Mrs Harris.

'Oh . . . yes.' Rona turned to signal and her pie was delivered. It proved to be as good as promised.

'You were saying about Mr Jesmond?' she prompted.

'Yes, well that's all, really.'

Rona sighed and gave up. 'Tell me about the classes, then. How were they planned? Did you do a complete menu at a time?'

The three of them talked while she ate, occasionally interrupting or correcting each other as they described how Nicole organized her lessons. At one point little Mrs Sloane broke off and dabbed at her eyes, apologizing as she did so.

'It's just so awful, knowing we'll never see her again,' she explained.

By the time Rona had finished her pie, the talk had slowed down and it seemed the flow of reminiscences had dried up. Probably time to make a move – Cynthia's train was due at four forty-five.

She bent to pick up her bag, and as she straightened a male voice behind her said, 'Good afternoon, ladies.'

'Oh, Mr Jesmond! Isn't it awful about Mrs Summers? We can't believe it!'

Rona turned swiftly and met the dark gaze of the man standing behind her. 'This is Ms Parish,' Mrs Harris added. 'She's doing a piece on her for the magazine and wanted our memories of her. Perhaps you could add something?'

Obviously they'd no knowledge of Jesmond and Nicole's relationship, but Rona flushed with embarrassment. Whether or not he noticed, he smiled gravely at her and held out his hand. 'Rory Jesmond,' he said.

'Rona Parish.'

Interest flickered in his eyes. 'The Rona Parish who writes biographies?'

'Well . . . yes.'

Her companions looked from one of them to the other in bewilderment.

'Then I'd be happy to talk to you, if you think I might help.'

Mrs Digby stood up decisively. 'Have my seat, I'm going anyway. I'm due at the chiropodist at two.' She looked down at her companions, still uncertainly seated. 'Are you two staying?'

'No, no.' They both stood up. 'I hope we were of some help, Ms Parish,' Dorothy Harris said.

'Very definitely, and thank you for allowing me to gatecrash your lunch.'

'We'll look out for the obituary,' Mrs Sloane added, and the three of them made their way towards the exit.

Rory Jesmond glanced at her empty glass. 'Can I get you some coffee?'

'Not if you have to queue for it!'

He smiled. 'I'm one of the regulars, I have perks.'

'Then thank you, I'd love one. White, please.'

He nodded and made his way to the counter. Older than Nicole, Amy had estimated, and Rona was inclined to agree: he looked nearer fifty than forty. A father figure, perhaps, to compensate for what had gone before? If, of course, anything had.

He was back almost at once, with her white coffee and a black one for himself.

'Rona Parish, eh?' he said, passing her the sugar, which she declined. 'Well, well! It's not every day one meets a famous author.'

'I don't answer to that description!'

'I read your work on Elspeth Wilding, one of my favourite artists, and enjoyed it enormously. Knowing more about her increased my appreciation of her art.'

'Thank you, that was the aim of the exercise.'

He stirred sugar into his cup, his eyes on the swirling liquid. 'You knew Nicole, then?'

'Not really, I only met her once.' She paused, then added impulsively, 'I'm so very sorry.'

He looked up, holding her gaze for a long moment. Then he sighed. 'Thank you,' he said, accepting her understanding. 'You know,' he went on thoughtfully, 'everyone thought she was aloof and self-sufficient, but she was actually extremely vulnerable.'

'To what?' Rona asked curiously.

He shrugged. 'People's opinions. The world in general. It had dealt harshly with her in the past.'

'You know something of her past, then?'

He smiled ruefully. 'Alas no, it was simply what I deduced. I was warned very early on to ask no questions.'

'Why do you think that was?'

'I assume it was too painful to remember, but whatever'd happened resulted in a multilayered personality which, as a hardened divorcé, I found intriguing.'

'I wish I'd known her better,' Rona said, and surprised herself by meaning it.

'As for memories of her, which I gather is what you're looking for, there's nothing very notable, I'm afraid, just enjoyable times spent in her company. She appreciated the finer things in life to an extent that made me wonder if she'd been deprived of them in the past, but again that's mere conjecture. Good food, good wine, good music, good conversation – she thrived on them all.'

He straightened his shoulders, took a sip of coffee, and sat back in his chair. 'So tell me, are you working on anything at the moment?'

She hesitated, reluctant to drop the subject of Nicole, but it seemed he'd nothing further to add. 'Yes, actually. I've been commissioned to finish Russell Page's life of Gideon Ward.'

'God yes! He mentioned that when we met.'

Rona's eyes widened. 'You knew Russell Page?'

'We were on an arts programme together about a year ago.' He shook his head sadly. 'It was a shock to realize I was one of the last to see him alive.'

Rona stared at him. 'How do you mean?'

'I saw him that day, and from what I read in the papers it must have been shortly before the accident.'

'You were at Merefield library?'

'Merefield? No, I was outside a country pub – the Blue Boy in Foxbridge, to be precise.'

Rona was puzzled. 'He told his wife he was going to the reference library, so as not to be disturbed.'

'Well, I assure you he was in Foxbridge. I saw him quite clearly, getting into a car with another chap.'

'There was someone with him?' she asked sharply.

'That's right. I wondered later at what stage he'd got out, because they'd driven off in the direction of the crash. He must have thanked his lucky stars he escaped.'

'That's really odd! Russell's wife didn't think he was meeting anyone, and no one came forward afterwards.'

'Well, there was no need to, was there?'

'I suppose not.' Her brain was buzzing with dozens of questions she'd not had time to formulate. 'You'd have thought he'd have contacted her, though, if only to say how sorry he was.'

Rory Jesmond leaned back in his seat, studying her face. 'Perhaps they were only casual acquaintances.'

'Did you get that impression? That they didn't really know each other?'

He gave a short laugh. 'My dear girl, I didn't get *any* impression. I didn't see the other man's face – he had his back to me – and at the time I thought nothing of it. Why should I? I don't know why you're attaching such importance to this. I'm beginning to wish I'd never mentioned it!'

Rona sighed. 'I'm sorry. It's just that when I met his wife, she said she'd give anything to know how he'd spent his last few hours, and this man might have been able to tell her.'

'I see. Well, I'm afraid there's nothing I can add.' He looked at his watch. 'I must go – the rehearsal starts in ten minutes.' He stood up and held out his hand. 'It was good to meet you, Rona Parish, and I apologize if I've raised more questions than I answered.'

And he had, Rona realized as she drove home. At the very least, he'd added another puzzle to the list she'd been compiling. Why was the Sedgwick DVD out of sequence? Why had Russell suddenly visited his old school? And now, who had he spent his last hours with? And why?

And, she thought suddenly, there was something else – something she'd not attached much importance to at the time. Esmé Page said their house had been burgled during Russell's funeral. Was that simply callous opportunism, or something more sinister? Nothing much appeared to have been taken, so perhaps the burglar hadn't found what he was looking for. And perhaps he'd try again.

EIGHT

The two secondary schools were on adjacent sites near the southern end of Alban Road. Catherine turned into the car park alongside the High School, retrieved her briefcase from the back seat, and made her way into the building. In view of her reaction to the St Stephen's photos, she'd brought only the histories relating to Buckford College and the grammar school as examples of what she proposed.

Having reported to the reception desk, she was approached by a tall, thin woman in glasses who introduced herself as Miss Dennis, personal assistant to the head teacher, and led her down a corridor to her office.

'I understand you're interested in researching the history of the school?' she asked when they were both seated.

'That's right.' Catherine opened her briefcase and took out the two bulky folders. 'During my headship of St Stephen's Primary in Buckford, I started a project whereby the children made up a scrapbook outlining the history of their school in the context of world events taking place at the same time. It proved popular and as a result I was asked to compile histories of both Buckford College and the grammar school, but – since I wasn't teaching at those schools – without student participation.'

She handed over the folders and Miss Dennis opened the first one, slowly turning the pages. 'What an interesting and novel approach,' she commented. 'We have our own archives, but nothing that puts them in context with historical events, which might well prove a useful teaching aid. Ours were collated years ago, and nowadays more information is no doubt available online.' She looked up. 'I don't know if you're aware of it, but this school opened in 1890, originally for the sisters of grammar school boys.'

She turned to the second folder and was silent for several minutes as she slowly leafed through it. 'I have to say I'm most impressed, Mrs Parish, but I can't give you an immediate decision. The proposal would have to be discussed in the appropriate quarters. Perhaps you could give me some idea of your fee?'

Catherine gave an embarrassed laugh. 'I'm sorry, I couldn't have made myself clear. There'd be no charge – it would be a labour of love, something interesting to research in my retirement. The only costs involved would be my expenses for possible travel, photocopying, and so on.'

Miss Dennis smiled. 'Then I can think of no reason why your suggestion shouldn't be welcomed,' she said. 'Permission would be needed for access to the archives and so on, but I'm sure such formalities could be easily dealt with. It will certainly be put forward with my recommendation.'

'So it looks as though I'll be getting the green light,' Catherine reported to Tom later. 'Actually being in the school made me impatient to begin on it straight away.'

She glanced across at him with a smile. 'So now it's your turn to stir your stumps!' she said.

'I seem to have been monopolizing the conversation with details of my lunch,' Cynthia apologized, 'and I've not even asked how you spent your day.'

They were seated in the window alcove at Dino's with steaming plates of the house special in front of them. 'Oh, nothing interesting,' Rona prevaricated.

She'd been only too glad to listen to her sister-in-law's account of her reunion; it had kept her mind off the treadmill of Nicole and Russell, Russell and Nicole. She'd also been agonizing over whether to pass on Jesmond's revelation to Esmé Page. Would it comfort her to know Russell hadn't been alone during his last hours? Or tantalize her not knowing the identity of his companion?

'You were working on your biography?' Cynthia pursued, belatedly interested.

'No, actually I went to Woodbourne. I had to interview some people about an obituary I'm writing.'

Cynthia pulled a sympathetic face. 'Oh, poor you! And there was I, enjoying myself! I hope it wasn't too grim.'

'It was . . . interesting,' she said.

Dino came bustling over, his shiny face wreathed in smiles. 'All is well, *signore*? The dish is to your liking?'

'It's delicious, Dino, as always.' Rona turned to her sister-in-law. 'Cynthia, this is the man to blame for my not cooking. Why should I bother when I can come here and enjoy food like this? Dino, this is my husband's sister, down from Northumberland.'

Dino bowed. '*Benvenuto*, *signora!* I am honoured to meet with the sister of Signor Allerdyce*!*'

To Rona's relief the interruption had distanced them from a discussion of the obituary, and for the rest of the meal talk centred on family matters.

The day's concerns were usually talked over during Max's bedtime call, but on this occasion it was shared with Cynthia, who wouldn't be seeing him again before she returned home. Later, as she tossed and turned, Rona resolved to write and despatch Nicole's obituary the next day, which would free her to give Russell and his aborted biography her full attention. She had the feeling they'd both have need of it.

Having seen Cynthia on to her train, she immediately put her plan into effect. She would, after all, have to concentrate on Nicole's culinary prowess, her efficient running of her cookery school and the popularity of her monthly pages in *Chiltern Life*. On the personal side, all she could add was her love of music and the dinner parties with friends that had led indirectly to the publication of her recipes.

By the end of the morning she'd completed it to her satisfaction and decided to deliver it herself. It was a warm spring day, too good to spend indoors, and Gus would welcome the exercise.

The offices of *Chiltern Life* were, like the restaurant, in Dean's Crescent, and she followed the curve of the pavement to the building that housed them. Polly the receptionist greeted them warmly, producing a biscuit for Gus from beneath her desk.

'I won't disturb Barnie,' Rona told her. 'This is Nicole Summers' obituary – perhaps you could do the necessary?'

Polly's smile faded. 'Wasn't that the most awful thing? Are they any nearer finding out who did it?'

'Not as far as I know.'

'I'll see Barnie gets this, but he's gone home for lunch. Some problem with one of the grandchildren, who are over from the States.'

With all that had been going on, Rona had forgotten Mel's precipitous return to the UK. 'Nothing serious, I hope?'

'I don't think so. He'll be back later.'

'Right. Well, I'll be on my way. Thanks, Polly.'

Out on the pavement the sunshine tempted her to extend her walk, and instead of turning for home she continued to the end of the crescent, crossed Guild Street, and turned into Dean's Crescent North, where Max had his studio. Friday was the only day of the week he had neither classes nor tutoring at the art school and could concentrate on his own work. She hoped he wouldn't mind the interruption, but with luck she could persuade him to have a lunch break.

Farthings was a small whitewashed cottage with a front door opening directly from the pavement. A blast of one of Beethoven's symphonies met Rona as she let herself in. She led Gus through to the back door and, unclipping his lead, let him out into the tiny walled garden.

Since Max wouldn't hear if she called, she walked up the stairs and emerged into the large studio that extended over the entire ground floor. He was standing at his easel by the windows, his back to her.

'Max!' she called loudly, and he turned quickly, switching off his iPod.

'Hello, love. To what do I owe this pleasure?'

'I dropped Nicole's obit in to *Chiltern Life* and decided to come on here, hopefully for a spot of lunch. We didn't get our usual chat yesterday.'

'It couldn't have waited till I come home?'

'It could, but I'd rather have it now.'

He put down his brush. 'Cyn get off all right?'

'Yes, the train was on time. She should be home by now.' She walked over to the easel and surveyed the painting of Guild Street in Victorian times, enlarged from an old photo propped up alongside. He'd been commissioned to do another calendar of local scenes, this time in a bygone age.

'With all the listed buildings, it doesn't look much different, does it?'

'Except for the mode of transport and the pedestrians' outfits. Come on, then, let's go down and see what's in the fridge. We can make the most of the sunshine and eat outside.'

Rona laid a tray while he cooked Spanish omelettes, and they carried it out to the rickety little table on the terrace. Gus came bounding up to greet them, and Rona set down a bowl of water for him.

'So,' Max said, as they started on their omelettes, 'what's been bothering you?'

Quickly she sketched in her meeting with Amy and Flic and their confirmation that Nicole had had a lover, a local musician. 'Then I had a call from one of her cookery students who was having lunch at the Community Centre, so I went to join her and her friends. And who should come up to speak to them but the man himself – Nicole's lover, Rory Jesmond.'

'Oh yes, the Woodbourne Ensemble,' Max broke in. 'I have one of their CDs.'

'Really? Well, much to my gratification he knew my name, and when we'd finished discussing Nicole – which produced little of interest, I might say – he asked what I was working on at the moment. And the incredible thing, Max, is that he actually *saw* Russell Page shortly before his death!'

Max raised an eyebrow. 'Why is that incredible?'

'I mean *really* shortly, like about ten minutes before the crash. And – this is the important bit – he was with another man, who got in the car with him.'

'So?'

'Max, it was just before the crash!' she repeated. 'And they even drove off towards where it happened. But there was no mention of anyone else involved.'

'So Page had dropped him off.'

'But the point is he'd told his wife he was going to the reference library so he could work all day without distraction.'

'Perhaps he met this bloke when he *left* the library. I don't see why you're making such a big deal of it.'

Which had been Rory Jesmond's reaction. *Was* she making too much of it? What was there about this reported sighting that had set alarm bells ringing? She couldn't define it, but felt instinctively that it was significant.

'Suppose,' she said slowly, 'he *had* arranged to meet him and didn't want his wife to know?'

Max sat back, shaking his head in despair. 'How did you dream that up? You're making an unremarkable incident into the mystery of the century.'

'But wouldn't it have been natural for this man, whoever he was, to have contacted someone – either Esmé or the police? If only to say how Russell had seemed when he left him. Was he in good spirits? Upset about something? In a hurry to get somewhere? Had he been drinking? Any of those things could have contributed to the accident.'

'Whatever mood he was in doesn't alter the fact that he's dead,' Max said baldly.

Rona laid down her knife and fork, somewhat deflated. 'I suppose not,' she said.

He reached over and patted her hand. 'Forget it, sweetheart. You don't have to worry about who Page did or didn't see. It's Gideon Ward's biography you're writing, not his.'

'I'd still like to know,' she said stubbornly.

Hugh Cavendish came to an abrupt halt, his heartbeat accelerating, then walked on quickly, swearing under his breath. After all this time it was humiliating that a glimpse of his ex-wife across the street should affect him this way. She was with that guy again, too, arm in arm, laughing up at him.

His fingernails dug into his palms. Why the hell had he come back to Marsborough? He'd moved away after their divorce, hoping to make a clean break but, unable to accept the finality of it, he'd soon slunk back, counting on the fact that their physical attraction was as strong as ever and refusing to admit that was all that had brought them together.

Yet, he thought grimly, if he'd not returned he wouldn't have been on hand to save both Lindsey's and Rona's lives when her murderous lover broke into her flat. That, at least, had earned him brownie points till someone else took her fancy; and the on-off relationship had continued, with Lindsey making use of him as the mood took her and he abjectly accepting whatever she was willing to bestow.

Until recently, that is, when the red-haired Mia Campbell had joined his accountancy firm. To his startled surprise, it had been she who made the first move and they'd swiftly become an item – though with well-defined limitations. They went out regularly, to concerts, meals and theatres, and just as regularly made love. But there'd been no suggestion of moving in together or putting their relationship on a more formal footing, and he accepted there never would be. Mia had a lovely home, an amiable ex-husband, a student son, and Hugh himself to supply her physical needs. Why upset the status quo?

So he continued to live in the flat he'd bought as a stop-gap till he and Lindsey got back together, and on the whole he too was content. Until, as now, he caught sight of her and all the old feelings flared up. Well, he'd have to learn to live with it – and let's face it, he'd a lot to be thankful for. Balance precariously restored, Hugh turned into the Five Feathers, where he was meeting friends for lunch.

* * *

Steve Hathaway had seen Hugh across the road and noted his abrupt halt on catching sight of them – before, almost immediately, walking on. This and other instances over the last few months seemed to confirm that he still loved Lindsey. A more pertinent worry was that, beneath the surface, she might still have feelings for him.

That concern stayed with Steve and later, when she'd returned to her office and he was back home, he sat for some time staring blankly at his reflection in his computer screen before, with a muttered exclamation, putting his head in his hands.

There was no point in denying it any longer: he couldn't escape the fact that he was in love with her himself – something he'd sworn never to allow to happen again. And now that he at last acknowledged it, it seemed to date right back to the weekend she'd spent with them after spraining her ankle.

God knows, he'd tried to fight it! The heartache following break-ups from his wife and, last year, Inga, his boss's daughter in the States, had plunged him into a depth of despair he'd determined never to be prey to again. But he'd reckoned without Lindsey Parish. He recalled how, immediately following her accident in Guild Street, he'd taken her to the Clarendon for a drink to steady her and she'd artlessly launched into a confession of the mess she'd made of her life following her divorce. He'd been touched by her vulnerability and assumed that, like him, she wouldn't lay herself open to further hurt.

Steve smiled grimly to himself. Despite that assumption he'd been unable to keep away from her, convincing himself that provided he kept things on a friendly footing it would do no harm. But that wasn't, and never had been, enough; he wanted her permanently in his life and the thought of losing her filled him with mindless panic. It was becoming harder and harder to keep up a casual front – but if she suspected his true feelings, it might frighten her away.

The ping of an incoming email jerked him out of his reverie and, with a deep sigh, he turned his attention to the work in hand.

Friday's sunshine had turned to showers and there was a cool breeze blowing across the cemetery. Chrissie Palmer, wiping away tears, turned to her husband, who was staring into the open grave. She touched his arm.

'Come on, love. There's nothing more we can do.'

He shrugged her off. 'Give me another few minutes.'

She glanced round, at her father-in-law shivering in his raincoat and the half-dozen elderly friends who'd attended the service and were beginning to stamp their feet.

'It's getting chilly, Alan, and it's going to rain any minute. Let's—'

'Go and sit in the car,' he said. 'I won't be long.'

'I don't like leaving you here—'

'I'm all right. Go.'

Reluctantly she turned to the others. 'I hope you'll all come and join us at the Bell,' she said. 'Refreshments are laid on, and I know George will want to talk to you. If you get there before we do, just ask for the Davenport Room.'

They murmured assent and started to walk down the path towards their cars. With a final glance at Alan, she linked her arm through George's. He gestured towards the small grave next to his wife's, which also bore a sheaf of flowers.

'She'll be with Tracy now,' he said.

Chrissie nodded and reached for Amanda's hand, surprised at how cold it was. The service had been a traumatic experience for her.

'Why isn't Daddy coming?' she asked.

'He's just . . . saying goodbye to Granny. He'll join us in a minute.'

Privately, Chrissie was concerned about her husband. He was taking his mother's death badly, though he seemed to have been expecting it; ever since her stroke he'd been withdrawn, sleeping badly and with no appetite. Perhaps now the blow had fallen, he'd be able to accept it and move on.

George was going back to London with them after the wake, for an indefinite stay. As they finally drove away from the cemetery he said quietly, 'I think now Mother's gone we should lay Tracy properly to rest. No more bedroom shrines and favourite meals. It wasn't healthy but it comforted Mother. Now, we can mourn them together and just be thankful for their lives.'

Alan nodded, his eyes on the road. 'That would be best,' he said.

'Rona?'

'Hello, Mags. How are things?'

'Fine. Are you doing anything this dreary wet Saturday?'

'Not a lot, no.'

'We were thinking of trying the Sedgwick for a meal. Care to join us? It's ages since the four of us were together.'

The Sedgwick! Rona's heart did a flip. Would the owner be there? And what would she say if she met him?

'You might even meet the famous Bruce!' Magda continued, as though reading her mind. 'Didn't you say you wanted to?'

'Well, yes, in the fullness of time,' Rona hedged.

'But you'll come this evening? Or do you need to check with Max?'

'No, I'm sure he'd love to. Quite apart from seeing you, it'll save him cooking a meal!'

'I'll book a table then. Eight o'clock OK?'

'Perfect. See you there.'

'Who was that on the phone?' Max asked as she walked into the sitting room.

'Magda, suggesting we eat at the Sedgwick this evening. I said yes.'

'The Sedgwick, eh? We've not darkened their doors yet, have we?'

'Probably time we did, though I'll feel a bit disloyal to the Clarendon.'

'It'll be good to see the Ridgeways.' He flashed her a teasing glance. 'As long as they don't bombard us with baby talk!'

The old Lansdowne Hotel had undergone a considerable transformation to become the Sedgwick, having been completely redecorated and refurbished, with the addition of a glass extension to the restaurant that almost doubled its size. In the foyer, immediately opposite the entrance, hung a large portrait of the founder of the chain, Jason Sedgwick, resplendent in his chef's hat. Instead of being sedate and traditional, as Rona remembered, the ambiance was now buzzing. She couldn't help wondering if Marsborough was quite ready for it.

As they entered the bar, though, it seemed her misgivings had been misplaced, since the room was filled with a well-dressed clientele, all holding drinks and talking loudly. Over in the far corner Gavin stood up and signalled to them, and she and Max went to join him.

'There was a crush at the bar, so I took a chance and got your drinks at the same time,' Gavin said. 'Hope I guessed right. Vodka and Russchian for Rona, whisky for Max?'

'Spot on,' Max confirmed as they sat down. Magda, Rona saw, had a ginger beer in front of her. Noticing her glance, she smiled.

'Worst part of being pregnant!' she said.

'So how are you? Slowing down a bit at work?'

'Not really. I do get tired, but I simply go into the back room of whichever boutique I'm in and rest for a few minutes. One of the perks of being the owner.'

'Well, you'll be a fine model for your latest maternity wear!'

Magda, at just under six foot, would stand out in any crowd. She laughed. 'I'm also starting on children's and baby clothes – a new line for me, but I saw this French catalogue and was hooked!'

A waiter materialized at their table. 'Will you be staying for dinner, sir?' he asked Gavin, and at his confirmation handed over four menus. 'You might like to make your choices now, and we can advise you when your table's ready. I'll come back for your orders shortly.'

The menus were flamboyantly set out, with illustrations of lobsters and crabs alongside the fish course and sundry other animals in appropriate places.

'That tends to put me off rather than tempt me,' Magda remarked, 'seeing them in the flesh, as it were.'

'But I think your scruples will be overcome, my love,' Gavin rejoined. 'I can see at least three of your favourite dishes at a glance. And don't tell me you're eating for two! At these prices, I'm only paying for one of you!'

Minutes later the waiter reappeared and noted down their selection. As he moved away and the men started to discuss cricket, Rona said, 'I half-thought we might see Lindsey and Steve. I know they come here fairly frequently, but there's no sign of them.'

'Nor of the manager. Talking of which, any more news on the murder?'

Rona shook her head. 'Not to my knowledge. I did meet Patrick, though. He kindly came round when he heard about the obit and gave me some background on Nicole. I honestly can't see him as a murderer, Mags.'

'Ah, but murderers don't *look* like murderers, as you have good cause to know.'

Rona shuddered. 'Well, now I've handed in the obit I'm trying to put it out of my mind and concentrate on the bio. I owe it to Russell Page to make it the best I can possibly do.'

A few minutes later the waiter returned and led them through to the restaurant. The glass extension lent the room the air of a conservatory, an impression reinforced by the potted palms and exotic plants that lined the walls. Most of the tables were already occupied, though a long one in the centre of the room stood empty.

Their chairs were pulled out, crisp napkins laid on their laps and the candle in the centre of the table lit, its quivering flame reflected in silver and crystal.

'I could get used to this!' Max commented.

Their first course duly arrived – a selection of scallops, oysters and prawns – and they had just begun on them when a slight disturbance over by the door made them turn.

'Well, well,' Gavin said softly. 'The man himself!'

Rona watched with unabashed interest as Bruce Sedgwick and his party were led with almost regal ceremony to the central table. He took his place at one end, which placed him directly in Rona's line of vision, and as he laughed and joked with his friends – there was an attractive woman on either side of him – she covertly studied him, trying to assess what, if any, changes the intervening years had made. It was immediately obvious that he'd put on weight – an occupational hazard, she assumed – and though he was now relaxed, whereas during the interview he'd been on his guard, he seemed altogether more polished, more sure of himself than when he'd just arrived in the UK. That, no doubt, was what a considerable inheritance did for you.

As the meal progressed she tried to confine her interest to her own table, joining in the general conversation and exchange of news. But when they'd finished their desserts and coffee was being served, Sedgwick excused himself to his companions, rose from his table, and began to circulate among the other diners, many of whom appeared to know him, and it was with a mixture of anticipation and apprehension that she watched him approach their own table.

'G'day folks,' he said breezily. 'I'm Bruce Sedgwick and I'm delighted to see you here. I hope you've enjoyed your meal?' And as they assured him they had, he turned to Magda with a slight bow.

'You're the boutique lady, I believe? Some of my guests are your customers and recognized you.'

Magda smiled. 'The recognition was mutual, Mr Sedgwick. Yes, I'm Magdalena Ridgeway, this is my husband, Gavin, and our friends Max Allerdyce and Rona Parish.' She paused, and with a jerk of her heart Rona knew what was coming and had no way of stopping her. 'Rona's a biographer,' Magda continued, 'and she's been commissioned to take over Russell Page's work on the life of Gideon Ward, which is quite an honour.'

Watching him, Rona was aware of a sudden stillness, so brief that she might have imagined it. Then he was saying smoothly, 'My congratulations. He was quite a character, as I know from personal experience, having been one of his victims when I first came over.'

He held her eyes a moment longer, then with a smile that encompassed them all moved on to the next table. Slowly Rona let out her breath.

'There you are!' Magda exclaimed, clearly pleased with herself. 'I've given you a way in, if you want to contact him later.'

Rona smiled and nodded, but something in those vivid blue eyes made her feel she'd have preferred Bruce Sedgwick not to know about her latest assignment.

NINE

The meeting with Bruce Sedgwick, brief though it had been, lingered unpleasantly in Rona's mind. And as she painstakingly went through the morass of notes, jottings and memoranda she'd inherited, she searched in vain for any mention of him. Furthermore, by the end of that week she reluctantly accepted that she'd have to reinterview all those to whom Russell had spoken, needing to assess their memories of Gideon for herself, rather than at second hand.

'More complicated that you thought, love?' Max enquired sympathetically on the Friday evening.

'Prue said all the groundwork had been done,' she replied, 'but Russell wouldn't have slanted questions in the way I would, so their answers might be completely different. The only real help he's been is to point me in the direction of whom to approach.'

'Well,' Max said bracingly, 'as someone once said, thank God it's Friday. And we have a family dinner to look forward to.'

'I'm apprehensive about that too,' Rona said gloomily. 'I really can't see Mum and Catherine exchanging niceties, but perhaps I'm wronging them.'

'Is Steve Hathaway coming?'

'No. Lindsey said Catherine apologized, and explained that as this was the first getting together she felt only family should be there.'

'Sarah and Clive?'

Rona shook her head. 'Only our side. They've nothing to do with Dad and Catherine.'

Max slid an arm round her. 'Don't look so worried, sweetie. I'm sure it will all be perfectly civilized.'

She smiled reluctantly. 'No pistols at dawn?'

'Not quite your father's style.'

The Parishes' new home was a fifteen-minute drive away, on the corner of Alban Road and Danvers Close, placing it midway between Hollybush Lane, where Barnie and Dinah lived, and Lindsey's flat in Fairhaven. Since the entrance was in the Close, its owners were spared the hazards of backing out of their drive on to the main road.

Guy's car was already at the gate and Lindsey's a little farther along, so Max drove through the open gates and parked in the drive. 'Looks as though we're the last to arrive,' he remarked, switching off the engine. 'With luck, any ice there might have been should have been broken.'

Tom opened the door to them. 'Come in, come in! Great to see you!' He kissed Rona and took the bottle of wine Max handed him. 'Thanks, Max – my favourite region, as you know. The others have only just arrived, so go and join them while I get your drinks. I think they're in the garden.'

Rona had been to this house several times, and was always struck by the air of warmth and welcome it generated. When Tom had left the marital home he'd taken only his books and personal effects, unwilling to denude what was still Avril's home. However, when she and Guy moved to Marsborough and the house in

Belmont was sold, she'd offered him the choice of ornaments and items of furniture and, after a spell in storage, it warmed Rona's heart to see them again.

She and Max walked through the sitting room – a replica of Catherine's at her bungalow – and joined the group on the terrace. Her mother, chic in a silk dress which Rona guessed had been bought for this occasion, was chatting to Lindsey, while the new puppy chased bees on the lawn. Rona hoped he wouldn't catch one. Catherine and Guy, meanwhile. were surveying the plants in a flowerbed.

'This year, we're just waiting to see what comes up,' she was saying. 'Then we'll decide what we want to keep or if we'd prefer to replan the whole garden.'

She turned as Rona and Max emerged from the house. 'Ah, there you are! Come and join the party! Is Tom getting your drinks?'

'He is,' Tom confirmed, appearing in the doorway with a tray. 'Incidentally, there's an interesting smell in the kitchen. Does something need turning down?'

'I'll go and check.'

The small groups reformed and conversation became general until Catherine called them in to eat.

'We'll leave Rex in the garden, if that's all right,' Guy said, closing the patio door just as the puppy reached it.

'Oh, let him come in!' Tom protested, as the little dog pawed the glass, whimpering.

Avril shook her head. 'Think of your new carpets!' she said. 'Really, once we're out of sight he'll be fine and probably fall asleep.'

In the dining room, sunshine glinted on the highly polished table and lit rainbows in the glasses. Their places were marked by cards in silver holders and they seated themselves accordingly – Guy and Rona on one side of the table, Lindsey, Max and Avril on the other. Cold watercress soup was followed by salmon en croute and to Rona's surprise and relief even her mother seemed at ease, no doubt aided by the copious wine that accompanied each course. She began to relax herself and, catching her eye across the table, Max gave her a wink.

'Did I tell you my wife has sent me back to work?' Tom asked humorously, topping up Rona's glass.

Catherine smiled. 'I've offered my services to the High School to research their history for them, like I did for the Buckford schools, and suggested Tom should do something similar for the bank. Not the local one, of course, but the group as a whole. It's been going for hundreds of years and survived amalgamations, takeovers and heaven knows how many financial storms in the course of them.'

'I resisted at first,' Tom admitted, as he continued round the table refilling glasses. 'But after Catherine got the go-ahead I went online to see what was there, and much to my surprise became hooked. She was right, my brain has been singularly inactive since my retirement and was starting to calcify.'

'I didn't say that!' Catherine protested laughingly.

'You hinted at it, and you were right.' He resumed his place, looking round at their interested faces. 'Would you believe the first National Bank opened in the sixteen hundreds? It'll probably take me years, and whether or not Head Office will be interested is anybody's guess, but I'm really looking forward to getting down to it. Who would have thought I was a researcher manqué?'

'Well, good for you, Dad!' Lindsey said approvingly. 'You too, Catherine. And if you'd like some unofficial history of the High to spice it up a bit, Rona and I could supply it!'

Rona said, 'I've fond memories of your Buckford histories. They were an enormous help when I was researching education in the town.'

Reminiscences of schooldays followed as the main course was cleared away and the dessert brought through. Then Guy, changing the subject, remarked, 'Awful thing about that journalist woman being murdered, wasn't it? I meant to ask, Rona, did you know her?'

Rona took a deep breath, willing Max and Lindsey not to elaborate. 'Yes, actually, I met her once. I was going to include her in my single-mothers series, so when she was killed Barnie asked me to do her obituary. It'll be in next month's issue.'

'I'll miss her recipes,' Avril remarked. 'I always cut them out and tried quite a few.'

'They still haven't found the person responsible,' Guy went on. 'Probably an ex-boyfriend – judging by her photo she was an attractive woman.'

'What was she like as a person, Rona?' Catherine asked.

'On the taciturn side, to be honest, which made it hard to do her justice.'

'You mean she was stand-offish?'

'Not exactly. Perhaps reserved is a better description. She didn't smile much and there was nothing to soften her image, like jewellery for example. No rings, earrings or bracelets. In fact her only adornment, if it could be called that, was a little tattoo on her neck in the shape of a butterfly.'

Catherine, who had started to serve the dessert, dropped the spoon into the mousse and sat down abruptly, the colour leaving her face. Everyone exclaimed in consternation and Tom jumped up and hurried to her side.

'Darling, what is it? Aren't you well?'

She made a dismissive gesture, turning to Rona. 'A butterfly . . . on her neck?' she repeated, her voice hoarse.

Rona, puzzled, nodded. 'Under her right ear, actually.'

'It was definitely a tattoo?'

'Well, it looked like one.'

'Could it possibly have been a birthmark?'

Rona hesitated. The rest of them were listening in bewilderment, their eyes going from one speaker to the other.

'I suppose so. All I noticed was that it was a butterfly. Why, Catherine? Why are you so interested?'

Catherine stared at her for a long moment but Rona had the strange sensation that it wasn't herself she was seeing. Then she seemed to snap out of it and gave a forced laugh.

'I'm so sorry, everyone. I don't know what came over me! I used to know someone with a butterfly birthmark, that's all. Now please, let's just forget it. Avril, would you like the mousse or the almond tart?'

Slowly, precariously, conversation started up again, but the relaxed atmosphere had been shattered and it never completely recovered.

'What the hell was that all about?' Max demanded rhetorically as they drove home.

'Goodness knows. The butterfly really spooked her, didn't it? I'm sorry I ever mentioned it.'

'Resurrected painful memories, perhaps, but it was a traumatic reaction. Remind me never to discuss insects when Catherine's around!'

* * *

The next morning Rona had a phone call from Phyllis Ward.

'I'm sorry to disturb you on a Saturday, Miss Parish,' she began, 'but I thought you'd like to know Gideon's sister is over from Italy. You said you were hoping to speak to anyone who knew him personally, and she'd be happy to meet you if you feel she might help.'

'That's kind of you, Mrs Ward, I should be delighted to meet her.'

'She's with me for the weekend, then going to spend a few days in London, staying at the Argyll Hotel in Mayfair. It would probably be more convenient for you to meet her there instead of trailing out here again. She suggests either Tuesday or Wednesday afternoon.'

'Tuesday would be fine.'

'At three o'clock, then? Her name is Mrs Hester Croft.'

'Thank you. I'll look forward to seeing her.'

Just the fillip I needed, Rona thought, switching off the phone. Gideon's sister should be able to fill in any number of gaps concerning his early life.

The Argyll Hotel was familiar to Rona for reasons varying from nights spent there with Max after theatre visits to confrontations with a murderer. This occasion, she thought whimsically, should fall somewhere between the two in terms of enjoyment.

Having asked for Mrs Croft at the reception desk, she was told the lady was awaiting her in the lounge. Afternoon tea was being served and the room was fairly crowded, but there was only one woman sitting alone and Rona approached her.

'Mrs Croft? I'm Rona Parish.'

'Delighted to meet you, Ms Parish. Please sit down. I've ordered tea – I presume you'd like some?'

'I should indeed.' Rona sat as instructed, slightly daunted by the woman opposite her. Hester Croft was, she judged, in her mid-sixties. She had silver rather than grey hair, sculpted close to her head, and apart from the slightly hooded eyes there was little resemblance to her brother. Her linen suit was obviously designer, her posture upright. She wore a long string of pearls that fell over her flat bosom, and her bony fingers were weighted down with rings.

As though he'd been awaiting Rona's arrival, a waiter hurried over with the pre-ordered tea – tiny scones, wafer-thin sandwiches, fancy cakes and a few slices of lemon arranged on a saucer. Mrs Croft poured tea directly into the china cups, using the strainer provided, and passed Rona milk and sugar. Then she slid a slice of lemon into her own cup and sat back, regarding her with interest.

'So. Phyllis tells me you've inherited my brother's biography?'

'I have, yes. It's quite a responsibility, taking over from Russell Page.'

Hester nodded. 'He and I never met, though we corresponded.'

That was something Rona hadn't yet come across. 'To be honest I've not had a chance to go through all his papers, so I hope you'll forgive me if I ask the same questions.'

'It wasn't question and answer he was interested in, so much as my recollections. But fire away, Ms Parish. What would you like to know?'

'Before I begin, would you mind if I record our conversation? It's a way of ensuring I don't miss anything.'

Hester Croft helped herself to a sandwich. 'So long as you can ignore the sound of my chomping, feel free.'

Rona extracted her ever-present recorder and laid it beside her plate. 'I suppose, like Mr Page, it's really your recollections I'm after. Were there just the two of you growing up?'

'We had a younger brother, but he died at the age of twelve, of appendicitis.'

'I'm so sorry.'

'Otherwise, it was just Gideon and I. We were born fourteen months apart and fought like cat and dog.'

'You grew up in Ireland, I believe?'

'That's right. We lived in this large, rambling house with masses of rooms that were never used, where we used to play hide-and-seek. It was set in an equally rambling garden, so we'd no near neighbours. Looking back, I suppose we were given a pretty free rein until we were nine or ten, when we were packed off to boarding school – quite a culture shock for both of us.'

'There are photos of the house among Mr Page's papers.'

'Yes, I sent him some.' She opened her capacious handbag, which had been on the seat beside her. 'I found a few more, of us as children, which you can reproduce if you care to.'

Rona lent forward eagerly. 'That's great – thank you!'

The snapshots were, of course, black-and-white and a little grainy.

She could only hope the printers would be able to revive them. One was of three children, the youngest a baby in a pram, presumably the lost brother. Another showed the two elder children, probably aged five or six, in front of a climbing frame. The boy's shirt was hanging out, the girl's hair blowing across her face. A moment in time captured about sixty years ago.

Rona flicked through the half-dozen, a couple of which included a woman, presumably their mother. 'I'll take good care of them,' she promised, pausing to look more closely at one of the boy, Gideon, on what was obviously a new bicycle.

'Did the family suspect early on that your brother was going to make a name for himself?'

'Oh, it was a foregone conclusion. Our father was a professor and former international rugby player, and our mother a member of Mensa. They expected nothing less.'

'And you?'

Hester sipped her tea. 'I fear they gave up on me. After I'd obtained my doctorate, admittedly at an early age, I was foolish enough to fall in love and throw it all away. But that, my dear, is the sum total of all you'll learn about me; it's Gideon we're here to discuss.'

'I'm sorry, I didn't mean—'

Hester waved a beringed hand. 'No need to apologize, it was only a warning shot.' She passed the plate of sandwiches and Rona took one. 'As a young man,' she went on, 'he was more interested in sport than academia, though that didn't prevent him getting a double first at Cambridge.'

'Mrs Ward said she accompanied him to sporting fixtures all over the world.'

'Indeed she did – to keep an eye on him, I suspect! Her hands were tied, though, once the children began to arrive.'

Rona waited expectantly, but when Hester showed no sign of elaborating she prompted, 'Then he became a foreign correspondent?'

She nodded. 'He spoke several languages fluently, so once again the world was his oyster. The more dangerous the place, the better it appealed to him.'

'It must have been hard, though,' Rona ventured, 'being away so much, especially when the children were young.'

Hester Croft regarded her with a faint smile. 'I fear my brother wasn't the uxorious man you seem to imagine, Ms Parish,' she said drily. 'It might surprise you to learn that he had affairs throughout his married life, right up until his death.'

Rona stared at her, her mind racing. This was news indeed! 'Did his wife know?' she asked after a moment.

'Of course. It would have been impossible for her *not* to have known.'

'And . . . she didn't mind?'

'She'd no choice in the matter. Her consolation was that his emotions were never engaged. He adored her – and her alone – all his life, and she adored him.'

'But he must have known he was hurting her?'

Hester shrugged elaborately. 'It was the way he was. To my sibling surprise, women found him very attractive. So he had his pick of them – famous actresses, politicians' wives, barristers, you name it.'

'But I don't understand – why wasn't it public knowledge?'

'Because everyone with whom he dallied had a very good reason for keeping it quiet. Oh, a few people knew, certainly, but there seemed to be an unspoken agreement that it should be kept under wraps. Don't ask me why! In my opinion it was more than he deserved.'

'Did you know who these women were?' Rona asked, her mind still reeling.

'Some of them. Quite a few really fell for him and thought they could inveigle him away from Phyllis, but they hadn't a hope.'

After a moment Rona said hesitantly, 'I'm not sure why you're telling me this.'

Hester raised an eyebrow. 'I understood you wanted a picture of the complete man, warts and all?'

'Well, yes, but I can hardly—'

'Don't worry, I discussed it with Phyllis and she's quite amenable for the truth to come out, now enough time has passed since his death. Her only stipulation was that none of the women should be named – and as I'm not going to tell you who they were, that shouldn't pose a problem.'

She raised the teapot enquiringly and Rona nodded, holding out her cup.

'It's not for the shock value,' Hester continued. 'His sexual drive was an integral part of him, and being aware of it gives a deeper understanding of his character.'

It seemed this was her last word on the subject, and Rona somewhat reluctantly moved on. 'Did you see much of each other in later life?' she asked.

'Not a great deal. My living abroad made it more difficult, but I contacted them whenever I came over and I was here for his sixtieth birthday. I'm thankful for that, because he died suddenly a month later.'

She sighed, looking down into her teacup. 'We were never particularly close, even as children, but blood is thicker than water and there are ties that bind. It saddens me, for instance, to know there's no longer anyone I can ask if I forget the name of someone we knew when we were young, or where we went on holiday in a particular year. But I suppose that's the penalty of growing old, family or no family.'

Rona longed to enquire about Hester's present circumstances – Mrs Ward had mentioned Italy – and whether or not she had children, but she'd been warned off personal questions.

'He kept a journal,' she said suddenly. 'I assume you know that?'

'No?' Rona was immediately alert. 'I haven't seen any mention of one.'

'Phyllis must have decided not to offer it. I'll have a word with her. It wasn't a regular day-by-day account. More jottings of his thoughts – who he'd like to interview, who he had dinner with, and so on – which I imagine would be more of interest to a biographer.'

'Invaluable!' Rona confirmed.

'Well, now she's resigned to the affairs becoming public perhaps she'll part with it. Or them, I should say – there were several over the years, dating back to his foreign correspondent days.' She threw Rona a sharp glance. 'So no doubt you'll discover *where* and *when* he conducted his liaisons – but, since he used a code, not *with whom*. It's up to you how you use the information.'

The room was emptying as, tea over, people went on to other engagements, and waiters were clearing the tables they'd vacated.

Hester Croft smiled. 'We'll be unpopular if we linger much longer. Unless there's something else you'd like to ask?'

'I can't think of anything. I'm so grateful for everything you've told me.'

'I know you'll handle it sympathetically,' Hester said calmly. 'And if you could ask Mrs Ward—'

'About the journals? Yes, I shall be going back to Richmond before I fly home. I'll speak to her while I'm there. Good luck with your book, Ms Parish. I look forward to reading it.'

And it would be all the richer after this meeting, Rona thought as she made her way to the Underground. A whole new section of her subject's life had opened up – one that it seemed Russell Page had not been privy to – and if she were allowed access to the journals she could give a far deeper portrayal of Gideon Ward than she had imagined possible.

TEN

Rona woke the next morning to the sound of Gus barking at the foot of the stairs. What was wrong with the dog? she wondered sleepily – he was usually content to await her in the kitchen. She burrowed more deeply under the duvet, but as she turned to face the window the strength of the morning sun penetrated her closed eyes and she opened them to come face to face with the clock on the bedside table. It showed nine fifteen! She sat up with a jerk.

It couldn't be! She was always up at seven thirty except when Max was home. She slid out of bed and checked her watch on the dressing table. It showed the same time. Just as well she hadn't any meetings scheduled for this morning! She ran down the stairs to the hall, greeting the dog, who continued barking and wagging his tail.

'I know, Gus! I'm sorry!' He turned and raced ahead of her down the basement stairs, pushing her aside as she opened the patio door. The kitchen floor was cool to her bare feet as she filled the kettle, still bewildered at the lateness of the hour.

She'd been glad to reach home after her London trip; it had been a hot, airless day and the Underground was suffocating. There followed an uncomfortable strap-hanging journey to King's Cross, and the main-line train hadn't been much better. She'd dozed off during the television programme she was watching, which was irritating, and had gone upstairs at ten immediately after Max's phone call. Which meant she must have had nearly eleven hours sleep!

She poured boiling water into the cafetière, let Gus back in and shook biscuits into his bowl, thinking over her talk with Hester. So the dishevelled, irritable man she knew from television had been a Lothario! That should help her sales! she thought cynically, remembering with sympathy the calm, dignified woman she'd met in Richmond. She doubted she'd have been able to cope with her husband's unfaithfulness as tolerantly as had Phyllis Ward.

Taking her coffee with her, she went back upstairs for a shower.

Rona spent the next hour or two sorting Russell's notes on Ward's early life. It was clear he'd been in touch with Hester, since he related some of the things she'd mentioned. There were reminiscences from school friends who'd known him both at his preparatory school and at Winchester, and tales of some of the escapades he'd got up to as a young man. She wondered at what age he'd begun to keep his journals and what she'd be able to make of them – provided Phyllis was in fact willing to part with them.

When her phone rang she reached for it automatically, and it was with a start of surprise that she recognized Esmé Page's voice.

'Good morning, Ms Parish. I hope I'm not disturbing you?'

'Mrs Page! How are you?'

'A little better, thank you. I returned from Scotland yesterday, and was wondering how you were faring with disentangling Russell's notes?'

'I'm working on them at the moment, actually.'

'I hope you're not blaming him for the state they're in. It was I who bundled everything higgledy-piggledy into the case.'

'Don't worry, they're falling into place.' Rona thought again of the sighting of him just before he was killed, and again vacillated about whether or not to mention it.

'Is there anything more I can help you with?'

'I don't think so, thank you. Oh,' she added on the spur of the moment, 'except that you said something was worrying your husband during his last weeks.'

'Yes?'

She crossed her fingers. 'Could it have been anything to do with Bruce Sedgwick?'

There was a pause. 'The hotel man, you mean? I suppose it's possible. Russell knew him when they were boys.'

Rona stiffened. 'Your husband *knew* Bruce Sedgwick?'

'Apparently. When the DVDs arrived he flicked through to see who they featured and exclaimed, "Bruce Sedgwick! Good God, I was at school with him!".'

Rona was floundering. 'But I don't see – I mean, he's Australian, isn't he? And I understood from the interview he'd never been to the UK, despite his uncle inviting him.'

'Oh. Then it must have been someone else with the same name.'

Rona said slowly, 'Might that explain his visit to his school?'

'Possibly, but if he'd wanted to get in touch, surely he'd have tried one of the hotels.'

There was no point in pursuing it, Rona thought in frustration; Mrs Page knew no more than she did. The simple answer, as she'd said, must be that Russell was mistaken – no doubt there were dozens of Bruce Sedgwicks.

For minutes after the call ended she continued to gnaw at the problem. Then, with an exclamation of impatience, she took the tape downstairs and played it for the third time, concentrating on every word Sedgwick said. As she'd thought, there was no hint he'd ever visited the UK and his education hadn't even been touched on. Perhaps the ex-Winchester man hadn't thought it of consequence.

She sat staring at the blank screen. Perhaps she'd read too much into the displacement of that tape; perhaps the only reason Page set it apart was because he thought he'd known the man. But had he? And had his visit to Buckford College settled that question one way or the other? And if she also paid a visit, would it settle it for her? And, perhaps more pertinently, did it really matter? Or was she going off at a tangent, as Russell Page seemed to have done before her?

She ran back upstairs and took her history of Buckford off the shelf. The series of articles on its eight-hundred-year history had appeared as central pull-outs in succeeding editions of *Chiltern Life*, and a binder had been offered for those who wanted to keep them. Rona sat down at her desk and started to flick through it, memories flooding back: its market charter dating back to King John, the

Royalists barricading themselves in the church during the Civil War, and old Miss Rosebury with her tales of ghosts and the Witches' Pond.

Although her research at the College had resulted in what Max called the usual mayhem and murder, the history itself had been well received and, with the exception of the headmaster, the staff had been helpful. Well, Richard Maddox was long gone, but hopefully some of the administrative staff would remember her.

Making a quick decision, she reached for the phone.

'Buckford College,' said a crisp voice.

'Could you tell me, please, if Miss Morton is still the school secretary?'

'Yes, madam, she is.'

Rona breathed a sigh of relief. The first hurdle cleared. 'Would it be possible to have a word with her? My name is Rona Parish.'

'One moment, please, I'll see if she's free.'

A pause and then, 'Miss Parish! How nice to hear from you!'

'Hello Miss Morton, I'm wondering if you could possibly help me? I'm trying to establish whether someone was at the College about thirty years ago.'

'My goodness! That's quite a tall order!'

'I was hoping there might be some records I could go through.'

'I'm afraid not. We have archives, of course, but as you'll appreciate it's a sensitive area and only the archivist herself is allowed access. However, you could submit a query and ask her to search on your behalf, if you know the exact year or term you're interested in.'

'Unfortunately I don't.' Rona paused. 'There's something else. I believe the biographer Russell Page was a past pupil and visited the school shortly before his death. Would it be possible to check if he had an appointment with anyone?'

'Ah, now there I can help you. Mr Page phoned a few weeks ago to ask if one of his contemporaries was still teaching here. They arranged to meet and I saw him briefly when he called to take Mr Spencer to lunch.'

'That's great, Miss Morton! Just what I wanted to know. Next question – do you think Mr Spencer would see me?'

'I can pass on your request and ask him to contact you, if that would help.'

'It would indeed. I'd be most grateful.'

'Is this for another article you're writing?' Miss Morton enquired interestedly, making a note of her number.

'It has links with what I'm working on,' Rona replied evasively. 'Thanks so much for your help.'

The call came at five o'clock that evening. 'This is Simon Spencer. Am I speaking to Miss Rona Parish?'

'Oh, Mr Spencer. Yes, thanks so much for calling.'

'I understand from the school secretary that you'd like to meet me, but I wasn't informed in what connection.'

So Russell hadn't been mentioned, which perhaps was all to the good.

'It's difficult to explain over the phone, but it concerns Russell Page.'

'You knew him?'

Rona bit her lip, but she owed him at least a brief explanation. 'No, but I've been asked to take over the biography he was working on, on Gideon Ward.'

His tone altered. 'Forgive me, you're Rona Parish the biographer? I hadn't made the connection, but I can't think that I—'

'It's about whether or not you knew someone at school,' Rona blurted out in desperation and heard him draw in his breath. When he spoke his voice had sharpened.

'May I ask what you know about that?'

'Not a great deal. I was hoping you could tell me,' she added frankly.

'I'm sorry, Ms Parish, but there's no point in going further. Any discussion Page and I might have had on the subject was sensitive and highly confidential.'

'There's another thing,' Rona persisted, playing what she hoped was her trump card. 'I have some information that might interest you concerning the last day of his life.'

There was a significant pause. Then Simon Spencer said drily, 'You're very persuasive, I must say. Very well, I'll meet you provided you accept that I'm unable to pass on anything he and I discussed. Twelve thirty tomorrow in the lounge bar of the White Horse. Do you know it?'

'I do, yes.'

'For purposes of identification,' he added ironically, 'I'm dark-haired, six foot two, and shall be carrying a rolled-up copy of the *Buckford Courier*.'

'Thanks so much, Mr Spencer. I look forward to meeting you.'

'It's been an eventful day,' Rona told Max over their pre-dinner drinks that evening.

Max sat back, crossing his legs. 'What have you been up to?'

'Well, the first thing is that Mrs Page phoned this morning. And you'll never believe what she told me – Russell was at school with Bruce Sedgwick!'

Max frowned. 'But he's an Aussie! What was he doing at school over here?'

'I've no idea. He certainly never mentioned it in his interview. She concluded it must have been a different Bruce Sedgwick.'

'Very probably, though I can't for the life of me see why you're so hung up on him. Why don't you concentrate on Gideon Ward?'

'I've not finished telling you the day's events! It seemed likely that the reason Russell suddenly went to Buckford College, which he'd not been back to since he left, was a direct result of watching the interview. So I rang them. And guess what? I learned he'd gone to meet a contemporary of his who's now a master there and they had lunch together.'

'Big deal!'

'Obviously it was to discuss Bruce—'

'Obviously!' Max agreed sarcastically.

'Just *listen*! The upshot is that I'm meeting this man tomorrow.'

'You're telling me you're going all the way to Buckford on this wild goose chase? What exactly do you hope to get out of it?'

'Admittedly he was pretty cagey on the phone, but with luck he'll open up. And if he still won't say what they talked about, it'll at least prove it was something important.'

'Or simply no one else's business.'

'Well, we'll have to wait and see, won't we, smarty boots?'

Max laughed. 'Have it your way. You're not happy, are you, unless you have some mystery to solve? I await the next instalment with interest.'

'I'm not sure you deserve to hear it,' she said.

* * *

During those four weeks of her research three years ago, Rona had spent two nights a week in Buckford and come to know the town well. Unlike Marsborough, whose spacious elegance was frequently compared with Bath and Cheltenham, Buckford's link with history was more palpable and in its narrow streets and winding alleyways the past lived side by side with the present. It wasn't only Miss Rosebury who was aware of ghosts.

She waited for the rush hour to pass before setting off on the two-and-a-half hour journey. Gus had settled on his rug on the back seat, and before meeting Simon Spencer she planned to walk with him round remembered haunts. If she'd had more time she'd have arranged to meet Nuala Banks, with whom she'd lodged, but since her lunch hour would be taken up with Spencer there wouldn't be an opportunity. Another time, perhaps.

The market car park looked ominously full, but as Rona hesitated a car obligingly backed out of a space and she slid smoothly into it. It was eleven forty-five and she opted for a three-hour stay. Since she wasn't sure the White Horse would accommodate dogs, she planned to settle Gus back in the car after his exercise. It was cloudy today, and with the window slightly open he'd be quite comfortable.

So she set off on a nostalgic walk down haunted Clement's Lane, looking prosaic enough in the midday light, past the ancient Counting House, the stone cross and, comparatively modern with its Victorian architecture, St Stephen's Primary School, where for twelve years Catherine had been headmistress. The centuries melded seamlessly together and Rona felt a surge of affection for the old town that wore its history so comfortably.

But time was moving on and she reluctantly returned to the car, where she poured water into Gus's travelling bowl, waited while he drank his fill, and let him back into the car. Then, already planning her approach to Simon Spencer, she made her way to the White Horse.

She saw him at once. Indeed he was hard to miss, with his height and the prominently displayed newspaper, and as she threaded her way through the crowd to join him she wondered how much, if anything, she would have learned about Bruce Sedgwick by the time she left.

He took her hand, studying her face as he did so. 'I apologize for the necessity but I shall have to eat while we talk – you'll appreciate my time is limited. I trust you'll have no objection to joining me?'

'Thank you,' she said, cursing herself for not foreseeing this slight embarrassment.

'Then let me take you to the grandiosely named restaurant, where we can at least sit down. The menu is the same as the bar's.'

The room he led her to was furnished with plain deal tables and chairs, most of which were already occupied, but he appeared to have reserved a place since the table he stopped at had a card on it to that effect.

'I can recommend the beef-and-ale pie,' he commented, handing her a menu.

'Then thank you, that sounds good.'

'And a glass of wine?'

She nodded. 'Red, please.'

'Excuse me while I place the order. They don't run to waitresses.'

She watched him leave the room, sorting out her first impressions. Tall and dark, as he'd told her, though strands of silver showed in his hair and there were deep grooves around his nose and mouth. An attractive face but one, she guessed, that would brook no nonsense. In other words, the face of a schoolmaster. With a slightly sinking heart, she suspected it wouldn't be easy to break down his reticence.

'Now,' he said on his return, setting down two glasses on the table, 'what exactly do you want to know, Ms Parish?'

Once again Rona explained about the DVD that was out of sequence and the questions it had given rise to. 'I've played it several times,' she finished, 'but I can't see any reason for its being singled out. Interestingly, though, when I saw Mrs Ward and asked if her husband had made any comment about Sedgwick, she said no, he hadn't, but Russell Page had asked the same question. Which, of course, increased my curiosity.'

'But not, surely, to the extent of seeking me out?'

'No, there were two other factors. Mrs Page also told me that Russell – sorry for the familiarity, but that's how I think of him – seemed to have been worried about something during his last weeks and had paid an unexpected visit to the College, which he'd never been back to, and wouldn't explain why. Then yesterday, when I asked her if his concern could have involved Bruce Sedgwick, she surprised me by saying they'd been at school together. However, we agreed that, as he's Australian and hadn't said anything in his interview about living in the UK, it was most likely someone with the same name.'

'But you wanted to confirm that.' Spencer's eyes were on his wine glass, which he was slowly turning in his fingers.

'Yes, which is why I phoned the College. I was told I couldn't go through the archives as I'd hoped, but when I asked about Russell's visit I learned that he'd called to take you to lunch.'

Spencer said wryly, 'You'll be thinking lunch plays a pivotal role in my activities.'

'Table nine!' called a voice from the doorway, and he raised a hand. Two appetizing plates of pie were laid before them and, picking up her knife and fork, Rona realized how hungry she was.

For several minutes they ate in silence, each mulling over what had been said. Then Spencer prompted, 'You referred on the phone to the last day of his life?'

'Yes. Quite by chance I met someone who'd seen him shortly before he was killed.'

'Go on.' His voice was tense.

'Well, he'd told his wife he was going to spend the day at the reference library, but when this person saw him he was in a country village, getting into his car with another man. Then they set off in the direction where the crash occurred shortly after.'

She waited expectantly for a response, and when none came continued. 'My husband thinks I'm attaching too much importance to that, but it seemed . . . strange to me.'

Finally Spencer cleared his throat. 'Did your friend give any description of this other man?'

'No, he had his back to him and at the time Rory attached no importance to it.'

There was a long silence, then Rona said suddenly, 'Oh, and there's another thing that, taken with everything else, seems a bit odd. Mrs Page told me their house was broken into during the funeral.'

Spencer swore softly under his breath. Then he looked up, meeting her eyes. 'I appreciate that you've been very frank, Ms Parish, and

I'm only sorry I can't be equally frank with you. What I can tell you, though, is that Page was convinced the man appearing on television was not the boy with whom he'd been at school.'

'But does it matter? He didn't claim to be.'

'That's a moot point. There were too many similarities to write it off simply as mistaken identity. And if the man on TV *wasn't* the Bruce Sedgwick we knew, then who is he and where is the real one?'

Rona thought for a minute. 'Did he *look* like him?'

'They both had fair hair and blue eyes, but faces change with maturity so it's difficult to say.'

'Then what made Russell so sure it wasn't the same person?'

'There were two things,' Spencer said slowly. 'One was that in the interview he didn't mention being at school in the UK, which would surely have been the natural thing to do. Rather, he implied he'd never been here before.'

'And the other?'

'That, unfortunately, I can't tell you.'

'Why not?'

'Because your knowing could have serious consequences.'

She drew a deep breath. 'Then at least tell me about the boy you were at school with.'

His meal finished, Spencer laid down his knife and fork and sat back. 'He came to BC in Year Six – at the age of eleven – for just one term. We were told he lived in Australia with his father, a single parent, and when said father was rushed to hospital with a burst appendix there had been no one to care for him. So his uncle, who was a chef and lived in this country, brought him over and enrolled him at BC as a temporary measure while his father recuperated. I'd forgotten, but Page reminded me how he used to boast about his uncle's cooking.'

Rona stared thoughtfully into her glass. 'You must have heard of Bruce Sedgwick and his hotel chain before this. Didn't it ring any bells?'

Spencer shook his head. 'Frankly, I'd forgotten all about the boy. As I said, he wasn't with us long and it was many years ago. In the meantime I'd met a number of Sedgwicks so I didn't make the connection till Page contacted me and told me his doubts, which I have to admit I found pretty compelling.'

He leaned forward suddenly. 'I'd strongly advise you, Ms Parish, not to pursue this any further. It has nothing to do with Ward – limit your investigations to him.'

Which was roughly what Max had said, but without the implied warning. Rona felt a cold shiver run through her. She moistened her lips.

'Why didn't you look into it further yourselves? Report your suspicions to the police?'

'We hadn't enough to go on, nothing that would make a credible case. And if we'd started voicing our doubts as to this well-known man's authenticity we'd have landed ourselves in the libel courts.'

She said slowly, 'You think it was important, don't you, that sighting of the other man?'

Spencer sighed. 'Against my advice, Page elected to meet Sedgwick, refer to having been at school with him, and gauge his reaction.'

'And did he?'

'I don't know, he was killed soon afterwards. Which is why I'm advising you to drop it.' He looked at his watch. 'I'm sorry, but I must go. Unless you're in a hurry yourself, please stay and have coffee. I've added it to the bill.'

'Thank you – and for lunch. And I'm sorry for inviting myself!'

'It was a pleasure to meet you, but please remember what I said.' And with a final nod, he was gone. Rona sat immobile, deaf to the shouts of laughter from a nearby table, and looked up only briefly as a cup of coffee was put in front of her. She nodded her thanks and reached automatically for the milk.

He was killed soon afterwards. Which is why I'm advising you *to drop it*. The juxtaposition of those two sentences was chilling. Did Spencer suspect that Russell's companion on that fatal day had been the man calling himself, either rightly or wrongly, Bruce Sedgwick? And that Russell's subsequent death had been, at the very least, convenient?

She hadn't mentioned that she'd met Sedgwick briefly herself.

She stiffened suddenly, and the cup she'd started to lift crashed down on its saucer. *Magda had told him, that evening at the hotel, that she'd taken over Russell Page's biography! Might he consider her, too, a threat?*

ELEVEN

'So was the trip to Buckford worthwhile?' Max enquired when he phoned that evening.

'It was certainly interesting,' Rona hedged.

'Was your informant able to add anything further to your suspicions?'

'I'd hardly call him an informant. He seems sure the two Bruce Sedgwicks aren't the same, though there are strong similarities between them.'

'Which, presumably, gets you precisely nowhere.'

Rona didn't reply. She was tired after the double journey and, although uneasy about what she'd learned, she hadn't the energy to argue with Max. He'd already advised her to drop her interest in Sedgwick. Now Spencer had done the same. The sensible thing was to follow that advice, but she'd give a lot to know what had aroused Russell's suspicions – it must have been something in Gideon's interview, but she'd not the slightest idea what it could have been.

The following evening, after supper at the Hathaways', Lindsey was, at her own insistence, helping Steve clear away. Luke was out at Scouts, and Frank had returned to the sitting room to check if there was anything worth watching on television.

She felt so at home here, she reflected as she washed the wine glasses in soapy water, so much a part of the family – but since most of the time Steve treated her as a family friend it was a mixed blessing. She felt a sudden overwhelming need to know his real feelings and, fearing she might betray herself, said abruptly, 'How's Patrick? Have you seen him lately?'

There was a brief pause and she realized belatedly that Steve had been speaking. Before she could apologize he answered smoothly, 'Not for some time. He seems to be spending every free minute out at Nettleton with Venetia.'

'That must be hard on Samantha.'

'I'm sure she understands.'

'Nevertheless, I might invite her to supper at the flat one evening.'

'That's a great idea, I'm sure she'd appreciate it.'

Lindsey rinsed a glass under the tap. 'You don't think he'd anything to do with it, do you?' she asked thoughtfully.

'The murder?' Steve sighed. 'I suppose anyone can snap, but I very much doubt it. He seemed very open about their relationship, didn't he? Didn't try to hide that they'd had a row.'

She was silent, and he prompted, 'What do you think?'

'I don't know him as well as you do, but it would certainly seem out of character.'

He gave a short laugh. 'Unless you're a serial killer, murder usually is!'

'I suppose so.' She set the last glass on the draining board, emptied the washing-up bowl, and rinsed it under the tap before reaching for a towel.

'Thanks for that,' he said. 'Now it won't be waiting for me in the morning!' He bent to give her a kiss – and Lindsey, suddenly unable to resist, caught hold of his face, turning his usual light caress into something much deeper and more meaningful. He gave a stifled groan as his arms went round her, pulling her closely against him, and they clung together for long minutes, acknowledging at last their need of each other.

'Oh my darling!' he said breathlessly. 'Oh my darling, darling girl! We've both been through the mill these last few years. I was terrified you wouldn't want to risk it again, and that if I told you how I felt, I'd frighten you off!'

'No chance of that!' she murmured.

He held her at arm's length, his eyes going hungrily over her face. 'I can't believe this is happening! I never thought I'd feel like this again!'

'I don't think I've *ever* felt like this,' Lindsey said. 'It must be because we got to know each other first, instead of suddenly being gripped by wild passion.'

'Speak for yourself!' he teased. 'I fancied you the moment I saw you, at Rona's with tears streaming down your face!' He smiled, smoothing her hair back from her face. 'Will you marry me, Lindsey Parish?'

* * *

Minutes later, wondering what was keeping them, Frank came to the kitchen doorway. Neither of them saw him, and a smile spread slowly over his face.

'Thank God!' he said quietly, and returned, unnoticed, to the sitting room.

Two hours later Max had just turned off the light when Rona's mobile trilled on the bedside table.

'For God's sake!' he muttered irritably, switching the light back on as she scrabbled for the phone. Lindsey.

Before she could speak, her twin's excited voice came spilling over the line. 'Guess what, Ro! Steve and I are engaged! Isn't it wonderful? I've only just got home and hope I didn't wake you, but I wanted you to be the first to know – apart from Frank, of course, who was there at the time. Well, not *exactly* at the time, of course, not in the same *room*!'

'Linz, that's absolutely great! I'm so happy for you!'

She glanced at Max, knowing Lindsey's voice had reached him, and he rolled his eyes.

'I'll phone the parents in the morning,' Lindsey gabbled on. 'Who do you think I should tell first? Mum, probably, or she might sulk. God, I'll never be able to sleep! Just as well tomorrow's Saturday. We're going to Tarltons to choose a ring!'

'I look forward to seeing it,' Rona said. 'I'm so glad for you, Linz.'

It was another ten minutes before she could get her sister off the line, by which time Max had pulled the duvet over his ears.

'Don't be a grouch!' Rona told him, when at last she lay down again. 'She's had a bad run, she deserves a break. I hope to goodness this one lasts.'

'Amen to that,' he said.

As promised, Lindsey and Steve called the next afternoon to display the ring – an emerald surrounded by diamonds – and seeing them together gave Rona hope that, after all the traumas, her sister now had the chance of a lasting relationship.

'We owe it all to you!' Steve told her. 'If you hadn't written that article on Dad, we'd never have met.'

* * *

During the following week Rona was able to make a start on the actual writing of the biography. Ward's early life had been well researched, and in some cases Russell's notes could be incorporated almost verbatim. Having determinedly closed her mind to Bruce Sedgwick, she felt she was at last making progress, a conviction strengthened by the arrival of a bulky package from Phyllis Ward containing half a dozen of Gideon's journals.

Hester feels these would be of benefit to you, read the accompanying note, *but I should of course be grateful to have them returned when you've finished with them.*

Rona opened them eagerly. The first she flicked through dated from thirty years ago, covering his assignments overseas. Peppered with personal comments on international events as they took place, it would make fascinating reading. Another volume, which was earlier still, detailed his international sporting career, and two more covered the last ten years of his life, notably his time in the media.

She was curious about the gaps between them, wondering if these were in fact the only accounts he'd written or if, for reasons of her own, Phyllis had chosen to withhold some. No matter, the ones she now had provided an invaluable insight into her subject's private thoughts on a variety of subjects and would add considerably to her portrayal of him.

Despite her new-found happiness, Lindsey had not forgotten her resolve to contact Patrick's girlfriend and accordingly phoned her on the Wednesday.

'It seems a long time since I saw you,' she began. 'How are things?'

'Pretty grim, actually,' Samantha replied. 'As you'll have noticed, the press have been hounding the police for lack of progress. Patrick's been questioned again, and according to the lunchtime news they're now saying an arrest is "imminent". And . . . well, there doesn't seem to be anyone else in the frame.'

'Oh Sam, I'm so sorry! How's he bearing up?'

'I don't know – I hardly see him these days. Neeshie has top priority, which is understandable.'

'I suppose so.' Lindsey paused, debating whether to mention her engagement, but in the circumstances it seemed inappropriate. 'I was wondering if you'd like to come for a meal one evening?' she said. 'We could chill out and catch up with what's been happening.'

'Oh, Lindsey, I'd love to! When were you thinking of?'

'Well, how about tomorrow, if you're free?'

'I'm free all the time at the moment,' Samantha replied ruefully. 'Tomorrow would be great. Where do you live?'

'Out at Fairhaven – a fifteen-minute drive, I'm afraid. It's a cul-de-sac and my flat is 6a, on the right-hand side. I can give you the postcode if you have a satnav.'

'That might help.' Samantha made a note of it.

'About eight o'clock, then?'

'I look forward to it.'

Samantha noticed the ring immediately on arrival, and caught hold of Lindsey's hand.

'Wow! This is new!' she exclaimed.

'Very,' Lindsey confirmed. 'As of Saturday, actually.'

'Congratulations! Nice to hear some good news for a change, and Steve's a super guy.'

'I agree! We're throwing an impromptu party at the Sedgwick on Saturday. I hope you and Patrick can come.'

'I can't speak for him, but I'd love to. Thank you.'

Lindsey led the way up the stairs and into the sitting room, glowing in the evening sunlight.

'What a lovely flat!' Samantha exclaimed. 'And what an original colour scheme!'

'It's all down to the interior decorators,' Lindsey confessed. 'Luckily they're friends of mine – Double N, in Guild Street. You might have come across them.'

'Afraid not.'

'I'd never have known where to start, but they bombarded me with colour charts and swatches of material. They did virtually the whole flat, and I have to say I'm delighted with it.'

'Will you live here when you're married?'

Lindsey laughed. 'Goodness, we haven't got that far yet! I doubt it, though – there wouldn't be room for Luke.'

'Ah yes, I'd forgotten Steve has a son. Do you get on with him?'

'Yes, very well. We liked each other right from the start, which is great. Now, sit down and let me get you a drink. G&T?'

'Please.'

When Lindsey handed her a glass, she raised it in a toast. 'Here's to you and Steve. Long life and happiness!'

'Thank you.'

'I envy you,' Samantha went on. 'Knowing that you'll both be together now, no matter what.'

'You have Patrick,' Lindsey reminded her.

Samantha's glance fell. 'I'm not so sure,' she said in a low voice.

'Sam!'

'He's not the same, Lindsey, since all this happened. Of course it's weighing on his mind – I understand that, but he's shut himself off and whatever I say seems to be wrong. I hope to goodness he's different at work, or Mr Sedgwick would have every excuse to sack him – he can't relish having a murder suspect as the manager of his newest hotel.'

'Patrick told us he'd been very supportive. What's he like? We often drop in for a drink, but I've never met him.'

'Nor have I. He's not often there – prefers the bright lights of London.'

'Poor Patrick,' Lindsey said reflectively, 'it must be a terrific strain.' She paused, wondering how best to frame her question. 'Do you know what this new evidence is?'

Samantha shook her head. 'When I asked him, he nearly bit my head off. Honestly, I don't feel I know him any more.' She took a quick sip of her drink.

'I shouldn't worry,' Lindsey said bracingly. 'Once the police find the culprit, he'll be able to relax and be his old self again.'

'Maybe, but I might not figure in his plans. Neeshie needs him more than ever, and the two of us don't really see eye to eye. I suspect she blames me for the marriage break-up, though I didn't meet Patrick till well after they'd separated.'

'I'm so sorry,' Lindsey said, fearing she might have flaunted her own happiness.

Samantha straightened her shoulders. 'No, *I'm* sorry. I'd no right to inflict this on you when you've been kind enough to invite me to supper. Let's just forget it – as you say, it'll probably turn out OK in the end.'

For a while conversation was a little strained, but by the time they went through to eat normality had been restored, and neither Patrick nor his problems were mentioned again.

*   *   *

'Hi, Rona!' It was her next-door neighbour on the phone.

'Hello, Monica. How are you?'

'Fine. We've just heard the news about Steve and Lindsey! Isn't it great?'

'It is indeed. You're going to the engagement party?'

'Yes, at the Sedgwick. That's why he rang.'

Rona bit her lip. 'I'd assumed it would be at the Clarendon, but only because that's where we've always held our celebrations.' She wasn't at all sure about braving the Sedgwick again.

'Steve knows the manager there, doesn't he? The one whose wife was murdered.'

'He does, yes.'

'Then it's probably for moral support. It seems a long time since we saw you, even though you are only next door! Perhaps we can fix a date tomorrow to get together?'

'That would be great, Monica.'

'See you then!' she said, and rang off.

Rona turned back to her screen, marvelling again at the series of coincidences that had brought the Hathaways and Furnesses together. It had been while researching her article on Frank that she'd read the account in his late wife's diary of how they'd been on a hijacked plane and befriended a child separated by the terrorists from her Jewish carer. And later that day, recounting the story to Monica over lunch, it had transpired that incredibly enough she had been that child. Over the years both sides had wondered what became of the other, and it had been wonderful to be able to reunite them.

When she saw Patrick Summers in the foyer, Rona was shocked at the change in him. His face was thinner, his eyes sunken, and a tic twitched at the corner of his mouth. Lindsey had described him as 'rather a hunk'; he certainly didn't look like one now, nor even like the charming, laid-back man who'd visited her. The ongoing strain was obviously telling on him.

He greeted her with a brief smile and she introduced him to Max.

'You're not coming to the party?' she asked.

'Unfortunately I'm on duty, but I promised Steve to make a token appearance later. They're in the Sundown Room, on the right at the top of the stairs.'

They thanked him and as they moved towards the staircase Rona reflected uncharitably that perhaps it was as well he wasn't free. He'd have been a spectre at the feast.

When inviting them, Lindsey had described the occasion as 'a small and select drinks party' and, since Steve was still fairly new to the area, Rona assumed it would be largely comprised of family and her sister's friends. It was therefore no surprise that the first people she saw were her parents and their new partners, chatting amicably with Sarah and Clive, Guy's daughter and son-in-law.

Avril caught sight of them and beckoned them over. 'Isn't this exciting, darlings?' she exclaimed, kissing them both. 'Just what we've been hoping for over the last four years! You've seen the ring, of course?'

'Yes,' Rona replied, returning her father's kiss, 'they called in on Saturday to show us.'

'It's probably too early to talk of wedding dates,' Avril went on, 'but I can't see any reason for waiting. Steve has his own house in Kent, which he rented out while abroad, and the lease is about to expire.'

'They're not moving away?' Rona asked sharply.

'Let's not try to pre-empt them,' Tom put in equably. 'They'll tell us their plans soon enough.'

The conversation continued, but Rona was suddenly desolate. Lindsey was a part of her, and the idea of being separated by a hundred miles or more appalled her. Ridiculously she felt tears come to her eyes, and hastily took a sip of champagne. But far from steadying her, the drink left an unpleasant taste.

'We little thought at your wedding, Sarah, that there'd soon be another in the family!' Avril was saying happily.

Looking about her a little wildly, Rona saw the Furnesses in the doorway. 'Excuse me,' she said hurriedly, 'I want a word with Monica.' And she threaded her way towards them as if they were a lifeline. To her surprise, their twelve-year-old son was with them.

'He's been invited as company for Luke,' Monica explained, and gave him a little push as Luke, smart in his school blazer, waved to him from across the room.

'Harriet not here?'

'No, she was invited but it's not her scene! She's gone to the cinema with a group of friends.'

Lindsey came hurrying over. 'Sorry, Ro, I didn't see you come in.' She gave her a quick hug and turned to the Furnesses. 'Lovely to see you both, and thanks for bringing Giles. It was the only way we could persuade Luke to come!'

She turned to a tall blonde woman who was standing to one side and pulled her forward. 'Let me introduce you to Samantha Duncan, Patrick's girlfriend. Unfortunately he's on duty but he promised to look in later. Sam, this is my sister Rona and my friends Charles and Monica Furness.'

The woman shook their hands. 'I don't need telling who *you* are!' she said to Rona. 'It's like seeing double!'

More people were arriving and Lindsey went to greet them, taking Samantha with her. Groups were re-forming and Monica commented, 'It's hopeless to try and fix a date here – I should have known! I'll phone you tomorrow.' Someone called to her, and with a farewell pat on Rona's arm she went to join them.

The small room was now oppressively hot and the noise level high. Rona put down her barely-touched champagne and, waylaying a passing waiter, requested a glass of water. She could feel her heart beating high in her chest – possibly due to the weather eye she was keeping open for Bruce Sedgwick.

Canapés of asparagus spears, smoked salmon and caviar were circulating and she declined one after the other, fighting down a wave of nausea as she looked round for a non-existent seat. What *was* the matter with her? Could one of the prawns she'd had for lunch have been suspect?

'Rona! There you are, my dear!' Frank Hathaway hurried up to her and kissed her cheek. 'Isn't it great that we'll shortly be family? You're not eating! Can I get you something?'

'Not at the moment, thank you,' she said hurriedly. She wanted suddenly, desperately, to go home. 'Actually, I was just looking for Max.'

'He's over by the buffet table.' Frank scrutinized her more closely. 'Are you all right, my dear? You look a little pale.'

'I'm not sure.' His face began to waver before her and she blindly reached out a hand. With a concerned murmur he caught it and, with his other arm round her, guided her out of the room to the blessed cool of the corridor, where he seated her gently on an upright chair.

'Put your head between your knees,' he instructed, but she simply drew a deep breath. 'I feel better already. I'm so sorry, Frank, I think the heat got to me.'

The waiter she had spoken to approached diffidently with the requested glass of water on a tray.

'Thank you.' She took it from him and sipped gratefully at the icy liquid. 'Sorry!' she said again. 'This isn't like me at all!'

'You've probably been overdoing it,' Frank said. 'Would you like me to fetch Max?'

She shook her head. 'I feel a bit of a fraud, actually. I think I'm OK to go back now.'

'Your colour's beginning to come back, but are you sure? Perhaps you should wait a few minutes.'

'No, really, I'm fine. And . . . please don't mention this to anyone.'

'Of course not, if that's what you want. And if you're sure you're all right, Vanda was looking for you.'

Vanda was Steve's slightly eccentric sister, a jewellery designer who lived in London. She had been far from happy about Rona's proposed article on her father, but misunderstandings had been ironed out and a truce struck.

'I'd love to see her.' Rona said. 'And thanks for the TLC.'

'Any time.' He escorted her back into the room and she drew a deep, exploratory breath. Yes, balance thankfully restored. 'And here's Vanda,' he added.

Vanda Hathaway was someone who turned heads wherever she went. With her cropped hair, her heavy make-up and the number of rings, bracelets and necklaces that festooned her (she was a walking advertisement for her wares, she'd told Rona), she could hardly avoid making an impact. This evening she was resplendent in a turquoise-silk trouser suit.

'Rona, my dear!' she drawled, 'I was convinced it was you standing next to my brother! The phrase "peas in a pod" comes to mind.'

'It has been quite useful at times!'

'So what are you working on now?' Vanda enquired. And as Rona, thankfully putting the blip behind her, started to reply, Frank, who'd hovered anxiously for a moment, moved away, satisfied that all was well.

* * *

The next morning she again slept late, and it was just after nine when she surfaced. Max's place beside her was empty and the sheet cold. He must have been up for ages.

She slipped on her dressing gown, washed her face, and padded down to the kitchen, where he was sitting with a pot of coffee reading the paper.

'Ah, good afternoon!' he greeted her.

'It's your fault – why didn't you wake me?'

'You were dead to the world, so I let you sleep. It's Sunday, after all. There's still some coffee in the pot.'

Rona took a mug from its hook and slumped into a chair, rubbing her eyes.

'Too much champagne!' Max said unsympathetically.

'Actually, I didn't have any.'

He looked up. 'Why not?'

'Just didn't fancy it. It was so hot in there – and incredible that relatively few people could make so much noise!'

'Now who's being a grouch?'

She smiled shamefacedly. 'Sorry. I've been feeling tired all week. Perhaps I need a tonic.'

'Was that woman dolled up like a Christmas tree the one who was so rude to you?'

'That's all water under the bridge, Max.'

He grunted. 'I presume she made all those geegaws herself?'

Rona reached for the coffee pot. 'Yes she did. And those geegaws, as you call them, would cost you a pretty penny.' She smiled. 'Rings on her fingers and bells on her toes!'

'I was spared her toes, thank God! But yes, from what I could see there were several rings on each finger.'

'She seems to have made an impression,' Rona said drily. She paused. 'Nice to see all four "parents" getting along so well. That dinner party certainly broke the ice.'

'Yes, and now the ever-expanding family will encompass the Hathaways – including, heaven help us, the Pearly Queen!'

Rona laughed. 'The more the merrier!' she said.

Later that morning there was a phone call from Dinah.

'Two things, Rona,' she said, her deep voice throbbing over the line. 'First, we read in the paper about your sister's engagement. Do please pass on our best wishes.'

'Thank you, I will.' It always came as a surprise to realize Lindsey had never met the Trents.

'And the second thing,' Dinah went on, lowering her voice, 'concerns Mel.'

'Oh, of course – she's with you, isn't she? So much has been going on that I'd forgotten.' She'd flown home, Rona remembered, the day after Nicole's murder, now over a month ago.

'I'm worried about her, Rona. She spends a lot of time in her room crying, and she won't really talk to us. Mitch has been desperately trying to contact her, so she's changed her email and mobile number.'

'I'm so sorry,' Rona sympathized. 'I remember how upset Lindsey was when she and Hugh were divorcing.'

'It hasn't come to that yet, but it seems to be heading that way.' Dinah paused. 'I know this is a lot to ask, specially when you're so busy, but do you think you could have a word with her?'

'Me?' Rona's surprise rang in her voice.

'Yes. She's always admired you, and you're more or less the same generation. She might find it easier to talk to you.'

'I don't know her very well, Dinah,' Rona hedged, alarmed at the prospect of being cast as counsellor.

'That might make it easier. I just feel she'd open up more readily to someone who wasn't family.'

Rona had planned to contact an old friend of Gideon's the next day, but twenty-four hours wouldn't make much difference. Sorry, Prue! she thought.

'OK, then. Suppose I call for her in the morning and we drive somewhere for a pub lunch?'

'That would be wonderful! Thank you so much, Rona.'

'I don't promise miraculous results, though,' Rona warned her.

'Can we say we were just talking and you said you'd like to catch up with her? I don't want her to know the suggestion came from me.'

'Fine. Suppose I pick her up about eleven?'

'She'll be ready. Bless you, Rona.'

'What was all that about?' Max asked, coming in from the garden.

'Dinah wants me to talk to Mel, heaven knows why. I'm not sure I want to be an agony aunt.'

'The best of luck!' he said.

A wet Sunday evening – surely the most dreary of times. Alan Palmer stood at his bedroom window gazing hopelessly out at the shining rooftops and the oil-prismed puddles lining the gutter. When, he wondered wearily, would this nightmare come to an end? Had his whole life been leading inexorably towards this moment? And if so, what was he supposed to do with it? Hadn't his family suffered enough? He couldn't bring fresh pain to them, he just couldn't!

The sound of the television drifted up from the room below. A burst of laughter rang out and in his present state it seemed alien, in some way threatening. God! Was he going out of his mind? Perhaps it was no more than he deserved.

He started at a tap on the door, followed by his father's voice. 'Can I come in, son?'

'Of course,' he answered dully.

He continued staring out of the window, heard his father's footsteps approach, felt a tentative hand on his shoulder.

'It doesn't do any good to brood, son,' George said quietly. 'Mother wouldn't have wanted that. It's time to move on now.'

Time to move on, Alan repeated inwardly. If only he could!

'Chrissie says supper's nearly ready. Shall we go down and perhaps have a glass of something to lift our spirits?'

Alan turned, staring into his father's worried face. 'I'm so sorry, Dad,' he said.

'No need for that, now.' George's voice became brisk. 'It doesn't do to shut yourself away, brooding over everything. Things always seem brighter when you have a spot of company.' He took his son's arm and led him firmly towards the door. 'There's some kind of talent show on the telly and Amanda's set on one lad winning. Come and see what you think.'

And, with nothing resolved, Alan allowed himself to be led downstairs to join his family.

TWELVE

Monday morning, and Rona had achieved her aim of arranging to see Rex Harvey, an old friend of Gideon's, on the following Thursday. He lived in Northamptonshire, roughly a half-hour's drive away, and he'd invited her to lunch at his golf club, which would make a pleasant change from the pubs and canteens where she'd conducted her other interviews.

She'd just noted the postcode for her satnav when the phone rang again, and she lifted it to hear Monica's voice.

'Hi, Rona. Sorry I didn't get back to you yesterday, but I was trying to juggle dates for that get-together, unfortunately without much success. It turns out Charles is attending a residential course up in Manchester over the next two weeks – a fact he neglected to mention – so could we possibly postpone it till mid-June? I'm awfully sorry about this.'

'Of course, Monica. No problem.'

'How are you fixed for the week beginning the thirteenth? I know Max's availability is limited, but either the Wednesday or Friday would be great.'

'Hang on, I'll run down and check the kitchen diary.'

'Sorry, are you working?'

'Only making an appointment. I'm taking the rest of the day off to take a friend to lunch.'

'Good for you.'

'Right, I'm now consulting the diary – which is supposedly kept up to date – and both the fifteenth and the seventeenth are free, but actually it's your turn to come to us.'

'Oh no, really—'

'Really. We've been meaning to ask you over for some time, but you've beaten us to it.'

'Now it looks as if I was fishing for an invitation!'

'Nonsense. But shall we say Saturday the eighteenth, rather than the Friday, to give Max more time to prepare the meal?'

'Well, if you're sure, that would be great. But I still feel guilty!'

'Eight o'clock,' Rona said firmly. 'See you then, and I hope Charles enjoys his course.'

It was just before eleven when she reached Hollybush Lane and drove through the open gateway. Gus sat up eagerly on the back seat, but she shook her head.

'I shan't be long. Stay where you are.'

He gave a protesting whimper but obediently lay down again, watching her with reproachful eyes as she walked to the front door and rang the bell. It was Mel herself who answered it.

Melissa Michelmore, the Trents' only child, always struck Rona as the unifying factor that melded them into a family. The wide divergence in her parents' heights (Barnie was over six foot, Dinah under five) had evened out to make her average; similarly, her mother's wiry black hair and Barnie's softer rapidly thinning thatch had merged into the cascade of brown curls that fell to her shoulders. She had to be in her late twenties now but, despite the baby in her arms and the three-year-old at her heels, seemed much younger.

'Rona! Come in for a minute. It was a lovely surprise when Mum told me what you'd suggested.'

'Well, I don't know when I last saw you, but it seems an age and I thought it would be good to get together.'

'It'll be a treat not to be encumbered with children!'

Rona smiled at the baby, who stared unsmilingly back. 'And this is Silas, whom I've not met before. He must be about a year now?'

'That's right, he had his first birthday last week.'

Feeling more was required, Rona bent to the little girl. 'Hello, Martha. Do you help Mummy with your baby brother?'

The child hid her face in her mother's skirt, and Mel laughed. 'Not so that you'd notice!'

Dinah emerged from the kitchen, drying her hands on her apron. 'Hello, Rona. You've brought a nice day with you!' She took the baby from her daughter, and, seeing Martha's face begin to pucker, went on quickly, 'We'll wave goodbye to Mummy, then we're going to the swings, aren't we? Go!' she instructed the adults in a low voice.

'You can tell me what you've been up to at teatime,' Mel said brightly, kissing the resistant cheek, and she and Rona went quickly to the car.

'Having said it would be good to be free of them, I now feel miserable!' she admitted with a half-laugh as she waved to her daughter.

'She'll be fine once we're out of sight. Where was Sam?'

'Upstairs on his iPlayer. I said goodbye, but he barely looked up! Anyway—' she settled back in her seat. 'Enough of that! Tell me where we're going.'

'I thought up towards Farnbridge. There are some lovely walks around there, not to mention several nice pubs!'

'Farnbridge! That takes me back – I went to uni there.'

'So did I,' Rona said, 'but I'm not proposing to go into the town. We'll park on the edge of the common and take off from there.' She paused. 'I'm sorry not to have touched base sooner, but things have been escalating workwise.'

'Dad said something about you being caught up in the death of one of his journalists?'

'Yes, Nicole Summers. It was pretty traumatic.'

Mel smiled. 'But not unusual!'

Rona laughed. 'Don't you start! Max says I positively attract disaster. But apart from that, I've been asked to take over a biography someone else started and . . . was unable to finish.'

'So the hard work's been done for you?'

'Some of it, yes, but there's a lot of sorting out to do. It's the first time I've taken on something like this, but given the choice I'd rather start from scratch.'

For the rest of the forty-minute drive they chatted about everything, it seemed to Rona, except the subject she'd been co-opted to broach. She'd been hoping Mel would raise it first; but if she didn't, she would have to bring it up herself, preferably before lunch. Difficult topics were best discussed when you weren't facing each other.

Having parked the car, Gus was let off his lead and they started to walk across the grass, the dog racing happily ahead. 'We were told at uni that in the sixteenth century the lord of the manor tried to fence off all this land and add it to his estate,' Mel said. 'But the villagers rose up in protest and tore it down, and he never bothered again.'

'Good for them!'

On this higher ground there was a breeze that lifted their hair and tempered the heat of the midday sun. They walked for several minutes in companionable silence then, totally out of the blue, Mel said, 'Mum asked you to sound me out about Mitch, didn't she?'

Rona, caught off guard, started to dissemble, but Mel shook her head. 'I'm not a complete idiot, Rona. Always before when we've been over here, either you've come and had a meal with us or we've been to you – you've never secreted me off somewhere all by myself.'

'*Would* it help to talk about him?' Rona asked.

'I don't know, we can try. But first, tell me how you'd feel if you found Max had been cheating on you.'

Truth to tell there *had* been a time when she'd thought his affections were straying. Thankfully she'd been mistaken, but she still remembered the hurt and rage she felt at the time.

'Betrayed,' she answered slowly, 'and . . . furious.'

Mel gave a choking laugh. 'That just about sums it up.'

'What exactly happened, Mel?'

'It's a girl he works with – the usual story, I suppose. She was with him in the Gulf that time when the kids and I stayed with the parents. She's married too, incidentally. I suppose they were both missing home comforts.' There was bitterness in her voice. 'I didn't know about it at the time, though I did notice how often her name seemed to come up during his phone calls. Cindy-Lou!' Melissa said with great scorn. 'Did you ever hear anything so stupid?'

Rona thought back. It must be three years since Mitch spent that extended time in the Gulf. If it had been going on that long, perhaps it was more serious that Barnie and Dinah were hoping. Mel's next words dispelled that fear to some extent.

'When we all went home,' she continued, 'his conscience got the better of him and he confessed the whole thing. To be honest, I wish he hadn't – what the eye doesn't see and all that. It took me quite a while to get over it, but he was so sweet and so repentant and thoughtful that we gradually teetered back and were actually closer than we'd been before.'

'So what happened?' Rona asked.

'For some reason, it flared up again a few months ago. God knows why – things were fine between us and I didn't suspect a thing. But her husband found out and it went viral. I felt so *humiliated*, Rona.' Her voice shook.

Rona was silent. She took Gus's Frisbee out of her pocket and threw it for him and he galloped after it, ears flying. Her intention of trying to see both sides was rapidly fading and her sympathies were totally with Mel. She doubted she could have given Max a second chance, and here was Mitch asking for a third.

'What did he say?' she asked at last.

'Begged my forgiveness *again*, and ranted at himself for being a bloody fool.' Mel's voice was tired. 'I'd heard it all before.'

'I'm so very sorry,' Rona said quietly. Then, 'How much do your parents know?'

Mel shrugged. 'The bare bones. I was too ashamed to go into details. They don't know what happened in the Gulf. Dad would have flayed him alive if I'd told them. They think this was just a moment of madness. And although they haven't said so, I know they want us to patch it up – for the sake of the kids, if nothing else.'

'And how do you feel?'

'At the moment? That I never want to see him again.'

There was a short silence, then Rona asked bluntly, 'Do you still love him?'

'Aye, there's the rub!' Mel quoted ruefully. 'Yes, damn it, I do. A first-class idiot, aren't I?' She reached into her bag for a tissue.

'What would you do if you decided to leave him permanently? Come back here?'

'I suppose so.' She glanced sideways at Rona. 'What would *you* do, if you were me? Would you take him back?'

Rona had her doubts, but felt it unwise to voice them. 'To be honest, I really don't know.'

'My friends in the States expect me to divorce him. They're surprised I've not already started proceedings.'

'Have you considered that perhaps the reason you haven't is because you don't really want to lose him?'

Mel sighed. 'I keep making up my mind one way, then the next day change it completely.'

'No one else can do it for you. It's good that you're having this time away to clear your head.'

'He was almost in tears pleading to come for Silas's birthday, but I just couldn't face it. I know the parents think I should have agreed. He's missing the kids, and Sam in particular keeps asking for him.' She sighed. 'So in the meantime I've severed communications. I've changed my email address and mobile, so he's having to use the landline and I refuse to go to the phone. Mum's beginning to lose patience with me.'

'She's worried about you, that's all.'

'She's very fond of Mitch, though she's mad as hell with him for what he's done. And she doesn't know the half.'

Gus brought back his Frisbee and Rona threw it again. They seemed to be going round in circles and she didn't know what else to say. She'd done her best, and she *had* warned Dinah not to expect too much. She was tired, hungry and a little dispirited, but thankfully they were now approaching the pub she'd earmarked for lunch.

Mel, too, seemed to have had enough of their discussion and, as if reading Rona's mind, announced, 'I'm hungry!'

'Me too!'

As Gus bounced back to them, Rona clipped on his lead. 'The Barley Mow's just beyond those trees. We're a bit late, but they serve lunch till at least two o'clock.'

The pub was still busy and they were lucky to find a table. As it was situated in walkers' territory, there were several other dogs around and Gus didn't pose a problem. He had a drink from the bowl provided and, used to such outings, slunk under the table and settled down, ready for a rest. They ordered their meal from the blackboard and Rona brought their glasses back to the table, wine for Mel and Coke for herself as she was driving.

'So, tell me how everyone is!' Mel instructed. 'What's Max working on at the moment?'

Rona outlined his latest project. 'And of course he's still giving classes, both at home and at the art school, so he's pretty busy.'

'And your sister's just got engaged, hasn't she? Do you like her fiancé?'

'Very much.' Rona explained how she and Lindsey had met the Hathaways.

'And Magda?'

It struck her that Mel was plying her with questions to forestall a return to the previous topic, though she had no intention of resurrecting it. Mel had met Magda during her prolonged stay with her parents, when she'd asked Rona's advice on where to buy clothes and been taken to one of her boutiques.

'Positively blooming!' Rona replied. 'In more ways than one. She's pregnant!'

'Oh, lovely! When's it due?'

'October, I think, so she should be over morning sickness, shouldn't she?'

'That's something I never had, thank goodness.'

Rona looked at her in surprise. 'Really? I thought everyone did – that it was one of the first signs of pregnancy.'

Mel shook her head. 'Not for me. I had blood pressure problems with Martha towards the end and Mum flew out to be with me the last few weeks, but at least I was spared morning sickness.'

'Then how did you know you were pregnant? Just a missed period?'

'Oh, there were other signs you start to recognize. I got tired very easily, and I was certainly more emotional. Burst into tears at the slightest thing! All hormonal, of course.'

Rona stared at her as memories and suspicions suddenly crowded in on her, accelerating her heartbeat and almost stopping her breath. Her unexpected tears when playing Nicole's tape, her panic that Lindsey might move away, her dizzy spell at the party . . . And she'd been so tired lately. God, she thought suddenly, she'd been so busy she hadn't been keeping track!

Their table number was called twice before she registered the fact, and when their meal arrived her throat momentarily closed. It was Mel's enquiring glance that forced her to take up her knife and fork, but once she started she was relieved to find she could eat, though she couldn't have said what was on her plate. *Don't think about it!* she instructed herself. *Not now, not till you're by yourself and can work things out properly.* She must concentrate on Mel. What was she talking about?

'Mum and Dad are taking a cruise this summer, just a short European one. They offered to take me along, but a cruise isn't for kids. Anyway, I'll probably have gone back before then – I can't hide here for ever.'

Rona made no comment, partly because she was still shell-shocked, partly because it seemed that, after all, Mel might have reached a decision, though 'going back' didn't necessarily mean back to Mitch. She made some non-committal remark and Mel chatted on. Having had the prescribed heart-to-heart, she now seemed more relaxed, even happier, so perhaps it had done some good after all.

Mel kept up her chatter during the walk back to the car, apparently satisfied with the monosyllabic replies she received. Rona's overriding desire was to get back to Marsborough as quickly as possible and visit a pharmacy, but on arrival in Hollybush Lane Dinah insisted that Sam wanted to see her and she must stay for a cup of tea. As the hands of the clock moved remorselessly round, she began to panic that the shops would close before she reached home.

When she was at last able to escape, Dinah walked out to the car with her. 'How did it go?' she asked anxiously. 'Mel seems decidedly less stressed.'

'I'm hoping she's starting to sort out a few things.'

'Thank you so much for seeing her, Rona. Even if nothing's resolved, it will have done her good to get away from us all for a while.'

As she finally drove away, Rona wondered how long it would have taken for suspicions to form if she'd not had that conversation with Mel.

Having garaged the car, there was no time to return Gus to the house, so the two of them set off up Fullers Walk at a brisk pace, passing a small pharmacy on their way. Rona was known there and since any unusual purchase would be noted she'd decided that, even though it meant a longer walk, she'd opt for the safe anonymity of the large Boots store on Guild Street.

Half an hour later her world shifted on its axis. According to the test kit she'd just bought, she appeared to be pregnant and among all the conflicting emotions, she was certain of only one thing: she would tell no one until she'd weighed up all the pros and cons, and perhaps taken another test. Though she ached to pour it all out to Max or Lindsey or her mother, she *must* wait until she was certain – there could be no false alarms. In any case, it was information that would have to be imparted in person rather than over the phone, and Max wouldn't be home till Wednesday.

She went slowly downstairs and, moving on autopilot, reached down the packet of dog food. Somehow, she resolved, she'd have to get through the next couple of days keeping her own counsel and try to come to terms with a future totally different from the one she'd always imagined. The dog, puzzled by her hesitation, nuzzled impatiently at her leg.

'Oh, Gus!' she said unsteadily and, crouching down, buried her face in his warm fur.

She didn't sleep well that night, managing only short snatches crowded with dreams before jerking awake again. It must be a mistake – it couldn't be happening to her! She thought of Magda's glowing face, of Mel's instinctive 'Oh, lovely!' when hearing of her pregnancy. Was there something wrong with her, that she wasn't filled with the requisite joy? Magda said she and Gavin had discussed starting a family; she and Max never had, not since the early days of their marriage when it had been mutually decided to 'wait awhile'. And that was now several years ago.

At six thirty she gave up trying to sleep and went for a shower, pausing in front of the mirror to rub her hand over the flat surface of her stomach. Was it possible that beneath it a new life was stirring?

Down in the kitchen she made some coffee and, aware of a feeling of emptiness, slid two slices of bread into the toaster. Then, with an exasperated sigh, she scooped up the Boots bag lying on the table, scrunched it in her hand, and threw it into the bin.

Two hours later she was at her desk, trying to concentrate on Gideon Ward's boyhood, when Lindsey phoned.

'Hi, sis!' she began breezily. 'How about joining me for lunch at the Bacchus? We've not really spoken since I got engaged.'

'Oh, Linz, I'd love to!'

Lindsey gave an amused laugh. 'I don't usually get such an enthusiastic response! Twelve thirty, then?'

'See you there,' Rona said, with a lifting of her spirits.

Lindsey was at her usual table when Rona and Gus arrived, and as soon as Rona was seated launched into an excited account of the plans she and Steve were making.

Taking her courage in both hands, Rona interrupted the flow to ask, 'Where will you live? Mum said something about Steve having a house in Kent?'

'Yes, that's right, but he doesn't want to move back there. It has unhappy memories and he likes it here – as, of course, do I! More importantly, he doesn't want to uproot Luke from yet another school, just when he's settling down so well. And as luck would have it, the people who've been renting the house are keen to buy it, so it's all worked out beautifully.'

'So you're staying in Marsborough?' Rona insisted, relief flooding over her.

'Yes, and the other piece of luck is that Frank, bless his heart, wants us to have the house in Alban Road! He said that when Steve and Luke moved out he'd rattle around in it and, would you believe it, he'd started looking at retirement homes! Vanda's quite happy with the arrangement, and of course we'll recompense her for what would have been her share of the house.

'But as you know, it's desperately old-fashioned, so we've decided to have it thoroughly modernized – rip out the kitchen and bathroom, new wiring and plumbing and so on – and Frank will have a self-contained flat on the ground floor. He's absolutely delighted. It couldn't have worked out better!'

She broke off, frowning. 'You're not crying, are you? What's the matter with you, Ro? That's the second lot of tears this month, and you never cry!'

'I'm just so glad you're not moving.'

'And that makes you *cry*?'

Rona brushed her tears away and took a deep breath. 'I think I'm pregnant,' she said.

Lindsey put down her fork and stared at her. 'Are you serious?'

She nodded dumbly.

'God, Ro! First Magda, and now you! Is it infectious?' Then, eying her sister closely, her voice softened. 'You never told me you were trying for a baby. Are you happy about it?'

Despite herself, Rona's eyes filled again. 'I don't know,' she whispered. 'I just wanted things to go on as they are. I love Max, I love our lives together. I'm not sure I want it to change. Is that very selfish?'

'Have you told him?'

'No, this only blew up yesterday and I wanted to be sure first.'

'But you presumably did a test?'

'Yes, but I'll do another, to be on the safe side.'

'And hope the results are different?'

'I don't *know*, Linz.'

'We'd better get married before you start to show!'

Rona gave a choked laugh, then abruptly sobered. 'What worries me most is not being in control. It's like being on a see-saw, and at the moment I'm down more often than up.'

'How did you find out?'

Rona told her about her day out with Mel, and how Mel's description of her own pregnancies mirrored how she'd been feeling herself. 'So when I got home, I rushed to Boots for a pregnancy kit. And bingo!'

'Well at least you and Magda can push your prams together!'

'Linz, you won't say anything, will you? I don't want anyone to know till I've spoken to Max and got to grips with it myself.'

'My lips are sealed. I was about to break my no-wine-at-lunch-time-rule to celebrate the engagement, but I suppose you're off the booze altogether now?'

'I hadn't thought of that, but yes.' She smiled. 'Funnily enough, I didn't fancy the champagne at the party.'

'I hope that's not a reflection on Steve's choice! Actually, you know, this is all rather exciting. I think I'll enjoy being an aunt.'

'I'll mark you down for babysitting, then.'

Lindsey smiled. 'That's better! A positive comment at last!'

'Give me time,' Rona said.

Wednesday evening came at last. Rona laid the table with the best china – Curzon, she acknowledged with a reminiscent smile. The firm had featured in her series on local businesses, and that particular article had caused her considerable heartache. Dismissing the memory, she set a candlestick in the middle of the table and stood back to admire the result.

In the hall above, the front door opened and shut. 'I'm back!' Max called, and Gus loped up the stairs to greet him.

'In the kitchen,' Rona called back. Her heart was beating high in her chest and her mouth was dry. Please let him be happy about it! she prayed.

Max's feet sounded on the stairs and he came into the room, stopping short when he saw the festive table.

'Have I forgotten something? Are we supposed to be celebrating?'

'You haven't forgotten anything,' Rona replied, returning his kiss, 'but I *hope* we'll be celebrating.'

He put down the carrier bag with ingredients for the evening's meal. 'That sounds very mysterious.'

'I think perhaps you should sit down.'

He turned to look at her through narrowed eyes. 'Now you're worrying me. I prefer to stand. Come on, love, put me out of my misery! What's happened?'

'I think – in fact, I'm pretty sure – that we're going to have a baby.'

There was a beat of total silence, then he moved forward swiftly, pulled her into his arms and held her tightly.

'You . . . don't mind?' she asked breathlessly.

'Mind? Of course I don't *mind*, you little goose. I'm delighted!'

'Really?'

'Really! I almost said something when you told me about Magda, but I bottled out. I wanted the idea to come from you.'

'Obviously it wasn't planned,' Rona said.

He held her at arm's length, searching her face. 'So how do *you* feel about it?'

'A lot better now I've spoken to you,' she said shakily.

'When did you find out?'

'On Monday, but I didn't want to tell you on the phone. And I did an extra test yesterday, to be sure.'

'You said you had lunch with Lindsey.' There was an unspoken question in his voice, and she answered it.

'I hadn't intended to tell her . . . but I started to cry and it all came out.'

He frowned. 'Cried because of the baby?'

'No, no, they were tears of relief. I'd been so afraid they'd leave Marsborough, but they're staying on in Alban Road.' She paused. 'But I've cried several times lately and Linz wanted to know why. Mel said it's hormones.'

'Mel Michelmore knows?' There was surprise in his voice.

Rona shook her head, and explained how her suspicions had been aroused.

'Well, well! This isn't what I was expecting when I walked in the door!'

'It's not what I was expecting either.'

'For one thing, I was looking forward to a drink – and now more so than ever! But I assume you're on the wagon?'

'Don't let me stop you. I don't really feel like one, anyway.'

'I can't drink alone.' He opened the fridge. 'We have apple juice, elderflower, or just plain tonic.'

'Elderflower and tonic,' she said. 'My tipple for the next nine months! Max . . .'

'Yes, my sweet?'

'It won't really change things, will it?'

'It will make them even better,' he said.

THIRTEEN

'Are you sure you're up to driving to Northamptonshire?' Max asked at breakfast.

'Of course – it's not far.'

'All the same, you were gadding about all over Buckfordshire on Monday. You mustn't overdo it, it's no wonder you've been tired.'

'Max, I'll be sensible, but I'm not an invalid!'

'I'll take Gus back with me,' he went on. 'That will be one less thing for you to worry about. You can collect him on your way home and let me know how you got on.'

'All right. Thanks.'

He buttered his toast. 'So when do you propose to make this public?'

'Not till the first three months are behind me. Magda said that's when things are most likely to go wrong.'

'You won't even tell the family?'

'No, and I've sworn Linz to secrecy. Fortunately, with the wedding coming up they've all got enough on their minds.'

'Well, at least you won't have to worry about Magda and her baby talk – you can join in.'

Rona smiled reluctantly. 'If you can't beat them, join them!'

She was due at the clubhouse of the Loganfield Golf Club at one o'clock, and turned into its gateway with ten minutes to spare.

Skirting the members' car park, Rona turned into the public one, which was almost empty. Presumably most of those using it would be at work on a Thursday, leaving the course free for retired members.

Having checked that she had her recorder, she locked the car and walked up the gravel drive to the long, low building. Pushing open the glass-paned door, she found herself in an impressive hallway. Several groups of easy chairs were dotted about, in which grey-haired men were either chatting to each other over drinks or reading newspapers, and the walls were covered with display cabinets full of silver cups. There were also boards listing competition winners and past captains, and a photograph of the current one. Glancing at the name beneath it, Rona was taken aback to see it was that of her host.

'Miss Parish?'

She turned quickly to find the man himself behind her, holding out his hand. 'Rex Harvey,' he said.

'It's very good of you to see me.' Her hand was completely enveloped in his. He was a big man in all respects, portly, over six foot tall and with a salt-and-pepper beard.

'Delighted, delighted. Would you care for an appetizer before we eat?'

'Thank you, no. But please don't—'

'No, no, we'll go straight through, then.' He waved her towards a door leading to the dining room, a large room with tables of varying sizes and a long one at the far end. They were all laid with white linen cloths, silver cutlery and wine glasses, but only a handful were occupied. The maître d' greeted them at the door and showed them to one overlooking a fairway.

Menus were produced, and again Rona had to decline the offer of wine and opt for sparkling water.

'I have to drive home afterwards,' she explained, thankful that this was sufficient explanation.

'Very wise,' approved Rex Harvey, ordering a half-bottle of Merlot for himself.

Their food order having been taken, he sat back in his chair and regarded her benevolently.

'So, you want to hear about that old reprobate Gideon, do you?'

She smiled. 'Is that what he was?'

'Oh, indubitably. I should explain that we were thrown together because our parents were friends and, although we came to know each other quite well, we were never that close. He was a competitive little sod, never happy to take second place in anything.'

Rona hastily took out her recorder. 'Do you mind if I use this?'

He glanced at it. 'Feel free.' He smiled. 'Would you like me to repeat my last remark for the tape, as they say on TV?'

She smiled back. 'I think I'll remember it, thanks. So when did you first meet?'

'When my family moved back to Ireland. I must have been six or seven, and I remember we fought the day we met. The first, I might add, of many fights! That's boys for you – little hooligans. For several years our families went on holiday together, and my sister and his became lifelong friends. And in the early days, of course, there was poor little Leo. You know about him?' He lifted a bushy eyebrow.

'The younger brother who died of appendicitis?'

'That's right. Bloody tragedy, that was. But as I was saying, Giddy and I were more or less thrown together and had to make the best of it.'

'But you didn't like one another?'

'Oh, I wouldn't say that. We *tolerated* each other, and as we grew older and slightly more sensible we got along much better.'

'Was he always good at sport? I know he later played internationally.'

'Yes, that was his main area of competitiveness. I was no mean player myself – but not up to his standard, which pleased him mightily.'

Their soup arrived – gazpacho, as befitted the warm June day – accompanied by a dish of croutons. Rona looked up as a family with two young children was shown to a table across the room. 'The dining room's open to the public, as you'll have gathered.' Harvey said, intercepting her glance. 'There's no age limit at luncheon, but no one under eighteen is allowed in for dinner. Now, what was I saying?'

'About his competitiveness at sport.'

'Ah yes. Mind you, it also extended to exam results, the relative merits of Oxford and Cambridge, and, as we got older, whose girlfriend was the better-looking. But it wasn't really serious by that time.'

'Did he have many girlfriends?'

'God, yes! Females flocked around him like flies, lord knows why.'

Hester Croft had said the same thing. Rona wondered if Harvey knew of the continuing string of affairs. If not, she thought with quiet amusement, he'd find out if and when he read the biography.

'We'd buried the hatchet sufficiently to be each other's best man,' he continued, 'and I admit his death rocked me to the core. I now regret we didn't keep in closer touch, but we were moving in different worlds by then.'

'Did you watch him on television?'

'Those chat shows? No, can't be doing with that kind of thing! And from what I hear, he came across as a pompous ass – which, let's face it, he could be.'

Their soup plates were removed and their main course brought. Dover sole for Harvey, Caesar salad for her.

'There was a time during our twenties when we corresponded fairly regularly,' Harvey said, neatly filleting his fish. 'It was while he was doing a lot of travelling, either for sporting fixtures or as a foreign correspondent, and I have to say his letters were remarkable. Full, as you'd expect, of his opinion on a wide range of subjects as well as vivid descriptions of the countries he was visiting. I kept a whole batch of them, I remember. I could look them out for you, if that would help.'

'It would be wonderful, thank you.' They should supplement the journals admirably.

'I'll set a reminder on my phone.' He took it out of his pocket and did so.

Through the window, Rona saw four men leave the clubhouse and set off with golf bags slung over their shoulders. They were all wearing hats – a wise precaution in the strong June sunshine.

Rex Harvey followed her glance. 'Do you play yourself?'

'Afraid not, and nor does my husband.'

'What kind of work is he in?'

'He's an artist, and also holds classes both at home and at the local art school.'

'That's interesting.' He paused to remove an errant fishbone from his fork. 'Does he paint animals, by any chance?'

'He has done, yes.'

'And presumably accepts commissions?'

'Certainly.'

'Thing is my wife has a horse she's very fond of. I've been wondering what to give her for her sixtieth, later in the year, and a portrait of it would be the ideal solution.'

'I'll ask him to get in touch. Then you can talk it over, have a look at his work, and decide whether or not you want to go ahead.'

'That would be excellent. Thank you.'

For the rest of the meal the conversation revolved round Max and his work, his methods, his famous sitters, and the galleries where his paintings could be viewed. It wasn't until they were finishing their coffee that Harvey remarked, 'You mentioned your drive home. You don't come from round here?'

'No, I live in Marsborough.'

'Marsborough.' He plucked thoughtfully at his lower lip. 'Now where have I heard that name recently? Ah yes, someone I used to know bought a hotel there.'

Rona felt a wave of heat wash over her. 'Someone you used to know?' she stammered.

'Well, that's stretching it a bit. We were at school together. Small, skinny kid he was then, with an Australian accent to boot. He's done well for himself.'

The room spun and Rona held convulsively on to her chair. 'I'd assumed you were at Winchester with Gideon . . .'

'No, no, I'm an Old Buckfordian and proud of it.'

'And . . . you *are* speaking of Bruce Sedgwick?'

'Sedgwick – yes, that's the name. He was quite a bit younger, but he stood out because he was different and the whole school took the mickey, imitating the way he spoke and so on. He wasn't there long,' he went on reflectively. 'In fact the only reason I remember him is because he was colour-blind. I'd never come across that before – and haven't since, for that matter – and it fascinated me. Couldn't distinguish between red and green, apparently – which led us to play all manner of tricks on him, little savages that we were. He must have been glad to go home, poor boy.'

Sedgwick was colour-blind! That was news to her, though it could hardly be the reason Russell had singled him out. She cleared her throat.

'Funnily enough he was interviewed by Gideon when he first came over, but I don't suppose you saw the programme?'

'No, as I said, never watched them. Read something about him in the press, though. Fallen heir to his uncle's fortune, if it qualifies as such. Well, good on him, as he'd probably say.'

Rona's thoughts moved on. 'Did you know Russell Page or Simon Spencer? They were at Buckford at the same time and were about his age.'

'Afraid not. We didn't have much truck with the junior boys. I only remember Sedgwick because of his colour-blindness and his accent.'

There was nothing further to keep them, and Rex Harvey escorted her out of the dining room.

'Thank you so much for lunch, and for all the information,' Rona said as she shook his hand in the foyer.

'I've enjoyed it enormously. I look forward to hearing from your husband, and perhaps when he and I meet I can hand over those letters I mentioned. Two birds with one stone, as it were.'

'That would be great.'

The heat struck her as she left the clubhouse, and when she opened the car door the interior was like an oven. She opened both doors and waited a minute or two, watching some players in the distance while the worst of the heat dispersed. It had been an interesting and worthwhile trip, she reflected, particularly if it resulted in a commission for Max.

It was nearly three o'clock when Rona drew into the little alley alongside Farthings. It gave access via a gate in the wall to the small triangular piece of ground that served as a garden, and hearing the car draw up, Gus started barking and jumping up at the gate.

'Just coming!' Rona called to him as she went round to the front of the cottage and let herself in. Since, as usual, she was immediately overpowered by music and knew she wouldn't be heard above it, she went first to the kitchen for a drink of water and to let Gus in. He'd emptied the bowl Max had put out for him, and she refilled it.

'I know, I know,' she sympathized as he nudged her legs. 'You've had a boring time, but we'll go for a walk later when it's a bit cooler.'

As at home, the dog wasn't allowed upstairs, so Rona left the back door open, giving him the option of sleeping on the rug or going back outside. A break in the music allowed Max to hear her approaching and he came to greet her as she emerged from the stairwell, switching the music off *en passant*.

'Hello, love. Not too tired after the drive in all this heat?'

'No, but I'd like to relax for a while before going home.'

'Of course. I've just finished the area I was working on, so let's go down and I'll get you an iced drink. Go into the living room and I'll bring it through.'

The curtains of the small room were drawn against the sunshine, bathing it in a green light that gave an underwater effect. Rona settled thankfully on the sofa as Gus padded in and settled happily at her feet. She lent back, closing her eyes, but almost immediately Max arrived, bearing two glasses of iced lemonade.

'So tell me,' he said, 'how did the lunch go?'

'Very well. He'd known Gideon Ward since they were boys and had some amusing anecdotes. They also corresponded while Ward was abroad on various assignments and he's going to look out Gideon's letters for me, which might well be a goldmine. Oh, and while I remember, he's considering asking you to paint a portrait of his wife's horse for her sixtieth birthday.'

'As long as he's not in too much of a hurry.'

'Later in the year, he said. Anyway, I said you'd contact him.'

Max nodded, sipping at his drink. 'Well, I hope there aren't any more of Ward's long-lost friends or relations scattered about the country requiring a visit.'

She smiled. 'Not as far as I know. Oh, and you'll never guess! Harvey was at school with Bruce Sedgwick.'

'Good God – another one!'

'He's quite a bit older, but he remembered him because of his being colour-blind.'

Max looked up. '*Sedgwick* was?' he asked sharply.

'Yes. I don't—'

'My God!' he said softly. 'Oh, my God!'

Rona sat forward. 'What is it? What's the matter?'

'Well, that's the answer to your question, isn't it? About why Page was interested in him.'

She frowned. 'I thought we'd settled that. It was because they were at school together.'

'He was *colour-blind*, Rona! And the man being interviewed very definitely wasn't!'

She stared at him. 'How can you know that?'

'Good lord, you've watched the tape more often than I have! OK, I picked it up because he was discussing paintings. You must remember him rubbishing modern art – *with all its garish reds and greens*?'

Rona's hand went to her mouth. 'So . . . what does it mean, exactly?'

'It means,' Max said deliberately, 'that the man calling himself Bruce Sedgwick must be an impostor, with presumably no legal claim to Jason Sedgwick's legacy. You said, didn't you, that the schoolmaster told you there were too many coincidences for it to be simply someone with the same name?'

'Wow!'

'Exactly – wow! Which also means this is dangerous ground. Accusations of that sort can't be made lightly. The man's a celebrity, God help us! But more than that, he'd have to be pretty ruthless to have gone through with this. And the sixty-four-thousand-dollar question is where is the *real* Bruce Sedgwick?'

'That's what Simon Spencer wondered.' Rona thought for a moment. 'So . . . what do we do?'

'*We* – and most particularly *you* – do absolutely nothing,' Max said with emphasis. 'Is that clear?'

'But Max, we can't just let him get away with it!'

'He already has.' He put his glass on the coffee table. 'You say Russell Page went to see Spencer after watching the tape. So it's not rocket science to guess what that was about.'

'Spencer told me that Russell was determined, strongly against his advice, to meet the man and challenge him. And,' she added, just above a whisper, 'Russell met his death immediately after they met.'

'Exactly! Which is no doubt why Spencer, who would be the obvious person to follow it up, hasn't done so. And one can hardly blame him.'

'Then you don't think Russell's death was an accident?'

'It was opportune at the very least, and I'd say there are few lengths to which the fake Bruce Sedgwick wouldn't go to prevent this coming out.'

'If he *did* kill Russell, he should certainly pay for *that*.'

'Agreed, but again the difficulty is proving it.'

Rona was silent for a while. Then she said ruefully, 'I remember telling Magda, back at the beginning, that this bio was a poisoned chalice. I didn't know the half of it.'

'The important thing,' Max said, 'is not to drink from it.'

Back in Lightbourne Avenue, Rona went straight up to her study and googled the web page for Buckford College. As she'd expected, members of staff were listed, together with their email addresses. Having noted Simon Spencer's, she opened a new email.

After a moment's reflection, she typed simply 'He was colour-blind, wasn't he?' and added her name. That should be cryptic enough if anyone else chanced to read it. Then she sat back, going over in her mind everything that could point to Russell's death having been deliberate.

One thing she'd not really looked into was the seemingly ineffectual burglary that had taken place during his funeral. It now seemed highly likely that the culprit was the bogus Bruce looking for anything that might incriminate him, so why hadn't he taken Russell's papers? He'd not have had time to go through them at the house, so the obvious course would have been to remove everything relating to the biography – which, since it was now in her possession, he clearly had not done. She needed another word with Esmé Page, and reached for her phone.

'I'm sorry to bother you again, Mrs Page,' she began when Esmé answered. 'This will seem a silly question, but did your husband have a study?'

Esmé gave a half-laugh. 'He did, yes. Why?'

'When your house was broken into during the funeral, was anything taken from the study?'

'Not that we could establish, although it had been turned upside down and all the drawers emptied out on to the floor. It was a terrible mess – which added considerably to my distress, as I'm sure you can imagine.'

'I certainly can,' Rona sympathized. 'I just wondered if anything relating to his work on the biography was missing?'

'Oh, he didn't do his writing there,' Esmé said. 'He used the study for general correspondence and accounts, that kind of thing. There's an old computer there, which I use more than he did, but the summer house was his writing domain. We'd put in central heating, and a little gas ring so he could make coffee, and so on, and he used to spend all day there.'

'Ah, I see! And that wasn't broken into?'

'Well, no. I mean, there was nothing of value there.'

Little did she know, Rona thought. 'That explains it, then. Thank you.'

'That's all?' Esmé asked in surprise.

'For the moment, yes.' Rona had no intention of telling her, certainly at this stage, that her husband had probably been murdered, though if justice was to be obtained she'd have to know eventually.

She was about to end the call when Esmé commented, 'Your phone's working again, then?'

'I'm sorry?'

'Well, it wasn't yesterday, was it? Your agent rang me because he couldn't get through to you. Said you weren't answering your emails, your mobile was switched off and there was a fault on your landline.'

'*My agent?*' Eddie had phoned Esmé Page?

'That's right. He wanted to confirm that you'd collected Russell's papers.'

A cold shiver traced its way down Rona's spine. 'Did this caller give a name?'

'Yes, but he spoke so quickly I didn't catch it, and when he explained he was your agent it didn't seem to matter.'

'Was the name he gave Eddie Gold?'

'It might have been,' Esmé said vaguely. 'He asked if I knew what progress you were making.'

Rona's mouth was dry. 'And what did you say?'

'That I'd no idea. You hadn't said much on the phone, had you? All I could tell him was that you'd been surprised to hear Russell was at school with Bruce Sedgwick, but that was nothing to do with the biography.'

Rona closed her eyes. 'What did he say to that?'

'Nothing really. He just thanked me and rang off.' She paused. 'Are you saying he *wasn't* your agent?'

'I'm pretty sure he wasn't, but I'll check.'

'Then why pretend to be? And if he wasn't, who was he?'

'I don't know, Mrs Page. Don't worry about it.'

'Well, I'm sorry. It never occurred to me he wasn't who he said he was.'

'Of course it wouldn't.'

'Just as well I didn't say anything important,' she said with satisfaction.

Rona's mind was reeling as she ended the call. With trembling fingers, she punched out Eddie's number.

'Dear girl! And how are you, this bright sunny morning?'

'Puzzled, Eddie. This might sound daft, but did you by any chance call Mrs Page yesterday?'

'Who?'

'Russell Page's widow.'

'No. Should I have done?'

'No – but someone did, pretending to be you.'

'Pretending to be *me*?' Eddie's voice rose in indignation.

'Wanting to know if I had Russell's papers and how the bio was progressing.'

'Bloody nerve! Who in the world could that have been?'

'I don't know, Eddie,' Rona said tiredly, though she had a pretty shrewd idea.

'Well, when you find out, let me know and I'll sue him for impersonation!' He paused. 'Now the question's come up, though, how *is* it going?'

'Don't ask!' she said.

She would not, she resolved as she switched off the phone, mention this when Max phoned later. She didn't want a tirade of warnings immediately before going to bed, and he'd be home tomorrow evening.

She was about to go downstairs when the phone rang again – a number she didn't recognize, and again she felt a frisson of unease. 'Hello?' she said cautiously.

'Where the hell did you hear that?' demanded Simon Spencer.

Rona let out her breath in a sigh of relief. 'Good afternoon, Mr Spencer,' she said pointedly, and he muttered a reluctant 'Good afternoon.'

'It was quite by chance, actually,' she replied, forcing her mind back to Harvey and his reminiscences. 'I met someone else who'd been at school with him.'

'Who was that?'

'A man called Rex Harvey.'

'Ah! A name from the past.'

'He didn't remember either you or Russell.'

'Well, he wouldn't. I knew him because he was a prefect, but prefects paid little attention to their minions. They still don't. So how did Sedgwick's colour-blindness come up?'

'That was the only reason he remembered him. He'd never come across it before.'

'You didn't tell him what we'd been discussing?' Spencer demanded sharply.

'No, it didn't seem important at the time. It was my husband who remembered that colours had been mentioned in the interview.'

'Which, of course, was what alerted Page.'

'Why wouldn't you tell me?'

'Because it's altogether too specific – if tackled, the man Ward interviewed would probably have an answer for about everything else. But that was something about the real Sedgwick that he hadn't known – until, we have to assume, Page challenged him. So now he'll be on tenterhooks in case he passed on his suspicions and, if anyone gives a sign of knowing about it, he won't hesitate.'

'To do what?' Rona asked from a dry mouth.

'I leave that to your imagination. He's got a lot to lose.'

Briefly she was tempted to mention the strange phone call, but what was the point? There was nothing he could do, and she'd no proof it had been Sedgwick anyway.

'Just remember what I said,' he ended. 'He has nothing to do with your biography, so avoid him like the plague. He could be dangerous.'

The sun had moved off the little garden in Danvers Close and, having spent the day on their respective researches, Tom and Catherine were sitting on the terrace enjoying a well-earned cup of tea.

Catherine was describing some incident at the High School that had happened eighty years ago, but Tom, whose mind was on more recent events, was only half-listening. Ever since she'd come across that photo of the child who'd been murdered, he'd been worried that she was keeping something back – something that profoundly disturbed her – and this conviction was strengthened by her reaction to Rona's comment about that journalist's tattoo. There had to be a connection, and for the last three weeks he'd been waiting for an opportunity to broach the subject and, hopefully, dispel the trauma, whatever it might be, for good.

'It really wasn't the school's fault,' Catherine ended. 'In those days playgrounds were paved in hard concrete, unlike the soft surfaces used today, and any fall could have serious consequences.'

Tom took a deep breath. It was now or never. 'Talking of schools, darling, I wish you'd tell me more about that little girl at St Stephen's – the one who died. I know it still upsets you, and I'm sure talking about it would help.'

Startled, Catherine turned to face him. 'Tom, no . . .'

He said gently, 'She was the one with the butterfly birthmark, wasn't she?'

Catherine stared at him, but he knew she wasn't seeing him. He waited patiently, and after a long silence she gave a shudder that shook her whole frame. 'No,' she said then, 'it wasn't Tracy, it was the child who killed her.'

FOURTEEN

Tom stared at her in horror. 'It was a *child* who killed her?'

Catherine's face had paled. She nodded. 'One of her classmates, Carrie Drake.'

Carrie Drake – the name was faintly familiar. 'But in God's name, *why*?'

'Because,' she said in a flat voice, 'Tracy had been given a part in the school play that Carrie'd set her heart on having.'

'That was reason enough to *kill* her?'

Catherine said reflectively, 'She'd always been difficult, Carrie, possibly because she was the only child of older parents who spoiled her. She'd been brought up to think she could have everything she wanted. She was bright enough . . . but there was something about her that was different, not that we ever dreamed she was violent.' She paused. 'The whole school was traumatized.'

Tom moistened his lips. 'So . . . what happened, exactly?'

She sighed. 'It's a tragic story in more ways than one. Tracy's mother always met her from school, but on that day she couldn't make it and her brother was told to take her home. And, being a twelve-year-old boy, he went off with his pals instead.'

She shook her head sadly. 'He was totally distraught – I've never seen a child in such a state. He had counselling, but it's a guilt he'll live with for the rest of his life. My heart still aches for him.'

'Did his parents hold him to blame?'

'No, thank God – they supported him all they could. It was herself the mother blamed, poor woman. I believe she attempted suicide at one point.'

'And what happened to Carrie?'

'She was sent to a secure care centre where she was able to continue her schooling, and later to an open prison to complete her sentence.'

'Which was?'

'Twelve years. Though it's "life" in that if she offends again in any way she'll be sent straight back to prison.'

'But she's out now?'

'Presumably. With a new identity, of course.' She gazed out across the garden. 'I read a survey once of three hundred young criminals aged between ten and eighteen. It stated that seventy-four per cent came from broken homes, one in three had borderline learning disabilities, and one in five an IQ below seventy. Carrie was an exception to them all.'

After a minute Tom said, 'And Rona's journalist had a similar birthmark.'

Catherine shrugged. 'She thought it was a tattoo and she's probably right – butterflies are a popular choice. It brought it back, that's all.' She smiled ruefully. 'Sorry I made such a drama out of it.'

Rona spent a restless night, but now it was Friday and Max would be home that evening. She could only hope that after hearing abut Esmé's caller he wouldn't try to talk her into dropping the biography.

She was having breakfast when Tess Chadwick phoned. 'Rona, I'll be in Marsborough today. Could we meet?'

'Of course, Tess.' Company would be welcome.

'Lunch at The Gallery at one?'

'Fine. See you there.'

In the meantime, she had the recording from yesterday's lunch to transcribe. It already seemed an age ago.

When, just before one o'clock, she set out for her rendezvous Rona was glad of Gus trotting at her side. Since hearing of that mysterious phone call she'd felt distinctly nervous, though exactly what she feared she was unsure. A dose of Tess's breezy company would be a welcome antidote.

Gus lolloped with her up the iron staircase and along the walkway to the café entrance. It was crowded as usual, but Rona caught sight of Tess's black-clad arm waving at her from the far end and went to join her at a table overlooking Guild Street.

'What brings you to Marsborough?' Rona asked.

'There's a story I'm following up, but to be honest I used it as an excuse. I needed to see you.'

Rona raised an eyebrow. 'I'm flattered.'

Tess shook her head impatiently, her chestnut curls bouncing. She still looked ridiculously young, though by Rona's reckoning she had to be well into her forties.

'There's something I have to tell you before tomorrow's paper comes out.'

'OK,' Rona said guardedly.

A waitress appeared within hailing distance and, as they were rarer than hen's teeth at The Gallery, Tess accosted her and reeled off their order. 'And two glasses of house red,' she added with an enquiring look at Rona, who shook her head. 'Just water for me, thanks. I've a bit of a headache,' she added by way of explanation.

Tess said grimly, 'Well, I'm afraid you'll have a worse one when you hear what I have to tell you.'

'Hey!' Rona protested, 'I was looking to you to cheer me up!'

'Not today, Josephine.' Tess leaned forward earnestly. 'Rona, we've got an exclusive coming out tomorrow, and I wanted you to have advance warning.'

Rona frowned. 'Warning?'

'Have you ever heard of Carrie Drake?'

'I don't think so.'

'Well, she was one of a handful of child murderers – a child herself, I mean, like Mary Bell and the boys who killed James

Bulger. Rod Jacobs, one of our journalists, decided to find out what's happened to those who've *not* been outed over the years.'

'I don't see—' Rona began, but Tess's raised hand silenced her.

'About six weeks ago he got a lead, and after a lot of digging and checking and rechecking he got the OK. It'll be headlines in tomorrow's edition, and strictly speaking I shouldn't be telling you this because it's being kept under wraps. However, at this late stage I doubt if anyone can pre-empt us. Can you guess what's coming?'

'Not a clue.'

'Then I have to tell you that for the last ten years or so Carrie Drake has been known as Nicole Summers.'

Rona stared at her blankly.

'Honestly. There's no room for doubt. It was a tricky one in the circumstances, but the editor reckons the police will welcome the story, rather than otherwise, as it could open up new leads.'

Rona cleared her throat. 'You're saying Nicole *killed* someone? When she was young?'

Tess nodded. The waitress appeared with their respective glasses and they both took a quick, much needed, sip.

'A classmate,' Tess went on, 'a little kid called Tracy Palmer. Stabbed her on the way home from school. They were nine or ten at the time.'

'I can't believe it,' Rona said flatly. 'All right, I didn't particularly take to her, but I just can't imagine . . .' Her voice tailed off.

'I know. Apart from anything else, you'd have thought she'd want to keep a low profile, wouldn't you, instead of making a name for herself in the cookery world?' She glanced at Rona's sombre face. 'At least by dying when she did she was spared this exposé.'

Rona took another sip of water, thinking back to her meeting with Nicole and trying to visualize her in this totally different light. Though she couldn't say so to Tess, she felt that, having done her time, Nicole should have been left in peace to live the new life she'd made for herself, without having the past dragged up to haunt her. As Tess pointed out, she'd been spared that. But how would Rory Jesmond react on seeing tomorrow's paper, let alone Patrick and poor little Venetia? And – oh God! – she'd have to warn Barnie.

'By the look on your face, you haven't a very high opinion of the press!' Tess said ruefully. 'Blame the insatiable public, my dear, who hoover up all the gory details!'

'I'm sorry, Tess, and I *do* appreciate your telling me. I was just thinking of the hurt it will cause those who are left. But I suppose if it leads to finding who murdered her, that would be something.'

Their mood remained subdued throughout the meal, though Tess tried to enliven it with some of the more amusing incidents she'd come across in her journalistic career, and it was with a certain sense of relief that they parted on the pavement.

'Thank you for taking the trouble to tell me personally,' Rona said, giving her a quick hug.

'It was the least I could do. Don't let it get you down, though, love. You can't take the cares of the whole world on your shoulders.'

With which philosophical comment she patted Rona's arm and set off in the opposite direction down Guild Street and, with a deep sigh, Rona turned in the direction of home.

When Max arrived home that evening, news of Esmé's unknown caller had been overshadowed by the bombshell about Nicole, and it wasn't until they'd discussed Tess's report in detail that Rona brought it up. His reaction was much as she'd expected: advising her to take Gus whenever she went out, to keep to crowded places, and not to answer the door without first checking through the spyhole.

'Though frankly,' he ended, 'I wouldn't take it too seriously. After all, even if it *was* Sedgwick, he was hardly after state secrets, was he? What does it matter how far you've progressed with the bio?'

'He might be wondering if I'd found out about the colour-blindness.'

'Why should he? He's got away with it for the last few years.'

'And if he was the burglar,' she continued, 'he could have been checking whether I had my hands on the papers he'd been unable to find.'

'If, if, if!' Max scoffed. 'If wishes were horses, beggars would ride.'

'A singularly unhelpful comment!' Rona retorted, and the discussion came to an end.

Early the next morning the *Stokely Gazette* dropped through their letter box alongside the daily paper, and Rona and Max sat down to read the lurid disclosures.

'Surely they didn't need to give Patrick's name!' she objected as she came to a reference to their marriage.

'It's already in the public domain,' Max said. 'Nicole was fairly well known one way or another, and it's no secret that she and Patrick were divorced. At least, although it refers to a daughter, *her* name isn't given.'

According to the account, from the day of her arrest Carrie Drake had refused to see her shocked parents, an incredible stance in so young a child. Neighbours who'd been around at the time reported that the couple, in their fifties, had been devastated almost as much by this rejection as by what they were told their daughter had done, which they steadfastly refused to believe. Over the next few years they'd made repeated attempts to see her until, accepting defeat, they'd left the district, cutting off all contact with friends and neighbours.

'Even when she met Patrick she wouldn't talk about them,' Rona said sadly. 'He told me so. If they're still alive, they don't know they have a little granddaughter.'

'Surely she'd have been *required* to cut herself off from everything and everyone she'd known,' Max pointed out, 'to safeguard her new identity. Though perhaps that only applied when she was adult. Now, though, all this publicity should help her parents trace the child, so with luck some good might yet come of it.'

'No mention of the butterfly birthmark,' Tom said, to break the silence. Catherine was sitting white-faced beside him, her hand grasping his. He shook his head disbelievingly. 'She must have thought she was safe after all these years. I wonder if her murderer knew who she was.'

Catherine moistened parched lips. 'I'm sure he did,' she said.

Lindsey phoned Rona later that morning. 'Have you seen the *Gazette*?' she demanded.

'I have indeed, though I met Tess yesterday and she warned me what was coming.'

'She could have killed *you,* Ro! You were alone in the house with her!'

'Linz, as far as we know she hadn't killed anyone for over twenty years. Why would she start now?'

Lindsey's mind had already moved on. 'We wondered if we should phone Patrick. When we had a drink with him last night he was looking forward to his free weekend. Which at least means he'll be with his daughter, thankfully. It's been one shock after another for them.'

'So are you going to contact him?'

'We decided to give him time to absorb it first.'

'Probably the wisest course.'

'It'll be a shock for *Chiltern Life*, too,' Lindsey said after a pause. 'First their columnist gets murdered, then she turns out to be a murderer herself!'

'I know. I was pretty shattered after seeing Tess, and rather than go over it all again on the phone I chickened out and sent Barnie an email.'

'How did he reply?'

'A return email, just thanking me for letting him know. I suppose there's not much else he *could* say.'

'Well,' Lindsey commented, 'that's another you can add to the list of murderers you've known!'

'I'm going for *The Guinness Book of Records*,' Rona said drily.

It was another warm day, and after lunch Rona and Max took Gus for a walk in the nearby woods. Halfway through, though, Rona began to flag.

Max was full of apologies. 'I'm so sorry, sweetheart, I wasn't thinking. We should have stuck to the park, where there are benches at regular intervals.'

'I don't know what's the matter with me,' she complained. 'We haven't come that far, I shouldn't be feeling like this.'

He looked about him. 'There's a tree trunk over there that looks fairly comfortable. You sit down and I'll go back and bring the car to that side road we crossed. I'll toot when I get there, and once you've got your breath back you can come and join me. I'll leave Gus with you for company.'

He whistled for the dog and, when he came running, reattached his lead and handed it to Rona.

'It seems such a shame when he was enjoying himself,' she said.

'He can enjoy himself nearer home for the next nine months!' Max replied.

He extracted a treat from his pocket and gave it to the dog, who sat down, panting, at Rona's feet. 'Shan't be long,' he said, and set off through the trees.

Rona eased her aching back, the main reason for her tiredness. This was something new and debilitating. Perhaps she should have expected it? She sat scratching Gus's ears, the sun warm on her back, and after a few minutes the sound of Max's horn reached them and they retraced their steps to join him.

Back home, Max suggested she lie down for a while, but she shook her head.

'I'm fine again now I've had a rest. I'm just sorry I spoiled the walk for you and Gus.'

'We'll survive.'

Half an hour later her world suddenly changed, as she stood in the bathroom staring unbelievingly at the ominous spots of blood. Surely this was not supposed to happen? A hundred thoughts clamoured in her head in the space of seconds. There wouldn't after all be any disruption to their lives; she wouldn't, as Lindsey had suggested, pram-push with Magda; there'd be no need to convert Max's study into a nursery. And a totally unexpected sense of loss swept over her.

'*No*!' she whispered. 'No, no, no!'

Moving cautiously, she went on to the landing to call Max.

Saturday afternoon in the Royal County A&E was surprisingly quiet – the lull, perhaps, before the storm of Saturday-night drinkers. Max parked Rona on a vacant chair and hurried to the reception desk. Minutes later he rejoined her, accompanied by a porter with a wheelchair.

'We've been told to go to the Early Pregnancy Unit,' he told her as she was helped into it. 'This gentleman will take us.'

They were conveyed through seemingly endless corridors, some with wards opening off them, some signposted with the names of departments. 'I could do with a wheelchair myself!' Max joked.

Eventually they reached their destination, where the porter left them and Max approached the desk. In the waiting area there were several rows of seats, most of them occupied by young couples sitting clutching each other's hands. Rona wondered if they were in the same boat. She watched Max anxiously as he talked with the receptionist, who glanced over in her direction before consulting a chart on the desk. She then spoke to a colleague before turning back to him.

He nodded his thanks and came over to Rona. 'It seems a scan is the usual procedure in these circumstances,' he told her. 'Normally we'd have had to come back on Monday or Tuesday but they've had a cancellation this afternoon, so we're in luck. They'll call us when they're ready for us.'

He sat down next to her. 'Don't worry, darling,' he said in a low voice. 'Apparently this isn't unusual, but it's best to check all is well.'

She could think of nothing to say – ever since seeing the blood she'd felt numb, suspended in a limbo between hope and despair. They sat in silence as various names were called and the appropriate couple stood up and were shown into a consulting room. Only yesterday, Rona reflected, she wasn't at all sure she wanted this baby. Now, the thought of losing it was unbearable. Please let it be all right! she prayed urgently.

'Rona Allerdyce!' a voice called, and Max stood up quickly and pushed her to the open door. The sonographer was a pleasant young woman who introduced herself as Maggie. When they were settled, she asked Rona a series of questions, including the date of her last period, which had begun on April 18th.

'Have you had any other symptoms before this spotting?'

'Not really, except feeling more tired than usual,' she replied. 'And a bit fragile emotionally.'

The young woman nodded. 'Well, let's get you up on this couch and we'll see what's going on.'

Rona was helped on to the couch, where she glanced rather fearfully at the monitor beside her. Her clothes were rearranged, exposing her stomach, which was spread with jelly, cold on her warm skin. Then Maggie moved the scanner slowly over her, her eyes on the screen.

Rona reached for Max's hand and gripped it tightly. The images were incomprehensible to her – she'd no idea what she was supposed to see or whether what she *was* seeing was as it should be. She glanced anxiously from the screen to Maggie's face and saw with a flood of relief that she was smiling.

'I don't think you've anything to worry about, Mrs Allerdyce,' she said, turning the screen slightly so that it was easier for Rona to see. 'Can you make anything out?'

Max and Rona shook their heads.

'So the baby's all right?' Rona asked, needing reassurance.

'Very much so. Look more closely. What can you see?' She waited a moment but they still looked blank. 'Then I have to tell you that we've picked up not one but *two* sacs.' She pointed to the tiny blips on the screen. 'Which means, Mr and Mrs Allerdyce, that you're expecting twins!'

FIFTEEN

At ten thirty on the Monday morning, Alan Palmer walked into Woodbourne police station and approached the desk.

'I want to confess to the murder of Nicole Summers,' he said.

The sergeant on duty didn't look up. 'Oh yes, sir?'

When there was no response, he raised his head and something in the man's eyes gave him pause.

'Sorry, sir,' he said quietly. 'There's been a positive avalanche of confessions since that article.'

'What article?'

'In the *Stokely Gazette*. Isn't that why you're here?'

'I live in London,' Alan said. 'I haven't seen any local papers.'

'You're telling me you coming in, today of all days, is pure coincidence?'

Alan frowned. 'What was this article?'

The sergeant looked at him through narrowed eyes, unsure whether his ignorance was genuine. 'About Nicole Summers being a child murderer.'

'Ah.'

'Ah? That isn't news to you?'

'Well, no. That's why I killed her.'

The sergeant sighed. 'All right, mate, you win. Sit down over there and I'll get someone to see you.'

* * *

Lindsey stood on the edge of the pavement, impatiently waiting for a break in the traffic. She'd an appointment with a client in ten minutes, and a phone call as she was leaving the office had already delayed her. They should put a pedestrian crossing here, she thought irritably; walking to the nearest traffic lights would take her in the wrong direction. With luck, after another three cars . . .

She turned, startled, as the car that had been approaching slammed on its brakes and skidded to a halt beside her. The driver leaned across and opened the passenger door.

'Miss Parish!' he said. 'Just who I was hoping to see!'

She stooped to look inside and was surprised to recognize Bruce Sedgwick. Though they'd never met, his was a well-known face. 'I don't think . . .' she began.

'I need a word with you,' he said.

A message for Steve, perhaps, from Patrick? Nevertheless . . . 'I'm sorry, but I can't stop now. I've an appointment in ten minutes and I'm late as it is.'

The driver behind him sounded his horn and Sedgwick said quickly, 'Look, we're holding up the traffic. Get in, please.'

Lindsey hesitated and a horn from two cars back blared a complaint. 'Well, provided you can drop me outside Netherby's,' she compromised. The department store was within yards of where she was going and a lift down Guild Street would save time. Forestalling the next hoot, she slid inside and pulled the door shut.

Alan was seated in an interview room opposite two plain-clothes officers, a recorder on the table between them. It was a scenario ludicrously familiar from countless television dramas, and he listened impassively to the routine of stating names and the time of day.

'Now, Mr Palmer,' began the man who'd introduced himself as Detective Sergeant Boxer, 'perhaps you'd like to tell us in your own words what happened.'

Alan took a drink from the glass of water in front of him. 'To start at the beginning,' he said, 'Carrie Drake, which is Nicole Summers' real name, murdered my sister, Tracy Palmer, in November 1990 on the way home from school.'

The officers exchanged a glance. It had already been established that Palmer, who'd arrived in Buckfordshire only that morning, was unlikely to have had access to the newspaper story. And Tracy Palmer was on file as Drake's victim.

Alan took his wallet from his hip pocket and extracted a creased snapshot, which he tossed on the table between them. Boxer picked it up. It showed two children, a boy and girl in school uniform, squinting into the sunshine of a long-gone summer day. The boy could pass as a younger version of the man in front of them, and if the identity of the children could be verified . . . He flipped it over. A blob of dried glue indicated that it had been removed from an album, and beneath it in fading pencil was written 'July 1990' – four months before Tracy's murder.

Boxer showed both sides of the snap to his companion, then handed it back without comment.

'A different world,' Alan commented, replacing it in his wallet.

'Go on.'

'We knew she'd been sent to prison and must have been released years ago, but she'd been given a new identity and we'd no means of knowing where – or who – she was now. Nevertheless, it was as if she was with us every day of our lives. Mum never recovered from Tracy's death, and every year on her anniversary we had to sit down to her favourite dinner. I never want to taste chicken again for as long as I live!'

He stopped, fished a handkerchief out of his pocket, and dabbed at his eyes. 'Sorry,' he muttered, 'Mum passed away a few weeks ago.'

'Our condolences,' said the DS perfunctorily.

Alan nodded, twisting his handkerchief in his hands. When he didn't immediately continue, Boxer prompted, 'So when and how did you manage to trace her?'

Alan shook his head. 'You make it sound as if I've spent my whole life tracking her down, but it wasn't like that. I came across her completely by chance.'

He took a deep breath. 'About six weeks ago we got a call to say Mum had had a stroke. And to make it even worse it was Tracy's birthday . . . the twenty-sixth of April. The parents moved from Buckford to Chilswood after her death – too many painful memories – so the nearest hospital was Woodbourne General. I drove up and we spent a pretty gruelling day by Mum's bedside. She couldn't talk properly, but we made out the word "Tracy" over and over again.

'Well, I spent that night with Dad, but when we went in the next morning they told us it was unlikely there'd be any immediate change, so Dad insisted I went home. There was a job waiting at work, so after arguing a bit I gave in, telling him I'd be back at the weekend. I left the hospital about mid-morning.'

His eyes dropped to the handkerchief he was twisting and he sat in silence for several minutes. The detective constable moved impatiently, but the DS shook his head – better to let him tell it in his own words, nothing would be gained by hurrying him.

Eventually Alan looked up. 'Well, I stopped for some cigarettes, didn't I?' he said bitterly. 'Would you believe a packet of fags cost Carrie her life? Doubly ironic since I'd given them up! But what with Mum and everything I badly needed a smoke, so I pulled into a service station on the edge of town.'

He paused again. 'And there she was,' he ended flatly.

'Is it about Patrick?' Lindsey asked, as the car started up.

'Patrick?'

'Look, whatever it is, could you please be quick? We're almost where I need to be. Please—' Her voice rose. 'Stop! I *told* you, I've got an appointment!'

Contrary to her request, he put his foot on the accelerator and they shot ahead, leaving the store behind them and forcing pedestrians at the crossing to jump back in alarm. She turned to him furiously, surprised to see the sheen of sweat on his face. 'What are you doing? You'll lose me my job! Stop!'

'Sorry, Ms Parish, we need to talk.' His voice held the undercurrent of a tremor and his hands were gripping the steering wheel.

'What about?'

He didn't answer and she looked about her, totally bewildered by the turn of events. Guild Street had rapidly become Belmont Road, and they were now driving through the patch of countryside that divided Marsborough from the suburb where she and Rona grew up. They used to cycle here to pick blackberries.

'Where are we *going*?' she demanded. 'Please, will you take me back?'

They were driving uncomfortably fast, his eyes fixed on the road. 'Tell me,' he said abruptly, 'how are you getting on with that biography of yours?'

She stared at him blankly – then, as understanding dawned, exclaimed, 'Oh, I don't believe this! It's not even me you want! I'm Lindsey, not Rona!'

'Yeah, yeah. Her twin sister, I suppose? As if I'd fall for that old chestnut!'

'But I *am*!' Lindsey protested.

'Look, I saw you at the hotel. Remember? So don't try to fob me off with that bizzo.'

'*That wasn't me!*' She fumbled in her handbag, extracted her credit card and held it in front of him 'See?'

He stared at it for a moment, his face changing, and swore fluently. Then the car swerved as, taking her completely by surprise, his hand snaked into the bag lying open on her lap, took out her phone, and dropped it into the door pocket beside him. Annoyance gave way to alarm.

'Look,' she said, her voice not quite steady, 'I'm sure you don't want any adverse publicity. You mightn't have known who *I* am, but don't forget I know who *you* are!'

'And that,' he said grimly, 'is where you're making a big mistake.'

'So,' Boxer said after a minute, 'was she buying ciggies too?'

Alan didn't answer directly. He was back there now, in the small shop at the service station. 'There were two cash tills,' he went on, 'one at each end of the counter. She was in one queue and I was in the other and we were keeping pace with each other. Then she half-turned to look at something . . . and there it was. The butterfly on her neck.'

'*Butterfly?*'

'A birthmark. Probably lots of people have them, but I knew it was her, even before she turned back. And seeing her more closely, I could trace the child's face in hers – the child who'd killed Tracy.' He drew a deep breath. 'There was even the little mole at the edge of her mouth which I'd forgotten about but which, when I saw it, I remembered.

'It was like . . . I don't know, as though I'd been punched in the solar plexus, knocking all the wind out of me. She moved to her cash till, then mine became vacant and the bloke behind gave me a nudge. Coming across her like that, just after leaving Mum, my brain was completely scrambled. How I paid for the cigarettes I don't know, I was just set on not losing sight of her, and when I got outside she was getting into a car a couple of pumps from where I'd parked. I flung myself into mine and went after her.'

He reached almost convulsively for the glass of water and drained it.

'You followed her home,' Boxer said – a statement rather than a question.

Alan nodded. 'She lived in an estate of wooden houses with open drives. I kept a fair distance behind her, without a thought in my head about why I was doing this. She turned into one of the driveways and I stopped several houses back. I thought I'd give her time to go inside, then go and ring her bell.

'But as I was about to get out, a car came zooming up and turned into the same driveway. A guy got out, went to the door and knocked, and after a minute she opened it and he went in. At first I'd assumed it was her husband, but then he wouldn't have had to knock, would he? Still, the fact he was there put paid to any idea of confronting her. I was still pretty shaken up, so I thought I'd stay where I was while I had a cigarette, hoping it would calm me down.'

DC Crawford said in an undertone, 'This statement should be in instalments.'

Boxer didn't reply. The suspect, if that's what he was, was voluntarily providing motive, means and opportunity, which would save a lot of hassle, and he was more than happy to give him enough rope to hang himself – metaphorically, at least.

Alan gave himself a small shake and resumed his account. 'I was on the point of leaving when the guy came storming out again, slamming the door behind him. He flung himself into his car, reversed out of the drive at high speed, and took off down the road away from me. So without really thinking about it I got out, went to the house, and rang the bell. It opened almost at once – I think she thought the other fellow had come back, because she opened her mouth, perhaps to continue an argument. But she recovered herself when she saw me, and just said "Yes?".'

Alan looked up then, holding the policeman's eyes. 'And I said, "Hello, Carrie!".'

Lindsey looked at him uncertainly. 'You're Bruce Sedgwick. We've not met but I recognized you at once, you're always in the news.'

In the door pocket her phone began to ring, startling both of them.

'That'll be my client, wondering where I am.'

He didn't comment and they listened as her voicemail kicked in: *This is Lindsey Parish. I'm sorry I can't take your call just now. Please leave your name and number and I'll get back to you.* Then an annoyed female voice filled the car:

'Miss Parish, this is Florence Frobisher; I was under the impression that we had an appointment for eleven o'clock. I postponed another engagement to fit you in, and should be grateful if you'd confirm that you're now on your way.'

'Oh dear!' said the man who wasn't Bruce Sedgwick.

But Lindsey wasn't thinking of Mrs Frobisher. She said, 'What did you mean "I'm making a big mistake"?'

He was silent for a while as the countryside flashed past and she grew increasingly apprehensive. 'Trouble is,' he burst out suddenly, 'you've thrown a dirty great spanner in the works. Or rather I have, by taking you for your sister.'

'Why did you want to see her?'

'She didn't tell you?'

They careered round a bend and Lindsey, clinging to her seat, momentarily shut her eyes. 'Tell me what?'

'About this bloody biography.'

She looked at him in surprise. What was Gideon Ward's bio to do with him? 'Well, obviously I know she's writing it, but we haven't discussed it. I don't see—'

She broke off as her phone rang again. Again the message kicked in, followed this time by the receptionist at Chase Mortimer. 'Lindsey? Are you there? It's Janet.' A pause, then: 'When you left here I understood you were going to Mrs Frobisher, but she's called to say you've not arrived. Could you contact either her or us as soon as you get this, please.'

'Another spanner!' commented her companion. 'But at least we can deal with this one.' And he one-handedly switched off the phone.

Lindsey gripped her bag. 'Will you please tell me what's going on?'

They were approaching the outskirts of Belmont, but instead of following the curve of the road he turned left on to a country lane that would eventually lead to the village of Shellswick. Her alarm intensified.

'Where are we going? Take me back to Marsborough – *now*!'

'Not,' he replied through gritted teeth, 'until I've decided what to do. And that will be a lot quicker if you'll stop bloody nagging.'

Lindsey bit her lip. Admittedly this was bizarre and totally out of order, but she must try to keep it in proportion. The man was unlikely to molest her – as she'd pointed out, he had his reputation at stake, not to mention bad publicity for all his hotels. And thankfully, having left the main road, he'd slackened his speed.

They drove in silence for several minutes between high hedges. Birds were flying overhead in a cloudless blue sky and far above them a solitary aeroplane droned, the sun striking silver from its wings.

Why, Lindsey was asking herself, was I fool enough to get into this car? But she knew the answer: because a lift along Guild Street would have saved minutes when she was running late. Never had she made a worse judgement.

Suddenly he smote the flat of his hand on the steering wheel, making her jump. 'This wasn't planned, you know!' he said furiously, as though she'd made an accusation. 'No bloody part of it! Maybe if Jack hadn't died . . .'

He broke off and Lindsey ventured, 'Who's Jack?'

He glanced at her quickly, as though unaware he'd spoken aloud. 'Jack Sedgwick,' he said after a minute. 'Bruce's dad.'

A creeping coldness crept over her. Was he losing his mind, talking in the third person? If that were so, then she *was* in danger. She said carefully, 'But you're Bruce.'

He shook his head slowly from side to side. 'No, I'm not. As I'm sure that sister of yours knows damn well.'

Lindsey's mouth was dry. Trying to keep her voice level she said, 'Then who are you?'

His mouth twisted in a mirthless grin.

'Grant Phillips, ma'am, late of Alice Springs, in the land of Oz. Happy to make your acquaintance.'

Boxer was leaning forward. *Now* they were getting to the point. 'What did she say?' he demanded.

'Nothing. She seemed . . . paralyzed. It was fascinating – the colour just drained from her face as she went on staring at me. Then she made a choking sound and reached for the door, but I caught it and stepped inside.

'I said, "Don't you recognize me, Carrie? I recognized *you* . . ." and she kind of licked her lips and said, "Who *are* you?" But before I could reply, she gave a sudden gasp and blurted out, "You're Alan, aren't you? Alan Palmer?"

'And she suddenly spun round and started to run. It was all open-plan so I couldn't think where she was going, but I went after her.'

He stopped speaking, and held Boxer's eye. 'I can't expect you to believe me, but honest to God I'd no intention of hurting her. Not at that stage. So when we reached the kitchen area and she seized a knife from the block and turned to face me I was . . . dumbstruck. She was half-crying by this time and she shouted, "How did you find me? I'm Nicole Summers now – I have been for years! Leave me alone! I've done my time!" And I said, "We're all still doing ours, and Mum is dying. I've just been to see her, and she's asking for Tracy." She kind of flinched and raised the knife. Then she suddenly cried, "Leave me alone, damn you!" and lunged forward. I caught hold of her wrist and held it up, our faces only inches apart.'

Alan wiped a hand across his own face. He'd begun to sweat. 'And suddenly – I can't explain it – a kind of haze came down. I looked at the knife still in her hand and thought of how she'd stabbed little Tracy and all the years of pain our family had suffered, and it seemed there was only one thing I could do. For Mum, for Dad, for myself, most of all for Tracy. So . . . I twisted her wrist so the knife was pointing towards her and just – pushed.'

He looked expressionlessly at the two men opposite him. 'And then,' he said flatly, 'I drove home.'

Which explained why there were only the victim's prints on the knife, Boxer thought. They hadn't entirely ruled out suicide, though the pathologist had insisted the angle of the wound was inconsistent with its being self-inflicted. There was a long silence. Out in the foyer a telephone started to ring. He cleared his throat.

'Why wait six weeks to come forward?'

Alan made a dismissive movement with his hand. 'I thought I could live with it. Mum died soon after and the whole thing just knocked me for six. It seemed like a bad dream, specially since neither Dad nor my wife knew anything about it and put my moods down to grief over Mum. But then I heard you were going to make an arrest, and I couldn't let someone else suffer for what I'd done.'

Boxer leaned back in his chair, looking at him. Poor bugger, he thought.

Rona was doing her best to concentrate on Ward's childhood relationship with his sister, but her mind kept drifting. Twins! Would they be identical, like herself and Linz, or fraternal – even, perhaps, a boy and a girl? Now they'd need two of everything! She wondered whether her mother had kept any of their baby things – the double pushchair, for example, she'd always hoped for grandchildren. She could—

The phone interrupted her musing and she started guiltily. 'Hello?'

'Rona Parish?'

She frowned, trying to place the voice. 'Yes?'

'I'm sorry to disturb you, but this is Janet Lawson, from Chase Mortimer.'

'Hello, Janet.' Rona had met her a couple of times.

'This is going to sound – well, I'm ringing to ask if Lindsey is by any chance with you?'

'No. Isn't she at the office?'

'That's just it. She left here about ten forty-five for an eleven o'clock appointment. She'd been delayed by a last-minute phone call and was in a rush.'

Rona waited, and after a moment Janet continued. 'So we were surprised, about half an hour later, to receive a phone call from the client saying she hadn't turned up.'

Rona frowned. 'And she'd have had time to get there by then?'

'Oh yes. If she hurried, she could even have made it on time. Mrs Frobisher – the client – was extremely annoyed, demanding to know where she was. She said she'd tried to phone her, but her mobile went to voicemail. So then I tried, with the same result.'

There was a pause and Rona was wondering what to suggest when Janet continued, 'And to add to the mystery one of the other partners has just come in and says he saw her getting into a car in Guild Street.'

'Whose car?' Rona asked sharply.

'He didn't recognize it, but he said it was a man driving.'

Steve? Rona thought in confusion. Could he have seen Linz hurrying and offered her a lift? But in that case she'd have arrived for her appointment.

'You're sure it was the right number you were phoning?'

'Definitely. She identified herself on the voicemail.'

Rona said slowly, 'This isn't like my sister.'

'I know, that's why we're concerned.'

'She can't just have disappeared into thin air!' Rona said a little wildly.

'There must be some simple explanation, but it's strange she's not been in touch with Mrs Frobisher. She's an important client.'

'I'm sorry I can't help,' Rona said from a suddenly dry mouth. 'You will let me know as soon as you reach her?'

'Of course, and may I ask you to do the same?'

She put the phone down, uneasiness gnawing at her. Then she punched in Max's number.

'Lindsey's gone AWOL!' she said without preamble.

'How do you mean?'

'Just that. I've had Chase Mortimer on the phone. They say she left to visit a client, but was seen getting into a car driven by a man.'

'Well don't panic, love, she's not a child. She knows not to accept lifts from strangers.'

'If it was someone she knew, why didn't he drop her off at the client's? I don't like this, Max. Something's wrong, I'm sure.'

'Now don't go all psychic on me!'

'I'm serious. Lindsey wouldn't just take off when she had a business appointment.'

'Well, I don't mean to sound unsympathetic, but what do you want me to do? Phone the police? How long has it been, for God's sake? Not even an hour yet.'

'But an hour during which no one knows where she is.' Rona could hear her voice rising.

'Let's just be sensible about this.' He spoke calmly, trying to allay her fears. 'Who on earth would kidnap her, if that's what you're thinking? It's not likely to be the white slave trade, now is it, in the middle of Guild Street on a Monday morning? And there's not much point in my going to look for her, because if they were in a car they could be anywhere by now.'

'Exactly,' Rona said bleakly.

There was a pause. 'Do you know what direction the car was going in?'

'No idea, but how would that help?'

'On reflection, I don't suppose it would. I should ring off, love. She might be trying to reach you as we speak.'

'Do you think we should let Steve know?'

'Know what, for God's sake?'

Rona's mind did a lightning switch from Steve to Patrick to Bruce Sedgwick, and for no reason she could pinpoint she went cold.

'I'm going to phone the hotel and ask Patrick what car Bruce Sedgwick drives.'

'What the hell has that to do with it?'

'I need to know, that's all.'

Max sighed. 'Fair enough. Good luck, and let me know when she turns up.'

'Sedgwick Hotel.'

'Could I speak to Patrick Summers, please?'

'I'm sorry, Mr Summers is on leave this week. Who's calling?'

'It's Rona Parish.' Of course – he must still be reeling from the *Gazette* article.

'Perhaps I can help you?'

She said carefully, 'Is Mr Sedgwick in Marsborough today?'

'Yes, but I'm afraid he's out at the moment.'

Rona quickly improvised. 'I thought I saw someone vandalize his car in Guild Street,' she said. 'It *is* a blue BMW, isn't it?'

'No, Mr Sedgwick drives a silver Mercedes,' the receptionist replied.

'Oh, that's a relief! I must have been mixing it up with someone else's.'

'Thank you for letting us know, but I'm glad to say the car wasn't Mr Sedgwick's.'

Rona promptly rang Chase Mortimer.

'It's Rona,' she said quickly.

'You've heard from her?' Janet Lawson broke in.

'No, but please could you ask whoever saw her to describe the car. And also which direction it was travelling in.'

'Hold on a moment.'

Rona waited, her heart thundering in her ears. Then Janet came back.

'Hello?'

'Yes?'

'He says it was a silver Mercedes and they drove west along Guild Street.'

Rona's nails dug convulsively into her palm. 'Thanks,' she said, and rang off before Janet could question her.

SIXTEEN

Lindsey said numbly, 'I don't understand.'

They were rounding a bend in the narrow lane, and a passing place opened up on their left. Grant swerved into it, coming to a halt with the passenger door hard against the hedge, making it impossible to open.

'I need to think,' he muttered and slumped forward, his forehead resting on the wheel.

Lindsey took a deep breath, assessing her situation. *Who was this man?* Was it true, what he said about not being Bruce Sedgwick, or was it some kind of trick? Perhaps she was marooned with a homicidal maniac? This, she thought with a touch of gallows humour, was the kind of thing that happened to Rona, not her. He'd effectively seen to it that she couldn't escape. If another car came along, would she have time to attract attention? Almost certainly not. And anyway, what could she do? Push him aside and lean on the horn?

As if she'd conjured it up, a car suddenly came round the bend behind them and passed before she'd time to register it. Possibly one coming from the other direction . . . She broke off her musings as her companion sat back in his seat, running both hands through his hair and over his face.

'Why the blue hell did he never *tell* me?' he demanded furiously. 'God, we'd got our passports and tickets and were set to go, but never a word of spending time here when he was a kid!'

Keep him talking. Wasn't that supposed to be the best strategy? 'Why didn't who tell you?' Lindsey asked.

'Mahatma Gandhi. Bruce, of course!'

So he was persisting with that line. She tried another angle. 'Why was it so important?'

'Because if he had, that biographer wouldn't have caught me on the hop. He'd been at *school* with him, for Pete's sake! How rich is that?'

Lindsey was becoming increasingly perplexed. She'd thought 'biographer' related to Rona but he must mean Russell Page, though how—

She'd not time to finish the thought. 'But he wouldn't have bothered to contact me,' Grant, or whatever his name was, was continuing, 'if I'd known Bruce was colour-blind! Something else he omitted to mention and I sure as hell hadn't noticed!'

She was now completely at a loss. 'And that was also important?'

'Too right it was! That's what started the whole bloody paperchase!'

Lindsey hesitated. 'So where is he now?'

'You might well ask!' he said bitterly. 'Just when luck was finally coming our way, it turned round and hit us in the face.' His hand raked his hair again, fingers splayed. 'Still, at least my old cobber died happy.'

A sudden chill. 'He's *dead*?'

Grant nodded. 'Bruce Sedgwick is dead,' he proclaimed ironically, 'long live Bruce Sedgwick!'

Had this man *killed* him? No, don't go there! 'So you . . . pretended to be him?'

'Well, damn it, wouldn't you, in the circumstances?'

She said aridly, 'I don't know the circumstances.'

He shook his head impatiently. 'Then let me enlighten you. I'd met old Jack six months before, in a pub in Alice. We got chatting, I told him I was out of work and down to my last dollar. He'd been laid off due to ill health and wasn't flush himself, but he took me home with him for a meal. Which is how I met Bruce. We hit it off at once, and the long and the short of it is I moved in with them. I'd no family of my own and Jack treated me like a second son. I got a job on a construction site with Bruce and for a while everything was ripper. Then within a few months we were knocked sideways by two bombshells.'

He was sitting up straight now, staring ahead of him at the English countryside, his mind thousands of miles away. 'The first was a bummer. Jack was more crook than we realized, and one day he just keeled over and died.'

'I'm sorry,' Lindsey said automatically. And then, curious in spite of herself, 'What was the other?'

'The other,' repeated Grant Phillips with deliberation, 'was Brucie getting a letter from London saying his uncle had also carked it and left the whole bang shooting match to him on condition he came to live in the UK . . . And he never bloody said he'd been at school here!'

'Why do you think that was?'

He shrugged. 'I've gone over it a thousand times, and all I can come up with is that he'd blanked it out for some reason. Perhaps he'd been unhappy here as a kid.'

'So what happened?'

'Well, he was insisting he wouldn't go unless I went with him, said we could live it up together – nightclubs, girls, no worries – and of course I went along with it. They'd forwarded enough dosh to travel first class and that, together with what we scraped together between us, covered two in economy.'

He was silent for several minutes, a small pulse beating in his temple.

'So,' Lindsey said at last, 'you both came over?'

His face contorted. 'No, that's where bloody fate intervened. Last night in Oz we went out celebrating, drank too much as usual and pranged the car into a tree. Bruce was killed outright, I barely had a scratch.'

He sighed deeply. 'Well, God knows that was enough to sober me up – and once I was over the initial shock and sure he really was dead, I reckoned I'd be a fool not to seize my chance. Jack always said we looked like brothers, both of us tall with fair hair and blue eyes. So I switched passports, didn't I? There was no one to mourn Grant Phillips. Reckoned I wasn't doing anything wrong either. No one else had a claim to that legacy and Bruce had wanted me to share it.'

While she was listening a worrying niggle had been growing in Lindsey's mind, and when he stopped talking she asked on impulse, 'But what happened to the biographer, Russell Page? Didn't he die in a car crash too?'

By twelve o'clock Rona, her anxiety mounting, could wait no longer. Lindsey had said Steve was working at home and, not having his mobile number, she phoned the house in Alban Road, praying it wouldn't be Frank who answered.

'Steve Hathaway'

'Oh Steve, thank God!'

'Lindsey?' he said sharply. No one could distinguish between their voices.

'No, it's Rona. Steve, I'm worried about Linz. She should have met a client at eleven, but someone saw her getting into a car in Guild Street – a car that I'm sure belongs to Bruce Sedgwick. And—'

'Hang on a minute, Rona. Are you saying something's happened to her?'

'I don't *know*!' Rona cried. 'Chase Mortimer tried ringing her mobile and got voicemail. And when I tried, the phone had been switched off. I'm *frightened,* Steve!'

'Why the hell didn't you contact me sooner?'

'I almost did, but Max thought I was making a fuss about nothing.'

'Max isn't in love with her. Now, go through it again from the beginning.'

Rona did so, adding that the car had been travelling west along Guild Street.

Steve said, 'In a way, you know, I agree with Max. This just doesn't make sense. Why ever should Bruce of all people kidnap anyone, let alone Lindsey?'

'He probably mistook her for me,' Rona said numbly.

'Then I'll rephrase the question. Why would he kidnap you?'

She closed her eyes. 'I haven't time to go into that – but please believe me, he might have reason to. What can we *do*?'

'Do you know his registration?'

'No, all I know is that it's a silver Mercedes.'

'Right. Well you mobilize Max, and I'll see you both at your house in ten minutes.'

Steve ended, 'In the hope it might give us a clue, I phoned the hotel and asked if Sedgwick had any engagements today. But his secretary said there was nothing in the diary. And for what it's worth, she doesn't know his car reg either. I had a job explaining why I wanted that.'

Max said unbelievingly, 'You're not suggesting we set off in a posse without the faintest idea where he might be or even if Lindsey's actually with him?'

'That's exactly what I'm suggesting. What other options do we have? The police won't be interested at this stage. So as I was saying, we drive west along Guild Street and when we come to a major parting of the ways, you go one way and I'll go the other. We'll agree a time frame and if we've had no luck we'll turn back and repeat the exercise at the next junction, keeping our phones handy so we know the score.'

Max said quietly, 'You do know this is useless, don't you, Steve?'

'We have to do *something*,' he urged. 'The alternative is to sit at home and wait for news, and I don't think either Rona or I could face that.'

'And how long do we give ourselves for this mad search?'

'Until we find her,' Steve said.

The lunchtime news contained an announcement that a thirty-nine-year-old man had come forward in connection with the murder of Nicole Summers and was helping the police with their enquiries.

Catherine's eyes met Tom's. 'Alan,' she said softly, 'I hope they go easy on him.'

There was a long silence, and when Grant finally spoke it wasn't a direct answer.

'It was easier than I'd have believed possible,' he said. 'At first I kept expecting to be rumbled, then I realized my great advantage was not having to pretend to know things, 'cos Bruce wouldn't have known them either. And as no one over here had any info on him, nothing I said could catch me out – or so it seemed.'

He shook his head, thinking back. 'Of course I grieved for him and the time we could have had together, but gradually I almost began to believe I *was* him.'

'And Russell Page?'

He sighed. 'Ah yes, Russell Page. I got a phone call out of the blue from this bloke wanting to meet me. It happens all the time and for a while I fobbed him off, thinking he was just another journalist wanting an interview. But eventually, to get rid of him, I agreed to meet him outside the library in Merefield. I parked in the multi-storey as he suggested, and thought we'd be going somewhere local for the interview – but instead he suggested driving out to a country pub he knew which would be less crowded and where they had real ale. I'd no objection and off we went in his car. I reckoned afterwards that he'd wanted to be sure I couldn't just storm out and drive away.'

He turned to look at her. 'God knows why I'm telling you this. I might as well put a noose round my neck.'

Goose-bumps came up on Lindsey's arms. The catchphrase 'If I tell you, I'll have to kill you!' came unnervingly to mind. No, she assured herself, he couldn't possibly mean that literally, but his comment brought home the fact that over the last hour his mood had changed from initial aggression to weary resignation. She hoped this was a good thing.

He gave a twisted grimace. 'Well, as they say on telly, I've started, so I'll finish. We parked outside this dinky little pub, all thatched roof and old rafters, and went inside. He ordered two beers and took them to a window table. A few people were scattered about, but none within hearing distance. So he puts down our glasses, looks straight at me, and says "You don't remember me, do you?"

'Well, I often get that, so I apologized, something along the lines of meeting a lot of people, and then he comes out with it and says we were at school together.

'That was something new, so I laughed it off, telling him unless he'd been in Brisbane forty years ago that wasn't likely. But he said no, he meant Buckford College.

'Well, I still thought he was mistaken, so I said, "No, mate, you've got the wrong bloke." Whereupon he knocks me for six by saying, "Another Bruce Sedgwick who stayed with his Uncle Jason, a chef, while his father in Australia recovered from appendicitis?"

'That's when the panic set in. All I could do was stick to my guns, so I kept shaking my head and repeating it wasn't me, that there were a lot of Bruce Sedgwicks out there, you only had to google the name and see how many came up. And he said again, "But they don't come from Australia and have famous uncles called Jason . . .".'

He ran a hand over his face. 'Well, I was pole-axed, I can tell you. I could see my whole world crashing down around me, all the high life I'd been living for the last ten years, and I knew I had to shake him. So I blustered, demanding to know why he wouldn't believe me.' He drew a deep breath. 'Which was when he dealt the final blow, told me that on the contrary he *did* believe I'd not been to school with him – because I wasn't Bruce Sedgwick.'

Lindsey was gazing at him, transfixed by this totally unexpected development. 'What did you say?' she whispered.

'Before I'd got my breath back, he went off at what seemed a tangent, saying he was writing a biography of that TV presenter, and I fervently thanked God he'd changed the subject. But he hadn't, had he? And when I said Ward had interviewed me, he said yes, he'd seen the DVD and that was how he knew I wasn't who I said I was. So I blustered, demanding what the hell he meant, and he said he'd been waiting for me to say I'd been at school in Buckford; but I was talking like I'd never been to the UK before – and to a kid of eleven, spending three months in a foreign country must have been one of the biggest events in his childhood and there was no way he wouldn't have mentioned it.

'And I thought, "Well, that's where you're wrong mate, because he sure as hell never mentioned it to me." Then he takes a long swig of beer and goes on, "But then came the clincher. You were describing your uncle's paintings and said you didn't like the garish reds and greens."

'And not knowing what he was getting at, I joked and said too right, I couldn't look at them when I had a hangover.'

He flicked a glance at Lindsey's intent face. 'Then,' he continued deliberately, 'he held my eyes and said very quietly, "But you see, the Bruce Chadwick at school, the *real* one, was colour-blind . . .".'

He paused, staring fixedly into space as he relived the shock. 'Well, it was like having a bucket of cold water thrown over me,' he went on. 'Literally took my breath away, and though I tried frantically I could think of nothing to say. I guess I could have called his bluff but I was too gobsmacked to make the attempt. In the six months I'd known Bruce this had just never come up – perhaps he didn't want to admit it, or maybe he didn't think it was important. But it sure was important now.

'And Page said, "So I'm wondering, if you're not the Bruce Sedgwick whose uncle died a wealthy man and left him everything, just who are you? And, more to the point, where's Bruce?"

'My brain was working overtime trying to find a loophole but nothing came, and he said calmly, "No, I didn't really expect an answer, but be aware I'm not going to let this rest. Either you explain yourself to the authorities or I report you myself. Now, if you've finished your beer, I'll run you back to your car."

'We went back outside and I got into the car like a zombie, my brain completely stymied. Then suddenly, as we turned into a country lane – not unlike this one, you've a lot of them in this county – I suddenly thought, God knows why, of the crash back in Oz and Bruce being killed instantly and me unhurt. And honest to God, on the spur of the moment I put my foot on top of his and pressed down hard on the accelerator, at the same time wrenching the steering wheel to the right, and wham! we went straight into a tree.'

He was breathing heavily, and in contrast Lindsey held her breath. 'It all happened in the space of a few seconds. It could have killed us both, and I wouldn't have cared if it had. But the devil's luck was with me a second time – like Bruce he was killed outright, and all I suffered was whiplash. So I got out and walked for miles till I came to a bus stop and caught the bus back to Merefield and my car. And all the time I was in denial. It just *couldn't* have happened.'

He turned to her again. 'I can't expect you to believe me, Lindsey, but I swear it's God's truth. Terrible and unforgivable though it was, at least it wasn't premeditated. I was in deep shock after the revelations in the pub and my brain just wasn't functioning. It was the association of ideas, acted on in a split second.'

There was a long silence, and finally Lindsey asked, 'What did you do?'

'Waited in trepidation for the report of his death, and to my enormous relief there was no suggestion he hadn't been alone. But I was worried he might have left notes that would incriminate me – so having seen the funeral arrangements in the press, I went to the house and looked for any reference to doubts about my identity.'

'You "went to the house",' Lindsey interrupted. 'You mean you *broke in* while his family was at his funeral?'

He moved impatiently. 'All right, I know. But it didn't do me any good. I searched the entire house without finding anything, so I assumed the Ward biography had been scrapped and I'd got away with it. Again.'

'Until?' Lindsey asked fearfully.

He nodded slowly. 'Until one evening your sister was dining at the hotel, and her friend informed me she'd taken over the biography. Which started alarm bells ringing. I reckoned she must have Page's notes, and all my fears were resurrected.'

'And then,' Lindsey said very softly, 'you thought you saw her standing in Guild Street, and more or less forced her – or rather, me – into the car. What were you going to do with her? Go for a hat-trick, with another car crash?'

He didn't reply and she persisted, 'And now I know everything and pose a much bigger threat, are you *still* going to?'

He flinched as though she had hit him.

'Well?' she demanded, her heart beginning to pound.

'To be honest,' he said wearily, 'I don't know *what* I was intending. That's why I pulled in here, to try to sort things out.'

She moistened suddenly dry lips. 'And have you?'

'Yes, regretfully, I think I have.'

A spasm of sheer fear lanced through her. 'There's no need to do anything stupid,' she said quickly. 'All right, you'll be penalized for impersonating Bruce – but as you say, you didn't rob anyone in the process. And while killing Russell Page is much more serious, you were in shock and it wasn't premeditated. You might get away with manslaughter, and that's not—'

He raised a hand to stop her, shaking his head. 'I've been living someone else's life for the last ten years,' he said, 'and let's face it, I've had a ball. All the wine, women and song I could ask for, and more money than I could spend in a lifetime. But now it's payback time.'

'It doesn't have—'

'Lindsey, I'm a cocky bastard, and after all this luxury and kowtowing I couldn't face the humiliation. As to prison, however long or short the sentence, no way. So – I'd rather go out with a bang.' His mouth twisted. 'Like Bruce and Page. Poetic justice.'

'*No!*' she said forcefully.

He restarted the engine and she saw his hands were shaking. 'I'm sorry you got involved,' he said jerkily. 'Wrong place, wrong time.'

As the car edged away from the hedge she dived for the door handle, but the click of the central locking forestalled her. She was a prisoner!

'Let me out!' she screamed as panic took over, and she started to pound at him with her fists so that the car, which was rapidly gaining speed, swerved drunkenly. 'They won't think it was an accident this time, and it won't do any good anyway if Rona knows you're not Bruce!'

'It doesn't matter who knows any more,' he said unevenly. 'It won't affect me. Or you.'

'Please!' she sobbed. 'I'm not involved in any of this! Let me out, for God's sake!' And then, in a fresh burst of desperation, '*I'm going to be married!*'

'Bully for you!' he said.

She scrabbled again for the door handle, but it remained rigidly unyielding. 'Oh God, please help me!' she cried, sobs tearing at her throat.

A tractor loomed up ahead of them in the narrow lane and Lindsey screamed again. Grant didn't slacken speed, merely swerved towards the hedge, its branches scraping with an agonized screech against the window. The shouts of the tractor driver reached them briefly, then he was far behind them.

Lindsey started to shake convulsively, struggling for some way of persuading him to spare her. 'You've not killed anyone in cold blood before!' she cried. 'What have I ever done to you?'

'Shut up!' he snapped savagely.

'Surely there's someone you wouldn't want remembering you as a murderer?'

'Shut up!' he said again, but his voice sounded choked and, glancing at him, she saw his eyes were full of tears.

'You don't even have to kill *yourself*—'

'For the love of God, will you shut *up*?' he shouted. Then, 'Oh, for God's sake go if it means so much to you! Get out!'

The central locking clicked again and, although he'd barely slowed down, she hurled herself at the door and as it swung back fell heavily on to the verge, painfully scraping her knees and elbows. A second later something came flying out of the car, landing on the grass ahead of her and she crawled towards it on all fours. It was her mobile phone. Bleeding, breathless, hardly able to believe she was safe, she manoeuvred herself into a sitting position and with fumbling fingers dialled Steve's number.

It was five days later, and Lindsey and Steve had come round for dinner. The story of Bruce Sedgwick's tragic death had filled the papers and television news all week, as his rags-to-riches story was rehashed and famous people who'd known him told of their memories. He'd have liked all that, Lindsey thought.

The four of them had debated long and hard as to whether or not to reveal the truth. But as Max said, what would be the point? It was only their word, and it was not as though a rightful beneficiary was waiting in the wings. Better, too, for Esmé Page to go on believing her husband's death was an accident.

'You must have got to him in the end, though, Linz,' Rona said as they sat over coffee, the patio doors open to the warm night and Gus basking in the last rays of the sun. 'He could so easily have taken you with him.'

'He almost did!' Lindsey shuddered, and Steve reached quickly for her hand.

'Let's just thank God he didn't,' he said grimly. 'But I'll never forgive him for what he put you through, not to mention the rest of us! I aged twenty years that day!'

Lindsey looked round at their serious faces. 'I must admit,' she observed, 'I hadn't realized quite how dangerous it is to be a twin!'

She exchanged a secret smile with Rona and on impulse raised her glass. 'So let's drink a toast to twins, past, present and future,' she said. 'God bless us, every one!'

'Twins!' they all repeated – and the sombre discussion ended, as she'd intended, in laughter.